Morris Island Lighthouse, Folly Beach, South Carolina

ISBN: 978-1-948370-00-4

Elucidate Publishing
PO Box 1262
Hermitage PA 16148

United States of America

Pier Lights

Ella M. Kaye

~ *One* ~

Gripping the cool, damp sand at the edge of the water with her toes, Caroline raised her foot from its hole, extended the leg behind her, and let her body drift forward in balance. Balance was difficult in the sand. Still she managed a decent arabesque with her arms extended, one over her head, reaching out toward the soft waves of the Atlantic ocean, the other reaching up to the sky. Relaxing her foot, the one she so often cursed these days, she felt the sand tickle through her toes as it fell.

Her polish would scratch, she supposed. As late as it was already, she didn't want to go home and repaint her toenails. Still, she dug. The lights of the pier sparkled in the dark to her right: a long string of lights beckoning her to join the festivities under the pavilion. Soft streams of jazz floated over along skimming waves.

She should dance on the pier. Normal dance. Not trained dance. Bringing her right leg and foot back to the ground, Caroline felt a long aching wail ready to stream forward from her tired soul. The soul that longed to dance. Trained dance. Not normal dance.

With a cleansing breath of briny ocean air, she decided it wouldn't hurt to at least get close enough to the pier to hear voices. There was no reason to make the decision until morning. He'd given her that long.

The sand shifted under her feet and she moved closer to the water until waves brushed up over her toes, over her ankles, and deeper still until it splashed up onto her calves. Normally, she would never walk where she couldn't see what her feet might find. Her feet were her lifeblood. Or they had been.

Now, she could walk where she pleased. Caroline did her best to convince herself the freedom would be worth it; it was the good side, where others had told her to focus. The good side. All in all, she would rather go back to watching every step. The good side had never been much of a friend that she'd been able to tell.

A pinch on her arch made her jump and she pulled her foot up to survey the damage. It was too dark to see whether there was blood or a protrusion. Rubbing her hand gently over the spot, she didn't feel anything other than moisture, and the pain felt only surface deep. A prick from a sea shell, Caroline guessed. Payback for her negative thoughts. Karma was, after all, a true bitch.

Swishing her foot around in the cool water to soothe the pain, Caroline continued toward the lights, the music, the voices. She wouldn't go up on the pier. That was far closer to people than she had any need to be. Instead, she made her way to the immense wooden support posts that looked to her like three rows of silent sentries leading from the base of the Folly Beach Fishing Pier, a long building held up by stilts, and extending a thousand-some feet into the ocean to an angled square platform featuring a two-story gazebo. As grand as the pier was, it was only a little speck of minor interruption to the ocean's flow. It always made her feel insignificant to walk along under the pier and realize it didn't matter to the ocean that she was there. It would still do whatever it was going to do, gladly taking out anything in its path along the way, without remorse.

Hand-in-hand couples nearly made her turn back. Caroline rolled her eyes. *Wait until reality slaps in, little ones.* Instead of turning back, she moved away from them, farther up the beach, underneath the long pier where locals and tourists talked and laughed and stomped against the wood planks above her head. Time to go home. She had an interview in the morning. Her looks mattered, and bags under her eyes wouldn't help any more than would scratched toe nails.

Home. Caroline laughed at herself. The bed and breakfast barely off the beach wasn't home. The three days she'd hidden inside didn't make it hers, especially since she sounded like a visitor to South Carolina, which used to be home. Her voice training had been worth the cost. Her accent was all but gone. If anyone guessed, they guessed she was Canadian. She refuted it but never said where she was from. Caroline from South Carolina was far too worn out to have to listen to it one more time.

A shiver urged her out from under the pier, but she remained just inside the water's edge, letting it splash her ankles. She'd gone farther than she realized. The outgoing path was always shorter than the return path. It was always true, whether or not it made sense.

Just before she moved out of the water to head back to her room, a flicker of light caught her eye. It was a moving flicker, similar to a lighthouse glow as it turned continuous circles, but far smaller. And far closer. She headed that direction. Caroline had always been too curious. Her mother had told her many times she was too curious. It killed the cat, so the story went. Caroline figured she was safe enough since she wasn't a cat. She'd gone well past her nine lives of curiosity and it hadn't killed her yet.

As she got close enough to find the source of the flicker, she decided it might not be all that safe. A man. A large man. With a sword. On a small boat. Alone.

Her gut told her to turn away, to go back to her room, to shower and redo her toe nails and sleep, in case her answer would be yes. Although in all truth, she expected it not to be. She only wanted the option.

The flicker came from the sword as he twirled it around his body. Twirled wasn't the right word. That was what Caroline did. Or what she used to do. It was a delicate, graceful movement. But then, so was this man. He was a delicate, graceful movement, if she could allow herself to stretch the definition of the word delicate. His precision was. As far as she could tell, the sword moved in exactly the same path, repeated, smooth, strong, graceful. It moved like a dancer, but more deadly.

Depending on its intent.

As she moved closer, Caroline found herself wishing it was not quite so dark, that the moon was more than half full or that the light emanating from the bottom of his boat was stronger so she could see him better. He was dark haired. Tall. Broad-shouldered. Muscular. His dark shorts hugged his hips and thighs. His thighs were broad but toned. The rippled muscles of his chest were occasionally highlighted by the moon's glint and the lights from the pier.

His face was mostly washed out by shadows. Only his chin showed. Odd.

The pattern changed, became faster, more intricate. His arm muscles surged and receded in imitation of the waves around him. By now, she was as close as she could get to him without getting her clothes wet. He was a good way out, standing up on the seat of the boat, balancing easily even while the small craft bounced with the gentle waves.

He stopped, chest expanding, shoulders circling, sword tip down between his feet.

Caroline stood in awe. His head was down. At rest.

A good time to leave. She stepped backward, slowly, tripped on a rock, and splashed into the water. Cursing, she righted herself, shivered from the shock of cold water and a slight breeze brushing against her still sun-heated skin.

He was looking her direction, as far as she could tell. His head tilted. Slightly. Held still.

She shuffled backward, slowly. The nick on the bottom of her foot pinched, so she curled her foot to take pressure off as she continued her slow creep away from the sword. He didn't move. He watched her. Or she imagined he watched her. It was dark. She was too far away, in black calf-length leggings and a long dark gray short-sleeved tunic. He couldn't see her.

To test her theory, she edged to the side, out of the water, still backward, away from the angle his face pointed.

His head followed.

Her stomach clenched and she turned, nearly jogging up the beach toward the sidewalk that would take her back to her room. Caroline glanced back several times, but there was no sign that he followed. As far as she knew, he was still on that little boat, with his big sword resting between his legs.

With her heartbeat calm again, she caught the spicy whiff of Taco Boy near the Beachside Bed and Breakfast and detoured that direction. When had she last allowed herself greasy tacos? She didn't remember.

Tonight, she would splurge, although she'd have to get them to go since she couldn't sit in the place soaked to the skin.

Tomorrow, she would decide whether to audition for the job.

~ *Two* ~

She'd expected a big, burly, slobby guy.

Why she did, Caroline wasn't sure. She'd never been in a strip club. Television, she supposed, not that she'd seen much television over the past few years. Still, the middle-aged, clean-shaven man with a friendly smile threw her. She'd been prepared for big, burly, and slobby, which would make it easier to turn the position down. This guy didn't look so bad to work for. Maybe she could do it.

Well, she *could* do it. But maybe she *would.*

The place didn't look shady, either. Of course, when the job paid between one thousand and three thousand a week, depending on performance, Caroline shouldn't have expected it to be shady or shabby.

Truth was, she had no idea what to expect.

"You've never done this kind of work before, is that right?" Hayes, who introduced himself only as that, walked fast and talked loud enough she could easily hear from behind as she followed, dodging small tables that dotted the slightly raised outer edge, with larger tables filling in the main floor.

"Not exactly this."

He stopped and turned to look at her. "Dance experience. I saw that on your resume. Let me guess, local theater?"

"No. I'm ... or I was..."

"Spit it out. I'm a busy man and you don't look the type for the job, so let's make this quick."

He was right on that mark. But she could be right for it. Caroline knew how to adapt. That was her specialty. "I'm a classically trained ballerina."

He laughed. "Okay, great sweetie. I have things to do..."

"I spent five years in Boston as part of the line and then moved up to understudy for the prima ballerina. From there, I went to New York and made one night's start in Giselle when the star was ill. I can give you contacts so you can check it out."

Mr. Hayes scratched his chin. "Why do you want to be a stripper?"

"I need a job."

"Of course. Why?"

Caroline raised her chin and threw out her prepared line. "I needed a change of direction, a new challenge. I'm good at challenges. I thrive on them. And I know you think I won't fit in here, but I will. If I decide to take the job, and I haven't decided yet if this is right for me, but if it is, I will do a good job, a great job, and you won't be sorry you gave me the chance."

With a thoughtful nod, Hayes paced away a few steps then pulled up a chair. "Prove it." He shrugged his head toward the stage in the distance. It was a large stage, complete with two poles at each side close to the front and a few props in the back. At least she assumed the chair and boxes of different heights were meant to be props.

"Without music?"

He threw her a sly grin and turned his head to yell to someone she couldn't see. "Charlie, turn on some music. Have an audition."

Scuffling of feet and the shrill bark of a speaker not treated right led to a blare of music. Techno.

Caroline placed a hand on her waist. "You're not serious with this?"

"Can't do it?"

"I could, but I won't. This isn't sexy. I don't believe this is what you use, so give me some real music and I'll dance for you."

"Dance? Sweetie, I don't want classical ballet. I want knock 'em off their feet sexy danceotica."

"That's not a word, you know."

He smirked. "It is here. Going to do it or not? Like I said, I'm a busy man and I don't like to waste time."

"Neither do I. Give me real music."

He skimmed her as though he wasn't sure she was worth the time. Caroline knew he would give in, so she waited him out.

"*Charlie*. Take two."

The music stopped. Strains of a rock beat started. Eighties rock, judging from the heavy sound. This, she could use, even if she didn't know it. The singer sounded familiar, a female with a deep voice and an edge, a Joan Jett edge, but not Joan Jett. She wasn't well versed in eighties rock enough to place her, but it was a good song.

Caroline weaved around the tables to the stage and dropped her bag on a chair up front. She could barely see Hayes where he'd wandered to the bar at the back of the room, which she figured would make it easier. It struck her that she saw him about the same as she saw Mr. Big Sword the night before on the beach. He was shadowed, but his form was still obvious.

The thought of the big sword and the body in control of it filled her thoughts as she melted into the aggressive beat and the lyrics that spoke of rockin' and letting go. Generally, Carolyn paid more attention to the words and danced to them, but the sword interfered. She danced to it instead, to the movements of the sword and its human body. And she danced the way she did in her apartment after a long day's practice, loose and free, unwinding, unleashing the tight control of sharp manipulated steps and forms and lines into soft sensual earthy movements.

As she relaxed into it, she made it more sexy, added more hip movement, more bends, with the facial expression to match. She tugged her slinky lightweight sweater off each arm, slowly, suggestively, never losing the beat or the movement. Under the sweater, her tight tank top showed her physique, the carefully kept dancer's shape and muscle. She knew her biggest obstacle would be her breasts. They were well-shaped enough, but they were ballerina size, not stripper size. Even with her red lace push up bra that showed through the thin skin-colored tank, they wouldn't pull much attention.

That only meant she'd have to make up for it with skill, and with attitude. She had plenty of both.

Hayes ambled closer, to just in front of the stage, eyeing her every move and different parts of her scantily clothed body. "Keep going." He glanced at her leggings.

Caroline stopped and faced him. "Not without a contract."

He snickered. "How do I know if I want to offer a contract if this is all I see first?"

"I have no scars. No stretch marks. It's all toned muscle and smooth skin. You know I can do it. I know you can see in my attitude that I can, and I will, if I decide to take the job. This is as far as I go without being on the clock."

Hayes continued to skim her body and stopped at her breasts. He frowned and scratched his chin. A power play. She knew it for what it was. "I've never hired a stripper that small."

"I bet you never hired one with as much talent as I have, either."

"Don't overestimate yourself. I have lots of talent here. Your kind is less valuable to me than most of theirs. Remember that." He picked up her sweater and tossed it back to her. "Let me show you around the rest of the place. We'll talk as we walk."

She'd taken the job.

Caroline was slightly sick to her stomach. She'd worked so hard to get as far as she had, and she'd been so close to being a prima ballerina, or principal dancer, as they now called it; she'd never been willing to switch the term in her own mind. And now this. She was down to being an exotic dancer in a club very close to her hometown which she'd tried very hard to escape. That song, *Gotta Let Go*, Charlie told her, by Lita Ford, would be forever burned in her brain as her road to perdition song. It was unfair of her, Caroline supposed, to brand the song that way. It was a good song and she planned to go back and search Lita Ford videos to see what else she did, since, at 27, Caroline would have been born around the time the singer was on the charts. Besides, she had no real reason or right to stigmatize someone else due to her own choices. And maybe, as Hayes said, she was overestimating herself. Her road to perdition started long before the audition.

Of course she could take the more normal road and look for something in an office job or in retail or... Caroline shuddered. She'd been there. It wasn't her. She was a dancer. Maybe she was no longer a ballerina, but she was still a dancer and she would be the best one at the club. How hard would it be to work her way up to top spot at a stripper club? Caroline set her goal to get there by the end of the month. On top, where she always told everyone she would be.

Her mother would be so proud.

She chuckled as she pulled into the B&B parking area. It might be worth stripping in the hope someone would find out and tell her mother.

The thousand a week wouldn't hurt, either, as a starter. Caroline had no doubt she'd soon work up to the high end pay scale instead of the starting end. Hayes was putty. Like most men. Putty and bluster. Once you learned that simple fact, the rest was easy enough.

For now, she would start small and turn on the charm. She'd learned that well during her professional days. Charm counted for a hell of a lot.

Three days.

Hayes wanted her to start in three days. Caroline hoped that would give her enough time to find an apartment. She couldn't stay at the B&B long term, no matter how much she loved the place with its odd architecture, loads of windows, and the big porch that connected what she supposed used to be two different houses where she often sat to read. It was casual and cozy and friendly, but it would eat into her small budget too fast.

Before she started to apartment hunt, Caroline wanted to celebrate. Lunch at Snapper Jack's and then a swim in the ocean. Or vice versa. And then tonight, she would walk back to the beach and see if Mr. Big Sword was out again.

~ Three ~

Amazed she found a nice furnished apartment barely in her budget and within walking distance from the beach, Caroline donned a tan bikini, wrapped a sarong over it, grabbed a towel, and headed back to the beach. Dusk approached. Her earlier swim was cut short by her growling stomach. As accomplished as she felt already, she figured a second swim would add to that. It was good exercise. And it was easy on her feet.

Her right foot ached although she hadn't walked as much as she used to walk. Walking was her thing. She'd had a reputation for it when she was in school. So many rides offered and none accepted. They thought she was too stuck-up to accept a ride when she didn't have a car of her own. She didn't have need of a car back when she lived where everything was walking distance from the house. She liked to walk. They could think what they wanted.

With a shake of the head to rid herself of the thoughts, Caroline crossed the street with a slow jog and sank into the sight of the water, the beautiful blue green gray expanse stretching to the sky, held back softly by the gray white brown sand. There were the irksome couples hand-in-hand again but she looked past them. It was quieter without the dance on the pier, a special occasion locals and tourists looked forward to and Caroline both enjoyed and detested. The music, she loved. The people, she didn't.

Caroline dropped her sarong and her towel near one of the wooden sentries and heal-toed into the water. She walked in up to her knees, waited to let her body get used to the cold, moved in up to her thighs, then bent and lunged in with an easy breast stroke. She swam under the pier, in between the large poles, her favorite place on the beach, even as a child. Her mother warned her to go out into the sun; there were more likely starfish to bother in the coolness of the shade from the pier. It only made her more determined to stay in the shade and keep an eye out for starfish to add to her collection. Her mother hated when she took the things out of the water or off the beach.

Not today. She didn't look for starfish today. She wanted the stretch of her muscles, the exertion of her body, the physical activity that was second only to dance on her love list.

Caroline told a fellow dancer once that dance was her first love and swimming her second as far as exercise went. Then walking. Giggling, the girl answered that sex was her first choice of exercise and dancing her second, but it was safer to get paid to dance and it all worked together well.

That had been her first and last conversation with the back line dancer, although Caroline knew many of the girls felt the same, or close to the same. Dance and sex. Sex and dance. The two filled their entire worlds. What was so good about it, anyway? Caroline had yet to understand their fascination with having a man in their beds all night. It only made it harder to sleep. They snored. Or they tossed and turned. Or they insisted on throwing a heavy sweaty hairy arm over top of her body. Or they got what they wanted and moved far away to the other side until they hauled their big asses out of her bed first thing in the morning.

Swimming was far more sensual.

The water caressed her skin as she stroked through its depths, dipping underneath for solitude and rising above for air. It both pushed against her and held her up. It rushed over her face to stroke her cheeks and made her close her eyes in defense and in pleasure. It made her heart beat fast, from exertion and excitement. It pumped blood through her system. And it was there for her to decide when she wanted it and to avoid when she didn't. Its soft splashing and rushing and receding and lapping was far, far better than a man snoring in her ear.

Caroline felt far more gratified lying on her towel after the intense swim than she had ever felt beside a man after a round or two in bed.

Maybe she was made wrong, or missing something. Or maybe she was mentally off, as she'd been accused of more than once. It wasn't like she didn't enjoy men at all. At times she did, for short times. Very short times. Too often she ended up trying very hard not to tell them to just finish already and get off.

She didn't have to tell the water that. The water was hers to manipulate as she pleased, when she pleased, for as long or as short a workout as she pleased. And it left her cool and refreshed, not sweaty and tired. It was hers only. Privately. As ballet had been, before she joined the dance school and had to abide by their routine, their schedule. Their rules.

If Hayes thought he would control her as much, he would learn fast how wrong he was. Some of the girls got to choose their own music. They had to work up to that privilege, he said. Fat chance of that happening. In three days, when Caroline went to DanceOtica and turned into Lina from New York, she would take her music with her. He would have to deal with it.

When she was dry enough to replace the sarong, Caroline shivered in the night air, shook her towel out, and headed toward where she saw Mr. Big Sword the night before. It was a long shot he'd be there again, she expected, and after it had frightened her, she didn't know why she made herself look again, but she had to look again. Or try.

More disappointed, *far* more disappointed, than she expected upon not finding him there, Carolyn sighed and walked back the other direction.

She supposed she should go on to her room. Tomorrow was moving day, not that she had much to move, but then she would have to shop for basics. Toilet paper. Food. A pan or two. A spatula. She had nothing but her clothes and her music, a few favorite books, most still stuffed tight in the trunk of her old gray boat disguised as a Montego, and her starfish collection. The car was a hand-me-down handed down several times. She picked it up in New York just before she left. New York was fine on foot or with public transportation and she preferred that, but on Folly Beach, outside Charleston, personal transportation was a must.

And the trunk made for good storage space while she needed it.

A sparkle in the water caught her eyes and she paused, then wandered closer, slowly. He was there. Out farther in the water and harder to see. But he was there. Caroline got as close as she could and spread her towel on the sand. Lowering, again slowly, so as not to catch his eye the way he'd caught hers, she crossed her left leg in front of her, the right leg out straight, and gazed out at his motion, his elegance, his skill. His dance.

He was a Man of La Mancha dancer except with more focus on the sword movements than on dance techniques. Caroline frowned. Maybe that wasn't true. The dance technique for him was the sword movement. The sword was an extension of him. His skill was every bit as trained as her own, his body every bit as controlled and precise. He would be a good dance partner.

And if his big sword, the shiny hard long extension of his body, was any clue as to the rest of him, he might be good at other things, also. She was tempted to swim over to his boat and find out if maybe nothing was wrong with her, if it had only been her partners who were lacking. Then again, he could be as much putty and bluster as nearly every other man she'd met. Better to admire him from a distance and make believe he would be worth sleeping beside, worth her energy and patience and skill.

Not that she was terribly skilled in that way. She had other skills she cared more about and skill in that department wasn't terribly necessary that she'd found. As long as she complimented her mate, she came off as skilled enough. They cared more about their own skill, real or not, than hers. She just had to be there and act like it was worth the energy.

Putty and bluster.

Maybe Mr. Big Sword wouldn't be either one. But some things were better left unknown.

She needed to leave. A yawn told her she'd reached her limit for the day. Rising slowly, still watching the man she could barely see, she froze when he stopped. He set the tip of his sword down, again between his slightly spread thighs, or just in front of them. And he stood still, faced her direction.

Caroline calmly walked away. At least mostly calm. Her heart rate increased only the slightest bit. He hadn't followed her the night before, so there was no reason to think he would tonight. And he was out farther in the ocean. By the time he could get to shore, she would be lost on the sidewalk with other night wanderers. It was dark. He'd never know who she was. Besides, she couldn't imagine he'd walk the sidewalks with that thing in his hand. It couldn't be legal. Could it? She doubted it. Not much was legal anymore, not like when she was a kid and the neighbor boys carried their BB guns around town to harass squirrels and discarded pop cans. They couldn't even carry water guns that had any resemblance to a real gun these days.

No way could Mr. Big Sword carry his weapon around town. She was plenty safe enough. Maybe she'd come back tomorrow night and … take another swim in return for making herself set up her apartment and tread through shoppers to get what she needed. The shopping itself she didn't mind. The loud pushy garish women who made a habit of shopping to the extent they believed they owned whatever store they inhabited at whatever time, she did mind.

She'd said once at the company that people annoyed her. It didn't gain her any friends among her fellow dancers, but then she wasn't there to make friends. She was there to dance, and to beat them out of lead positions she wanted. There was no point in acting otherwise, although most of them did.

Caroline was glad to be away from the falseness of girls acting sweet to each other the whole time they had every intention of stepping right over their "friends" on their way to the top if at all possible. They all had the same goal. She simply admitted it. They hadn't liked it much.

She supposed her fellow strippers wouldn't, either. And she supposed they'd be just as determined to walk over each other to get to the top. Such was life.

~ *Four* ~

"Yes, I'm coming." Dio set the rake aside and wiped his hands on his jeans. On the porch, he shoved his shoes off using the toes of the opposite feet. He didn't have the energy to have to sweep and then wash the old wood plank floor, which he'd have to do if his shoes so much as touched it and she noticed.

"What took you so long?" His mother shuffled from the heavily varnished maple counter to the matching kitchen table and set a platter in the middle atop a black metal potholder. Steam rose from the dish and he smelled cheese and ... spinach. Again, spinach. He supposed there was rice or noodles at the bottom. Always rice or noodles. And spinach. She said it was healthy and she needed him to stay healthy.

He didn't mind it. Or he didn't use to mind it. At this point, though, nearly anything dark green made him cringe.

"Well?" His mother's drawn-in wrinkled face met his.

"I'm not done raking the weeds."

"No matter. Do it after dinner."

"I work tonight."

She sighed. "Must you? Why can't you find a normal job instead of letting all of those horrid females gawk at you? If I'd known you would turn around and do that, I wouldn't have fed you so healthy."

"A normal job is daylight hours. I need those for the farm work. What do you want me to do? Let it all go to weeds and rodents?"

"You should, yes. A young man should set up a house of his own, not look after this awful big place. God love your father, but I will never understand why..."

"He loved it."

She stopped adding silverware beside the plates and looked up again. "Yes. But you don't."

"I love the place. It's the constant work I have to do alone I don't love."

"Then hire someone..."

"We've tried that. It doesn't go well."

"Then sell the place and get yourself something that's less work."

"Mom, it's what we have left of him."

"Oh, Diomedes." She shuffled over and reached up to set her hands along his face. "Of course that's not true. You have your memories. And when I leave this earth, which won't be much longer, I don't want you here alone working day and night for what? For some land you work only because your father loved it? A few animals? There's no sense in it. Skip work. Go somewhere you'll find a nice girl and settle down so I don't have to worry about you being alone."

"A nice girl won't take me and you know it."

"That's not so, and I know it's not so." She backed away. "Go and wash up now. The weeds will wait."

Bless her soul, she wouldn't give up. Dio obeyed orders and went to scrub the black dirt off his hands and face. Drying, he caught himself in the mirror. No. A nice girl wouldn't want him. A nice girl wanted someone to hold hands with on the beach, to show off to her friends. She wouldn't want ... this, what reflected back at him.

Why had they waited so long to have him? His parents were over fifty by the time he came along. They hadn't the energy or patience to look after a too-curious uncontrolled three-year-old. And Dio was only twenty-six when he lost his father. His mother was closing in on eighty. She was holding up well for the life she'd had, but like it or not, he knew the years were ticking fast.

And he had nothing else. The farm. The night job, on occasional nights. The occasional flings after the night job. It was his life. He wouldn't expect more from it.

On top of his dreadful face, there was his mother. She'd always been an odd bird, always stood out everywhere she went, dressing far too fancy just to run to the store, dragging Dio with her. He supposed the good thing about her being so flamboyant was that he got less attention. Of course, if she'd just let herself fit in, maybe no one would have paid any attention to the way he always had his hair down over his face as much as possible and kept his face to the floor, trying not to be seen.

He didn't have to work the second job. They didn't need the

income. What he needed was the human interaction, and hiding behind his disguise, as part of the job, was the only way he could get it without scaring people off.

Dio didn't bother anymore to tell his mother as much. She thought he was being ridiculous, but then opinions had never bothered her whatsoever. A nice trait to have, he supposed, but he did not have it himself.

Caroline pressed her face close to the mirror, in the dressing room of DanceOtica, and carefully lined her eyes with thick black liner edged with thin rust liner that complemented her hair color. She loved the contrast of the black lines against her pale greenish brownish flecked eyes and her pale pinkish sallow skin. Many of her fellow ballerinas groaned at the idea of doing their stage makeup. Caroline loved it. She'd always loved to play in makeup, to change it around, to make herself look older and more polished than she was. With the right combination, she could turn herself into the beauty she needed to be on stage.

During the day, she left herself unmade, with no more than shiny gloss for her lips. She also liked the contrast of her dull paleness with the shiny lips. Contrast amused her, captured her imagination and interest. It was an obsession. It was part of what attracted her to ballet. The contrast of the beautiful delicate graceful movements as they appeared on the exterior to the tight controlled strong muscle coordination she felt inside. It had delighted her as a child. It still delighted her.

The best reason to enjoy this new job was the contrast with ballet. Ballet was elegant and sophisticated. Stripping was primal and raunchy. She looked forward to the challenge, and to be honest, she looked forward to being more who she felt she was inside. Ballet was always a grand act, the perfect show that disguised what went on behind the scenes. Here, they simply took off the polite disguises and let the vulgarity of life shine through.

Life was vulgar. At least hers always had been.

Caroline didn't, however, look forward to the audience reaction. That would be opposite, as well, she expected. Polite applause and polite standing ovations from the well dressed was unobtrusive. She didn't notice it any longer. It was easy to block out. Blocking out the raucous crowd in the club could become her nemesis, if she allowed. She wouldn't. Caroline Corinth was well known for always being in control of her emotions and reactions. She wouldn't let it to get to her.

It was that simple.

She'd told many people many times it was that simple. You don't want something to bother you? Then don't let it. They said it wasn't that easy. She said it was if you wanted it to be. Could be she'd just had more practice at it, but if she could do it, they could.

"Hey, good luck tonight." A short busty girl wearing a bright orange glittered bikini set a hand on Caroline's shoulder. "And watch the guys on the far left. They're the rowdy ones, here every Saturday night, and always mouthy. Don't let 'em bother you."

"Thanks. They won't."

A brunette in dark red glanced over. "Aren't we over-confident for our first night? Not as easy as you think, honey. Don't get cocky."

"I didn't say it would be easy, but I'll be fine, thanks."

The woman with deep lines under her eyes and on her forehead gave her a half snarl and turned away to rub on a heavy coat of lipstick that matched the tiny strappy ridiculous outfit.

"Don't mind her. She never likes newcomers." The orange girl slipped into high orange heels and a few stage clothes she would soon take off.

"That's 'cause she's been here forever and us younger girls make her feel her age." A voice from somewhere behind Caroline snickered.

"Careful not to trip tonight, Lovey." The dark red woman pursed her dark red lips in the mirror. "Gonna be a hard fall if you do."

Caroline blocked them out. At least they didn't act sweet to her face. She much preferred this. Maybe. She'd heard a few names. Some of the girls offered them. She gave her own as Lina, admitted she'd never stripped but she'd danced plenty, and told them nothing more, no matter how a couple of them pried. They were work acquaintances; they would not be more to her.

At least she was on early. The best girls were the closing

entertainment, along with some guys thrown in here and there to entertain the few women who came to the club. It was the only strip club in the area. Hayes said they had to entertain in both directions, in all fairness.

Fairness had nothing to do with anything. It was about money.

Either way, she figured she'd go out and earn her paycheck and then wash the makeup off, push her hair into a ponytail and her body into jeans and a sweatshirt and join the crowd to watch the other acts. Any tip she could pick up would only help her progress to becoming one of the girls at the end of the show with the higher paychecks.

Dio sat in the shadows just behind the side curtains. They had a new girl. He'd rushed through dinner, to his mother's chagrin, and come in earlier than he normally would bother in order to see how bad Hayes screwed with her. The worst part of working at DanceOtica wasn't the drunk loud men in the audience or the women who tried to ignore the *no touching the dancers onstage* rule. It was Hayes. On the outside he looked okay, decent. On the inside, the guy was a huge asshole. Not many girls stayed long enough to pass his test. Once they did, they were in and he didn't bother them. Word had it the girl who should have started on a week night had never danced anywhere public before. She was not only new, but very new. Hayes would eat her alive.

Dio figured he'd keep an eye out and see if she was one who needed to be talked into a different business or convinced Hayes would back off once she proved herself. Twice already he'd talked with young girls after their first night who thought they had no other options but didn't have the heart for stripping into finding other jobs and used his contacts to make that happen.

The girls called him the white knight of DanceOtica. Some called him the black knight. He wasn't either. He was gray. Through and through gray. Bland. The only interesting thing about him was his build and his one talent, a talent only useful in a strip club entertaining drunks like a side show freak. He stayed quiet enough, enhancing the tall, dark, and silent image they found intriguing, that they would never know how gray he was inside.

"This new one's gonna fall straight on her face." Sandy slid a hand up his arm, her normal way of greeting him.

Dio scanned her. "Ever going to wear anything but pumpkin orange?"

"Hey, it's my thing." She shook her shoulders to tease, made her ample breasts jiggle over top her bikini. "Ever gonna take that mask off and let me see you?"

"No." Dio turned back to the stage. Lights dimmed. Music started. Not music he recognized. Didn't sound like anything Hayes would choose. It was edgy, but sultry. He let her use her own music? Already? He recognized the voice but couldn't place the singer, a female with an earthy tone. Not one of the new little twits who could only hold a tune with a producer's help, but one with a good strong voice. And passion. Deep sultry passion.

"Ohhh, he's gonna flip big time. He told her not to do this. Bet this'll be her first and last strip." Sandy laughed.

"Can't you all be nice to the new girl for once?" Dio rolled his eyes. "You're kind of in this together, you know."

"Like hell we are. We're all in it for ourselves. And if Little Miss Cocky don't know that yet, she better learn fast. *If* he lets her come back after this stunt."

Dio decided to ignore the comment about being cocky. Sandy wasn't the best character judge. She was about the worst at reading people he'd ever met.

The new girl was pale under the bright lights. Except for her overdone eye makeup, she had very little color of any kind. Even her costume was tan with a black scarf-like accessory she used to imitate the words. Something about a black crow and shadows. Hayes wouldn't like that, either. He liked bright and showy. But her movements were stunning. She was controlled but fluid. Graceful but aggressive. Her hip movement was maybe the best he'd seen. She was small busted for a stripper and some of the audience reaction reflected that, or reflected her tan costume that still hid a lot of her. A long thin skirt. A loose flowing blouse.

Tan. Up and down tan, to include her hair.

But this music was her. Or she became the music, the song. Her dance fit the words. She released the black "wings" and her hands flitted over her body, promising, teasing. She tugged on the blouse, untied it as she moved without throwing herself off the beat. Tossed it out of the way. Definitely small for a stripper. But her arms were well toned, thin, not skinny, and her abdomen was perfect.

Sandy had started to heckle quietly but stopped. This girl wasn't going anywhere. She had a hell of a lot of potential, although obviously inexperienced. Not with dance. She knew dance. Even small and tan, she yanked attention and had them pulled in to her movement. Her back bends were fabulous: her head nearly brushed the floor and she came up slowly, very slowly, perfectly in control of her body.

She played with the skirt, rubbed it away from one leg as a hand slid up from her knee to her inner thigh to her outer thigh, up her hip. Someone yelled at her to take it off. She eyed the screamer directly and moved away, to the other side, teased with her skirt, her body, her gaze. She looked at them. Most new girls didn't dare. They kept their gaze anywhere but at the audience.

No wonder Sandy called her cocky. Dio would call her confident. Sexy. Sensual. Beautiful. Intriguing. He could think of a hell of a lot of names to call her, but he'd missed her introduction through Sandy's chatter. He bent toward her to ask.

"Lina. From New York. And wow, I doubt she's going anywhere, no matter how mad Hayes gets."

No. If he had been mad, Hayes wouldn't be now, not after this performance. The girl probably lied. She wasn't inexperienced. Not by far. Not even the other closers were this good, this confident.

"What singer is this?"

Sandy shrugged. "I only listen to men. Can't stand girl singers."

Sadly, Dio was not at all surprised, although the singer's voice was fairly deep and every bit as polished and controlled as Lina's movements.

The skirt slipped from around her waist. Unlike most of the girls who wore skimpy bikini bottoms, Lina wore what looked like the new swim bottoms, short and skin-tight. She played with the band by running fingers along the top edge, pulled them down only enough to tease. Screeches from the audience told her to take more off. She could only take so much more off. Most of the girls took off their tops. Bottoms had to stay on, as per club policy. Dio was just as glad. He preferred a little something left to the imagination, and he didn't want to see quite that much of his coworkers.

She ended the song still technically covered, and they yelled for her anyway.

Dio had planned to introduce himself when she was done, but he changed his mind. Not tonight. He was too turned on by her, and he had to be able to perform later.

~ *Five* ~

Caroline was ready for a night off by Tuesday. Saturday and Sunday, she'd left before the end, although she wanted to see the closer. She found the experience more exhausting than she expected. It was part mental, since it was such an adjustment from the long days of practice and barre work and hearing the clap clap of hands keeping time through calling out choreography, through large groups of dancers memorizing the same dance and the same or complementing parts, from costume fittings and dress rehearsals and show days which were the escalation of the work and not the work itself, not to the same extent.

At DanceOtica, they practiced on their own time and chose their own costumes and saw each other only when it was time to get ready for the show, and the show went on every night.

Her foot was starting to object, so Caroline badly needed the night off. And she badly wanted to hit the beach, to unwind.

Okay, she might as well be honest with herself. She'd wanted to catch her swordsman if he was there. He hadn't been. Caroline tried to convince herself she wasn't really as disappointed as she felt she was. It was just a guy with a sword. So what? Honestly, she could be so childish at times.

Monday night, last night – had it only just been last night? – she stayed until the end. Again she was disappointed. The older lady in dark red closed on Monday. Caroline wasn't too impressed. She was flirty. She was very flirty, and very open. And her breasts were still in good shape for her age, not too saggy, no stretch marks, at least not apparent from stage. But she was a bad dancer.

Of course, she was a stripper, not a dancer. They weren't the same. Some girls were both. Most were only strippers.

Spreading her towel on the sand, Caroline slipped out of her sarong. She'd worn a very small bikini this time, and she relished the way men nearby turned to leer. It was a little disconcerting to realize she already enjoyed putting on a show with her body in this different way, allowing appreciation of what she'd worked so hard for so many years to have. Not that she'd ever been shy about it. Her biggest splurge was swimwear. She had far more than she needed, and many were barely there suits.

Taking the elastic band off her wrist, she bent her head back enough to gather her medium length boring-colored hair and twirled it into a ponytail high on her head. Then she tossed her head so it swished like a horse's mane and settled on her towel, on her back, her feet propped flat-footed and her knees up and parted, slightly, not vulgar. Dark sunglasses shielded her eyes from the glaring sun. It would lower soon. She would enjoy the heat for a while, take a long swim, then return to lie on her front and leave her barely covered rear to catch whatever rays were left for the day. It was time for a tan. Ballerinas didn't have tans since they spent so much of their time inside, but strippers did.

As dark descended, Caroline would sip at her thermos of red wine that would look only like she was drinking water, and munch on the few things she'd thrown in her little cooler. Fresh cut veggies. Rolled up ham and cheese. Crackers. And she'd wait for a glimpse of him.

Dio looked forward to being at work.

He worked Saturday and Sunday nights, had Monday off, and worked Tuesday. Then not again until Saturday. Most often he loved Wednesday, Thursday, and Friday when he could go to bed early and recover from the rest of the week. This week, he resented not being there, not being able to see her. The new girl. He'd missed her last night. He looked forward to her tonight.

Sandy slapped his rear as she walked past. "Gonna come home with me tonight?"

"Same answer as last time."

"Yeah, yeah, no coworkers. Don't know why, though. Think I can't be as good as some bimbo you take home after she sticks money down your pants? I can do better than that." She slid her fingers into the waistband of his elasticized black pants.

Dio didn't stop her. It had been some time since he took a woman back to her place. Never home. He would never take them home. Even if it was just Sandy, the touch helped him prepare for the show. It turned him on, only enough, as he watched her tease. When she teased far enough he considered hauling her to a back room, he leaned down, pulled his mask up just enough to avoid getting her stage makeup on it, and kissed her neck, not enough to leave a mark, but close. Her body relaxed, her head dropped back.

And he walked away.

If she wanted to tease, he could play that game. He chuckled as she cursed him.

Caroline gave up. It was after one in the morning and she shouldn't have let herself sit out there and wait for him for so long. The ocean air had turned chilly. Sick was the last thing she needed. She'd danced sick plenty often. Unless you were near death as a ballerina, you danced. Otherwise, those just below you swooped in fast, got a chance to prove they could do it if you couldn't. She wouldn't take that chance. She danced sick. She danced in hellish pain. She danced. And she never let it show on her face.

The girl at the club the night before had irked her to no end as she whined like she'd never had cramps before and never had to work through them. Caroline barely kept herself from telling her to shut up and get the hell over it. She managed to hold her tongue. The girl got Hayes to let her go home early.

Baby.

Caroline never danced anymore without pain. Never. That was part of dance, of the job of dance. You get over it and get through it and that's how you get on top, where she was, or had been, very nearly on top. Pain or not, though, some things kept you from getting there. It didn't matter anymore. She would get there this time. All the way there.

Although tonight, she wouldn't mind being on top in a fully different way. Could be the job was getting to her. Or it had just been too long. Either way, maybe next time Mr. Big Sword showed himself, she would make that intention known.

Payback was pure hell.

The new girl was off. He would miss her again. It had to be payback for giving in to Sandy's level of torment. Dio tried to stay above that level, above the nastiness and jealousy and game playing in the club. Most nights it worked. Some nights, though, his frustration took hold and he gave in to it.

The thought of not seeing her again made his own performance far more lackluster than it should have been. Hayes bitched at him. Dio didn't argue. It wasn't the first time. Far from it. But no one had the skill he had. So many women, and some men, too, came only to watch his sword dance. They liked the danger of how close it came to his body, to scarring him or worse. They came for the fear. The thrill.

No one could provide that in the same way.

One of these next nights, the new girl would be there long enough to see it. And he may be damned to hell for it, but Dio was going to make sure she had the thought of going home with him. And then he'd say no. She was a coworker. He didn't do coworkers. Just the thought of it would add more spark to his shows.

~ *Six* ~

Caroline woke up thinking of him. What was wrong with her? It was just a guy with a sword. So what? The men at the club, her fellow performers, were also well built, not quite as well, but well enough, and talented with their bodies. The one she hadn't seen yet she'd heard was the biggest draw, but he only worked a few nights and his next night wouldn't be till Saturday.

Why did the guy on the boat pull at her? She didn't get obsessed over men. She never had. When other girls in school could talk about nothing else, Caroline happily left them to their talk in order to get to dance class or to go practice her dance before she had to do chores and homework and dinner dishes and then take a hot bath to soothe her always tired muscles.

Maybe that was her problem. She was always too tired to obsess over something that turned out not to be that big a deal, anyway. Even her first time wasn't a big deal. It was just a thing. It happened. The end. She moved on. Maybe she hadn't reacted well enough. Maybe he expected her to sob and beg when he said he obviously didn't turn her on enough and had found someone more interested. Whoever the someone was probably didn't have so many hours of physical work every day of her life in order to try to get where she wanted to be. What did he expect when her muscles ached or a charley horse set in because her legs had relaxed for the night and she insisted on using them? The stupid thing always hurt for a good three days after a charley horse night, and still she practiced.

Too much ambition for a girl, he'd said. Screw him. Who cared what he thought?

Shoving her blanket away, Caroline got out of bed and cursed. Her foot hurt. A lot. She knew she'd turned wrong the night before, in the sand, when she thought she saw a glimmer as she left the beach and pivoted toward it. Too fast. Too careless. She'd felt the pop, had to sit down long enough to massage it back to where she could walk home. And damn it hurt today. It would be a long night at work as she forced herself to hide it.

It nearly pulled her thoughts from the sword guy, though. Not quite. It was too intense, her vision of him. Of course, as always, her thoughts made him far more intriguing than he would be if she got to know him, if she knew what he did on a daily basis. She always did. She always fantasized men into more than they were and the reality, when it whacked her in the face, always knocked her over.

So this time it wouldn't. This time she would enjoy her fantasy and never meet him. Her fantasies were always kick-ass. Their reality couldn't ever compare. She didn't ever expect it to compare, unlike a lot of naive women who thought they could have a fantasy man in real life.

Caroline hobbled to the shower and turned it as hot as it would go. At least she could separate fantasy from reality. At least she learned from her earlier mistakes. That was more than many women did. They just kept on looking for Mr. Perfect who would never exist.

Let them. If that's what got them through their days, let them have at it. She would find something more real, something temporary and fleeting and passionate ... and then she'd move on first.

Not with Mr. Big Sword. Him, she would not meet. She would not use and leave him. She would admire him from the shadowy distance and make him into anything she wanted and refuse to let that burst into nothing by actually meeting him. Although she did have to wonder if the control and technique he showed with his unique kind of dance might reflect his other techniques.

Of course they did. He was a fantasy. She would make him anything she pleased. He was magnificent. Big. Broad. Muscled. Controlled. Oh, so very controlled. And so very uncontrolled.

Damn. The pain couldn't even begin to distract her from that.

As a reward for unpacking through her foot screaming at her to get off of it, Caroline put on her sturdy walking shoes instead of her sandals and went out to prowl Folly Beach. It was a gorgeous day, warm but not too warm, sunny but with a few clouds here and there breaking the sun, and breezy enough to feel the ocean air wisp across her face and the back of her neck.

Her pain pills and fifteen minutes of icing her foot made it at least bearable to walk with supportive shoes, and she knew she should be home resting it, but the walls of the tiny one-bedroom apartment had closed in while she unpacked, a task she hated, and she needed to be out and about.

As was her habit by now, whenever Caroline stopped to window shop along Center Street, she raised her right foot and propped it behind her left ankle for a moment of rest. At one stop, a young girl holding the hand of a woman with half gray hair pointed and said she looked like a stork. The woman hushed her and apologized, but Caroline laughed. She was wearing coral and white, a tank top with flowing maxi skirt, so the comparison was fair. When the girl asked how she kept her balance, she said she was a ballet dancer and then wished she hadn't since the girl thought it was really cool and asked twenty questions until Caroline lied and said she had to go meet someone.

The thought of it both amused and annoyed her as she turned off Center onto Huron and parked her aching foot, and the rest of her, on the outside deck of Lost Dog Café. The name pulled her in. Maybe she'd get a dog. Good, loyal companionship, she wouldn't mind. But she'd have to move since her place didn't allow pets, so that would have to wait at least a year until her lease was up. By then, she hoped to afford something bigger and brighter.

Unable to resist the lure, Caroline ordered fruit covered pancakes and a chocolate muffin. Too many carbs, but she didn't care. Her foot was shooting prickles up into her ankle and it was going to be a long walk back to her apartment. She considered going out to the beach and working on her tan, but it would be twice the distance, and if she was going to keep working, her foot absolutely had to function. So, back to the apartment it would be, for more ice and elevation, but only after a long lingering early dinner of a high-carb breakfast.

And a stop at the wine store.

~ Seven ~

Dio rowed toward the pier. Tomorrow he could go back to work. He was tempted to go tonight, to see her. But the day had been long, too long, and he needed time alone to unwind under the stars.

He'd waited later than normal, until his mother was finally asleep through her congestion. He worried when she got sick, even a little summer cold as she called it. She told him again to find a nice girl so he'd still have someone around for him once she wasn't, someone to cook for him and to look after things for him, to talk to at night.

He told her he could cook and look after things and he'd rarely talked to a girl who held his interest enough, or agreed with his views well enough, to be worth the trouble. He only needed one for his physical needs and he could do that with women from the audience, while in costume, when they didn't know who he was.

He wouldn't again risk trying for more, not with the way things were. It wasn't worth the heartache.

Anchoring his boat to his normal spot since he wasn't interested in exploring tonight or in seeking new waters, Dio stripped out of his clothes, other than the black shorts, and picked up his sword. He started with easy warm ups, rotations, thrusts, bends that rocked his boat but only as far as it would still hold him. He knew exactly how far he could push and when he had to rein in and shorten his movements.

There was something exhilarating in taking it almost all the way to the edge and then pulling it back. It was something perverse in his nature, he expected. Or it was learned.

Either way, it was part of him. And it would drive a "nice girl" right over the edge. His mother didn't understand. She saw only his good side. She didn't know what dwelled within that would be unfair to lay on some nice girl's shoulders. He couldn't do it.

Moving farther into his routine, his exercise, his release, Dio put his full concentration on his movement, on the power, on the danger of the sword as it zipped around his body, around his head. It spiked his adrenaline, and he brought it in even closer to his body, made it more dangerous. He scanned the area on the shore, saw nothing. No one. She was in his mind's eye, only a shadow, a graceful movement, but he let himself see her the way he wanted to see her, the new girl at work, on stage, her backbends so deep her medium-length hair bent its ends onto the floor, her hip movements so fluid they looked detached from her body, like a wave rolling over the ocean, in and out, back and forth, foaming up and receding.

Dio stopped. Set his metal tip down on the wood plank seat of the boat. Dropped his head. Focused on his breathing, on the need to release his tension, on the control it took not to allow it, to savor the moment. He stood still until it waned. Until his body relaxed.

He congratulated himself on his control. Most nights, he would now go home and focus on his frustration. He was also perverse to enjoy the frustration of the unallowed release. But he enjoyed it. It took his mind off other things, off everything else. Except the girl. So far it had not taken his mind off the girl at work, or on the girl that kept coming out to the beach at night, watching him. She moved the same. It had to be the same girl. He'd never seen anyone else move quite like that.

When he'd calmed enough, he started again, warmed up quick, got into the groove quick. Swung the sword hard and fast. He got to the edge too fast. He'd wanted to enjoy the buildup longer.

He stopped. Put the tip down. Forced control. But it didn't work. The girl's face was in his thoughts. Her body. The way she moved.

Giving up on his practice before he got too distracted, Dio set the sword aside, pulled up the anchor, and rowed back to his dock. Tying the little boat, he stood on its bench seat and dove into the water to cool himself off.

He wanted a nice girl, but not too damned nice. He wanted a girl he could show himself to, be himself with. And he hadn't let himself acknowledge that in months.

He needed to see her, the trained and controlled dancer.

To calm his urges, Dio did a hard, fast front crawl out into the Atlantic, then turned back. Hauling his tired body up the ladder, he sat panting on the dock until he could make himself drive home.

~ Eight ~

Unloading the last of the hay bales from his supplier onto the old flatbed trailer, Dio thanked him and hopped into his small tractor to take them over to the stable. Sweat rolled down his neck under his shirt and from his lower back down into his jeans. As he downloaded them again, into the stable far enough they wouldn't get wet if it ever rained, Dio wished for at least a break in the humidity. Heat, he didn't mind. Normal humidity, he hardly noticed anymore. But this sweltering humidity where it was wet enough to feel nearly like rain and invaded his lungs enough it was hard to breathe, that was another story.

It would be hot backstage at the club, also. The audience area stayed well air-conditioned so they wouldn't lose customers, and nasty humid days seemed to drive up their audience earlier in the night than normal. No surprise, he supposed. After dealing with this kind of swelter during the day, it only made sense to want to unwind with cool air, cold drinks, and good entertainment.

All of it sounded good about now, as Dio gripped the ropes holding the hay bales and carried them into the stable, tossing them into a neat stack.

"All right, Titian. I hear you. You can just hold on a few minutes. I only have two hands." And tired shoulders before the day was through and he'd have to go do the second job. He needed to hire help. Dio knew it as well as his mother knew it. There were all kinds of complications that came with that, though, starting with the most obvious...

When the dog jumped up and ran, barking a warning, Dio set the bale down he'd just grabbed and wandered out to see what was bothering him. A car pulling into his drive. Why in the hell would a car be pulling in when the sign out front clearly told them not to bother?

His mask was in the house since Dio never wore it to work around the farm. Trying to decide whether to ignore them and let them go away, his mind got made up for him when his mother stepped out on the porch and greeted them. Two men. One in shirt and tie, the other in jeans and a T-shirt. Whatever they wanted, if they thought they only had an old woman to get through, they were about to find out they were mistaken.

With Estrela at his side, Dio walked up behind them, quiet enough to hear the conversation. The men stopped at the bottom of the porch, luckily for them.

"Can we come in and look around a bit?"

"Well, of course." His mother waved them up.

"Hold it." Dio stopped them and as they turned to his voice, they both took a step back. "Dog won't bite unless I tell him to." Not that it was the dog that had them worried. "What do you want?"

"Oh, Diomedes." His mother gripped the rail and came out to him, in her slippers. "Go on about your business. I was expecting them."

"For what?"

"Do I have to explain everything I do?"

"If you're inviting people into the house, yes. What's this about?"

The man in the tie warily approached and offered a hand. "You live here, as well?"

"It's my place. What do you want?"

"Yours?" He glanced at Dio's mother.

"Mine. This is my mother. She lives here, but I own it."

He handed Dio a card as he introduced himself. A realtor. "It is up for sale, is it not?"

For sale? "It is not." He clenched his jaw to keep from yelling.

"Your mother gave us a call. This gentleman is interested in the place. So maybe we could..."

"My mother has no legal right to list or sell the place. It is not for sale. Leave my property now." Dio heard her fussing at him, heard her tell the men not to be hasty, slowing their retreat. She also told them not to worry, he wasn't as gruff as he looked.

"The hell I'm not. Mom, go back inside, and if you've called anyone else, you better call and tell them to stay off my property." When the men hesitated, Dio eyed them. *"Go."* As he expected, between his size, his face, and the gruffness of his voice when he decided to make it that way, they turned tail and left in a hurry, with Estrela following down the lane to be sure.

"What do you think you're doing?" He had to force his voice to lower, although there was a part of him that wanted to be as gruff with her as he'd been with those men.

"Diomedes, this is too much work for you..."

"That's my business. Don't bring anyone else out here."

"Don't you order me around as though..."

"As though, what? I own the place? I do own the place. I pay the bills. And I do the work of running it. I'm *not* selling."

She shoved her fists against her waist, about to let him have it.

"You realize you're out here in your house slippers."

With a glance at her feet, she gave up the lecture and started fussing to herself about having to take them off on the porch and having to wash them and her feet being cold. How her feet could possibly be cold in this heat, Dio couldn't fathom. Either way, it stopped her tirade and sent her back inside.

He'd hated to do it, to remind her he owned the place, but she could not keep bringing people out here and offering to let them inside. Truly, the woman was losing whatever sense she'd had, not that she'd ever had any to spare.

Caroline heard the applause, the yells, the offers, the requests. She had to admit, now that she was used to it, this was more satisfying than ballet at least in the way the audience so fully connected to the performance. Most ballet audiences appreciated the beauty of the dance but they didn't understand it, at least not fully. They couldn't name more than one or two of the French terms used to describe what she did, if that many, and they didn't understand how many years and how much work and what kind of pain it took to get up on that stage. Night cramps in her feet and calves were often excruciating. Blisters. Spasms. And those dreaded charley horses.

She had nearly quit when she first went en Pointe because of the charley horses nearly every night, thinking she wasn't cut out for it, that her body was telling her she wasn't meant to be a ballerina. But then she overheard another dancer who'd been en Pointe for a few months complain that she couldn't practice that day because of a charley horse the night before. Caroline started to listen better. It was common. There was nothing wrong with her.

So she didn't quit.

Since then, any pain she had, she knew others had it too and if they could get through it, so could she. It was her mantra. If anyone else could do it, she could do it. She would not accept any other possibility.

She'd been far too full of herself.

But then, it did get her far. Even now, it was getting her far. Hayes was putty in her hands. He knew Caroline could walk out if she decided to walk out, and he knew she would. She knew he didn't want her to walk out.

She also knew he desperately wanted her to sleep with him.

It wouldn't happen. Not even the younger men, the ones her age or close to it, the sexy handsome mobile and virile-looking men had talked her into it. Caroline was there to dance. To strip tease, but to dance in the only professional way she now could.

Her stupid foot.

After so many years of putting up with the aches and…

It didn't matter. She wouldn't let herself dwell on it. She was dancing, with a paycheck.

And the audience did relate better to her current job. There were no fancy French names. Technique didn't matter as much as showmanship, as moving well, as shaking her hips and bending and … whatever her body felt like doing. They understood that. Anyone could do it. Anyone could stand up and move to the music in the way they felt it, in a way that made them feel desirable, at least for that moment when they danced and let themselves go. Even if they didn't feel desirable at any other time of their lives, they could when they danced while fully absorbed into a sensual song. You had to make yourself think you were sexy in order to look it. They could see she thought she was. At least when she danced, she thought she was.

As Caroline made her way backstage to wash off the overdone makeup and put a decent amount of clothes on, she was pulled to movement nearby. It was him, the man in the mask she hadn't yet seen. A closer. And my, no wonder he was a closer. In his black skin-tight trousers and black skinny vest with no shirt underneath, showing off his massive chest and arms, he was hot as hell. Even standing doing nothing, he was worth a look or two. He might even be worth a good daydream. He was tall, a whole head taller than she was, as best guess. And she wasn't short, at 5'7".

From the distance, his hair looked nearly as black as his clothes. His thin stretchy mask was also black, like the Lone Ranger except it covered more. It covered far too much of his face, in a diagonal rather than straight across. One side of his jaw showed and it was a beautiful strong swarthy jaw. Half of his forehead on the other side showed youth but not too much youth and strength and ... and she wanted to see the rest.

Of his face. Caroline told herself it was the rest of his face she wanted to see.

He turned and caught her staring.

She didn't look away. She'd taught herself long ago that if she admired a man enough to stare, she could let him know she did. He was too far away to see his eye color, but close enough to see he didn't pull away, either. He skimmed her with a slight tilt of the head, in appreciation. She knew the look.

Caroline grinned and continued her path. She would dress quick, skip washing off the makeup, and get back out to where she could see his act, see whatever it was he had to show off other than his body.

She guessed his body was about it, and enough.

Dio forced himself to breathe again. She smiled at him. Teased. And walked away.

He wanted to say the hell with the show, his act, and follow her, ask her for coffee or... He nearly laughed. Coffee. Right. Like he was just any guy who could ask a girl to coffee, and like she was a regular girl who would accept just to see if it was worth it.

He wasn't. Neither was she.

On the other hand, maybe that would make it work.

Chastising himself, Dio forced himself to put it out of his mind and went to get set for his appearance. He was only a farmer with a secret double life. Nothing for her to see. Nothing for her to want.

One of the other girls stroked a hand down his shoulder and arm as he waited to go on. He didn't remember her name. He'd told her before he didn't do it with coworkers but he repeated it in case she forgot.

"This is my last night. I have another gig. So how about tomorrow night? Wanna get together tomorrow night?"

"No. But good luck to you." He turned back and watched the current girl perform with her baton. She wasn't a good baton twirler. The moves were basic. But she was a good tease, which part explained how she was so late in the night's line up. Mostly it was because she gave in to Hayes whenever he wanted company.

Dio found himself wondering if the new girl would.

Lina. Her name was Lina. And he let himself think she wouldn't. She had attitude. She had plenty of self-respect. Regardless of her job, she did, and he could see it. So did he. He understood it. The baton girl didn't. She was an easy target.

He realized the girl on her last night at the job was still talking to him, still touching him. It was slightly disconcerting that he hadn't noticed either. He brushed her off, said he had to focus on his act, although he already knew tonight's act would be on the simple side.

Dio had different routines for different nights, for what he felt up to each night. Lina had thrown him, so tonight would be a simple night. He couldn't afford to mess up. The last thing he needed was one more hurdle he gave himself.

Caroline found a spot behind a curtain close enough to the stage to be able to see the guy well. Sandy stood with her, to see Caroline's reaction, so she said. Orange girl had hyped this guy so much, Caroline nearly wasn't interested any longer. She hated hype. She avoided anything too hyped. Books, movies, music. Didn't matter. She hated it.

When his music started, she considered leaving, letting her imagination make it better than she assumed it would be. An old song. He was using an old song, from the same era as Lita Ford,

Caroline assumed, by the sound of it. Was that his normal music? No one else in the club used Eighties music. It was all new stuff. Was he mocking her choice..?

A flash of a sword made her gasp.

He was on stage. Her Mr. Big Sword. It was him. How could she not have recognized him? She heard Sandy speak at her side but she couldn't hear the words and she didn't want to hear the words. He was there. She'd grinned at him, stared, teased.

It wasn't supposed to work that way. She was supposed to be able to stalk him at the beach whenever she could get there and enjoy who she thought he was and not have to find out she was wrong. Caroline supposed she still could. She didn't have to talk to him.

Damn was he good. She'd seen him do more complex moves on his little rowboat and yet seeing this close up with full light made it ... more intense, more sexy, more ... just more. And this song. At the chorus, she recognized it: *Talk Dirty To Me*. She didn't know who sang it. She didn't care, either.

Caroline walked away.

It was time to go home. She couldn't do this.

Dio dressed fast and rushed out the door. Maybe she was still around. He could say hello, ask how the job was going. Welcome her to the club. That would be innocent enough. He just wanted to speak to her. He wanted her to speak to him. Even just once.

"Who are you looking for, sweetie?" Sandy sidled up against him.

"Good night, Sandy."

"The new girl left during your act. Guess she wasn't impressed."

He turned to her and wondered if she was being truthful.

"Some girls just can't handle dangerous weapons. Their loss. Me? I think they're extremely hot. I like a guy who can defend me."

"I have to head out."

"Aw Dio, one of these nights you'll give in to me."

Not a chance in hell. He kept himself from saying it as he walked away to his truck. No sign of her in the parking lot, either. She hadn't wasted any time leaving.

~ Nine ~

She called off?

Dio paced backstage while Hayes ranted. Sandy assured him it was fine, she'd do a double set. Hayes gave in and let her do it, since it was Sunday and she'd be "good enough" for the smaller crowd.

Lina called off. And she left early during his set the night before.

But she'd smiled at him.

Maybe Sandy was right. Maybe it was the sword she didn't like, didn't approve of. A peacenik type. Dio had a hard time believing it, not that he'd seen her long enough to know. Not that he'd talked to her. What made him think he would know what type she was?

It was only frustration. A broken fence section on the farm, escaped sheep he had to rustle back in, minus one he couldn't find, and his mother was coughing. Too hard. She said she was fine and he should go on to work and not worry about her, or not work and go somewhere he could find a nice girl.

Maybe she'd agree, Lina, if he asked, to act like a nice girl interested in him for his mother's sake. Right. Huge problem with that. He couldn't wear his costume at home. His mother already bitched that he let women leer at him because of his skill. If she knew he was only half dressed at the time, in thin black stretch pants that left little to the imagination, that he teased and flirted while he kept the sword swirling, she would have a heart attack.

And he couldn't let Lina see him as he was.

He was too vain, his mother said. He was being ridiculous. An actual nice girl wouldn't care. Problem was, he'd tried. He knew better. He would not accept a girl who would take him out of sympathy or because she was that desperate. He'd make do with club patrons forever first. The whole thing was frustrating as hell. Dio was just frustrated, all the way around.

He needed to watch Lina dance. He'd told himself during the hellish day that it didn't matter, he only had to get through the day so he could go to his night job and watch her dance.

And she'd called off.

Lina walked along the beach with her arms crossed in front of her stomach.

He'd ruined it. He was only a strip club side show for the few women in the audience who didn't really appreciate what he did, who only wanted to leer at him. The way she had. But different. She respected his skill. She watched the ebb and flow of his arm muscles, his abdominal muscles. She watched his face, what she could see of it, the concentration. Along with her enjoyment of his physical attributes, Caroline respected the work and practice it took to get to where he was, to the level of skill he had.

And he threw it away on drunk women at the strip club.

Like she was one to talk. What was she doing?

Dio. Sandy called him Dio. And now he had a name, too. He was too human, too real. She didn't want him to be real. Real ruined everything.

Dio. Like the band? The *Holy Diver* band? Was that where he got his stage name? If so, why did he not use the music? She made Hayes allow her own music from the beginning. Surely he could do the same. Why Eighties? She only used it because Charlie had played it during her audition. Why had he played that instead of something more modern? Charlie was an old guy, probably in his seventies. It wasn't his era. It was ... Hayes's era, according to how old he looked. Did Dio let Hayes choose his music? Could be. It wasn't right for him. He needed ... more dangerous music. Like ... the *Last of the Mohicans* soundtrack, which Caroline had always wanted to dance to.

She'd had thoughts of finding the right background and a good videographer and composing a whole DVD of dance to that soundtrack. Not that she could afford it, or that anyone would want it. Although, with Dio added, maybe they would. A nice contrast combination that would be... Exquisite. They could do it together, with his sword work and her ballet.

Except he used Eighties music. Caroline was right. Her thoughts of him, of who he might be inside, were better than reality. The infamous Dio was more showman than fighter.

Too much reality. It was all blown out of the water now.

Lina took her shoes off and treaded along where the waves could brush up on her feet. He'd ruined it. She called off to spend the day at the beach, to brush it off, to swim and sun and swim more and maybe to talk to someone. She hadn't done any of it. She'd walked along the shore. She sat on the pier and looked out. She couldn't get in the water.

Allowing the waves to splash her feet was the most she could make herself do.

He ruined it. Typical man.

~ *Ten* ~

Caroline stretched her arms over her head and debated whether to get up. It was after ten. She wouldn't normally let herself sleep so late, but she had nowhere to be, during the day, or tonight. Maybe she would try to change her schedule to work only on the four days he didn't. But she supposed that wouldn't be the way to move up in the business, to get a raise. A different career might be an option. Anything else. Anything that didn't relate to dance, that didn't make her mourn what she should still have. Caroline supposed that wasn't possible. Ballet was in her soul. It always would be. She's already learned the hard way she couldn't escape from herself.

She could get away from him, though. From Dio. Caroline adored his name, fake as she expected it was.

Maybe she would spend the day hunting for a new job. A day job would allow her the time at night to wander the beach and watch him from a distance. And it wouldn't make her foot ache. At least if she found the right job, it wouldn't. It likely left admin work as her only option.

With a sigh, Caroline rolled out of bed and gave herself a moment to let her foot realize she would put weight on it soon. She had to start slow, so it wouldn't crumple out from underneath her. Sitting on the edge of her bed, she put some weight on it, raised to her toes, felt the sharp pain and rolled back down to flat, pressed the ball into the floor and gritted her teeth, then returned it to flat. Waited. Got up carefully. Tested it.

She was glad it held today. More often than not now that she'd started to dance again, it didn't. She had to sit down, wait longer, massage it, try to convince the foot it was fine.

Making it to the top would be a hell of a lot harder if her foot refused to cooperate, but maybe she could change her routine, figure out a way around the thing.

"There you are."

The lamb bleated at Dio from where it lay down a deep ravine, but it didn't get up. Probably injured. Dio hoped it wasn't bad.

Hooking his rope around a nearby tree, he made his way down to the little beast and checked out his legs. "Come on, stand up now." He tried to help it up. It stood, started to walk, sat again. Not a bad injury, he figured, since it had the ability to walk but not the interest.

Dio scanned the ravine from his new angle. Getting the creature back up on solid ground wouldn't be easy. Good thing it was a young creature. "Up." He pushed it to its feet, shoved his head beneath the beast's underside, and wrapped the thing over his shoulders. Good thing Dio had big shoulders. They occasionally were put to better use than to let women leer.

With the extra length of rope, he tied the legs together, careful with the one the lamb favored, and made his way back to the rope around the tree. He had to keep one hand on the animal since the thing fidgeted and bleated in his ear. Stupid creature. Dio had half a thought to just leave it be if it wanted to be so obstinate.

He wouldn't, of course.

Wrapping the tree-held rope around his arm several times, he started up the hill, pulling himself with the one hand and gripping the lamb's wool at his neck in the other, as though it wasn't hot enough without adding a thick wool scarf, one with body heat added.

At the top, he dropped to his knees and wrapped the rope over the creature's neck. It sat again. Dio caught his breath and gave his muscles time to relax. He pulled the leather work gloves off to survey his palm where the rope bit into it. Red but otherwise fine. If not for the foresight to wear his gloves when he went to hunt for the little beast, it would have been blistered. Again. It happened. Made it hard to use his sword well that way. But he'd done it.

He tried again to get the creature to stand. It took several steps then sat again. With a heavy sigh, Dio got it back to its feet and shoved the thing over his shoulders. It was easier to keep it still with the rope around its neck and its legs. Still, it was a long walk back to the fenced pasture.

Damn good thing it wasn't a work night. Dio was spent by the time he got back and put the lamb in a separate stall, small enough it wouldn't run around, and away from the others so they wouldn't bother him. He'd have to wrap the leg and keep an eye on the thing and hope it would heal. It was young. It didn't look badly hurt. He'd give it a couple of days and watch a bit before calling a vet.

"All right, Estrela." Dio scratched the dog's ears. "I'm done for the day. Keep watch over them for me."

Caroline should have taken her car. She'd spent a couple of hours wandering Folly Beach looking for other job opportunities. A cashier position was open, but standing so long would be as hard on her foot as stripping and it paid far less. She wouldn't see Dio there, though. Or if she did, he'd be dressed in regular clothes and without the mask, she assumed, so she might not know him.

She rolled her eyes at herself. She would know him.

When her stomach growled, she grabbed a sandwich and walked down to the Pirate Cove playground to relax on the wood bench around the big oak tree. It was a school day, she realized, which explained so few kids on the premises. A couple of little ones were there with their mothers but they were too small to climb up inside the big white and blue play boat. They did crawl through the little tunnel and run around in a half circle to crawl through again from the same side like Follow The Leader. Their mothers talked to each other. Old friends, she assumed. She could almost see herself someday standing and chatting with a friend while her kid ran up in the play boat and climbed across the horizontal ladder.

She rolled her eyes at herself again. She was more suited to be a pirate's wench than a mommy.

With her sandwich gone and her foot slightly rested, she got up to wander along the murals that depicted Charleston's pirate history. When she was young, she used to dream of being a pirate, of living out in the water on a huge ship. Instead, she became a ballerina. At this point, she wasn't sure there was a hell of a lot of difference. Pirates looked out for themselves first while plundering for booty, didn't they? If they had to stab a mate in the back to get a leg up, they'd do it, as far as she knew about pirates. The movies. Which, of course, were only movies, some guy's imagination mixed with old stories which may or may not have been spread truthfully.

She expected the stories were more story than truth, in which case, who knew the truth? Maybe pirates were less cutthroat than dancers, at least than some of the dancers, the "too ambitious" dancers such as herself.

Charleston. She could skip job hunting in Folly Beach and drive into Charleston. It would mean she'd have to keep driving every day and she wasn't sure how long her old car would allow that, but the opportunities would be better. Maybe she'd go in and finally visit the Porgy House as she always thought of doing and job hunt while she was there.

Fat chance she would run into Dio in Charleston other than at work.

After the drive into Summerville and back for his monthly grocery supply restocking, Dio was half glad he didn't have to work tonight, but only half. Lina worked tonight. He could go in and... No. He couldn't, not without his costume, and he was too easy to spot in costume.

He checked on his mom and was disheartened to hear her cough was worse. The time she spent each day in bed to "regain her strength" hadn't worked. He assured her the trip was fine, argued again that he did not want to shop in Charleston instead because it was too close to home and work, and said he picked up more of her white tea with raspberry and would go put the water on to simmer.

The only local place he stopped was a farm down the road where they already knew him and where few others shopped and those few others were used to him. He often picked up their homemade honey and jam along with the milk, cheese, and homemade bread they stocked in their little convenience store. His mother used to do the canning and bread making. Homemade bread fresh from the oven was one of Dio's most favorite things, but buying it from the neighbors was nearly as good.

As the tea simmered, Dio put the rest of the groceries away and added a large teaspoon of honey to a delicate tea cup, the only kind his mother would use. Adding the tea, he stirred it well and took it to her.

"Diomedes, dear. Give me a hand up, if you would. And sit with me to tell me about your day."

She coughed as he helped her sit and propped a pillow behind her back. It was a deep rattling cough. He would have to call the doctor in. She'd told him every day not to bother, it would only cost money they didn't need to spend on a little cough, and that if it was time, it was time and he shouldn't worry about it.

Easy for her to say, he supposed. She wouldn't be the one left with a farm to run alone. Speaking of which, he had work to do. But it would have to wait. Cleo Troy rarely felt like sitting and talking. Generally, if she was awake, she was up trying to do something or other, whether or not it needed doing.

Dio had always appreciated her energy. There were many things he didn't appreciate about his mother, but she at least always kept him on his toes.

~ *Eleven* ~

On her way in to Charleston, her objective changed. Because of a song. Switching between stations as she always did, Caroline stopped at a Caribbean-style tune. About a coconut. And a lime. The words made no sense whatsoever, but she loved the beat, the simplicity, and a hidden sensuality in the bass line. So, instead of job hunting, she decided to shop for a costume that would match the song.

She stood backstage wearing a tan bikini topped with a fake grass skirt and bright multi-colored lei. She'd even found a coconut bra to go over the bikini and an ankle bracelet made of shells. The other girls either rolled their eyes or laughed at the cliché costume, but they wouldn't be laughing later.

Letting her music start before she went on, she strutted in to the beat, walking, but swinging her hips more as she went, adding shoulders, then arms. At the front of the stage just out of reach of the guys lining it, she turned circles like a hula dancer. She'd taught herself years ago how to move her hips like they did. As the music got faster, she revved up the sensuality of her movements, taking off the coconut bra and getting plenty of whistles and hoots.

And then she did three pirouettes, ten fouette turns, and three more pirouettes. Smoothly, she switched back into the hula and then strutted off the stage opposite the way she'd come on, letting her movements decrease as the audience reaction went from surprised silence to loud applause and whistles.

"That was really cool." Sandy's eyes were wide. "Hayes will hate it, of course, but it was cool. How did you do that?"

"Years of practice." And she could have done it better in her toe shoes and what used to be her stronger foot. Caroline had easily done five pirouettes and thirty-two fouettes back when.

"What in the hell was that?"

When Hayes moved in front of her, she swerved around him heading toward the dressing room. "The coconut song. I think it's just called *Coconut*, though."

"I'm not talking about the music." He grabbed her arm.

Yanking away from him, she met his glare. "*Don't* touch me like that again."

"Calm down. I didn't hurt you. I told you I don't want that kind of dance in my club."

"So fire me. I am what I am." She waited, refusing to back away from his warning. It was bluster, nothing more.

His gaze dropped down her body. "Tell you what. Take off more and you can dance any damn way you please. Without me jumping down your throat. Might even move you to a later spot."

"Thought you didn't want that kind of dance."

"Do it half naked and it's a whole different thing, isn't it? Otherwise, keep it out of my club."

"I read my contract, Hayes. I don't have to take my top off. And there's nothing in it that says what kind of dance I have to do. So you might as well stay off my back. Fire me or leave me the hell alone." Tossing her head, she went back to the dressing room, pulled off the grass skirt, and pulled her clothes on over the bikini.

Part of her had been hoping to be fired. She knew she'd never get a closing spot or the raise she wanted if she didn't give in to him and strip farther. She had yet decide if she wanted it quite that bad. It wouldn't be much different, as skimpy as her bikini was. Still, her nipples were covered. Maybe she would practice without them covered, in her own apartment, and think about it.

Dio stopped to catch his breath. He didn't see her. It was plenty late enough that if she was coming, she would be there.

He'd caught her act. Those turns she'd done were outstanding, so beautiful. He heard Hayes bitch at her, but he also heard the audience reaction. They'd loved it. It was something of a shock value, going from the casual and slightly raunchy moves matching the song – and no one would convince him that song didn't have hidden raunchy elements – to such elegance and back again without effort. It showed two very different sides of her and echoed his own two very different personas.

Hayes wouldn't fire her. It was a bluff to get her to show more.

Dio vacillated between hoping she would for his own sake and hoping she wouldn't for her sake, because she didn't need to show more. She was beautiful, tasteful but with those necessary raunchy elements, fiery as all hell but defensive, showing a side that could easily get hurt if she allowed, which she obviously had no intention of allowing. It would be hard to break through her guarded wall.

He understood that wall. Plenty well.

And he very much wanted her to show up on the beach tonight.

With a check of the time, he shook his head, set the sword down, and pulled in the anchor to head back home.

Caroline had stayed for his act, but dressed in her street clothes and hidden at the back of the club at the bar. With her makeup washed off and her hair in a ponytail with a baseball cap over part of her face, no one recognized her. A couple of women were talking about Dio as he performed, and one of them talked as though she knew how he performed off-stage, as well. The other one was trying to decide whether to believe she actually knew.

With the thought of telling the woman it was highly tacky to kiss and tell, she had bit her tongue. She'd wanted to be only part of the audience, to watch him.

He'd used a Nickelback song, only a few days after she had. She hadn't seen him that night. From what she heard, he often came just before his own act and left as soon as he was done. Had he been there? Coincidence, maybe, since many of their songs lent themselves well to the mood of the club. She'd chosen *Shakin' Hands* as a bit of a slam to those looking down on her while they were there watching her show. An odd concept. It was perfectly fine to watch girls strip, but somehow, the one stripping was automatically a lesser being, or less moral. Like all the men out there that made a habit of searching for porn online, usually in secret, and then ranted about how degrading it was for a woman to take nude photos, even tasteful nude photos.

Some people just couldn't see their own faults or judgment errors if you hit them right in the kisser with them.

Caroline at least recognized her faults, her insecurities, her possible lack of moral aptitude. She didn't care much about them, but she did recognize them.

Dio at least hadn't used the same song. *Feeling Way Too Damned Good* was one of her favorites, and the one he used. A few days after she used their music. Very odd coincidence.

She had halfway considered going out to the beach to see if he was there, but to what end? It was ruined. She'd met him, knew his name, worked with him. Too close.

Instead, she went home and showered and iced her foot so she could make it through the next night's show.

Twelve

Dio wasn't at all sure what Lina would think about him again grabbing an artist she'd used. He meant it as a way to get her attention, since when she did see him at the club, she only gave him the barest acknowledgment. He'd thought she missed it since they said she left as soon as she was done, but the bartender let him know she stayed. Not only had she stayed, but she watched him, not like the other women in the club, but seriously watched his moves.

He hadn't seen her since Tuesday, three days ago, but her act stayed in his thoughts while he was hauling hay, feeding the animals, exercising them, training them, cleaning pens, checking on the injured lamb's leg that was coming along fine. He thought of her through all of it. The strong and delicate turns. The fire. The attitude, both on stage and off, while letting Hayes know who was in charge. The smile she'd given him.

Although he was late into the house to clean up before work since the big fan in the sheep's shed had stopped working and had to be jerry-rigged until he could fix it better, and he had to rush through dinner as his mother complained about him rushing through dinner, Dio got there in time to catch her act again. She'd been moved after Sandy, giving her a better time slot, closer to his own with only one act between them.

Sandy threw him a look as she came off stage, catching him watch Lina waiting to go on. With a roll of her eyes, Sandy turned her chin away from Dio, a purposeful snub, and sauntered down the hall, pouting.

Lina caught his eyes, just for a moment, and headed out to her music. Unable to refuse a chuckle as he recognized the song, Dio figured it was her "check" to his move. Poison. *Cry Tough*. She'd returned the favor and grabbed a band he used, but a different song. A good song for her. She was also calling Hayes's bluff since she was mixing more ballet moves in than she had last time, but also with plenty of suggestive moves using the poles. Her costume matched the song with a black leather-look halter and wrap-around mini skirt that she took off halfway through to reveal a strappy bikini bottom.

His gut tightened when she played with the halter. A few men in the crowd yelled at her to take it off. Again, he wished she would and then again, wished she wouldn't. Possessiveness and no more than that. He had no right in the world to feel that way, but the more she teased, the more he wished she wouldn't.

He wasn't at all sure Lina even knew whether or not she would. Maybe it was more debate than tease.

She ended with a running jump that fell into a turning collapse onto the floor, her head tucked under an arm. Still covered. He felt a huge sigh of relief and chastised himself for it, but when she came off stage and again caught his eyes, he gave her a light nod.

Caroline was trying hard not to let the pain show as she made her way off stage catching her breath. And he nodded at her with a slight grin on his face, or was it a smirk? An amused smirk or a making fun of her smirk?

Amused. He'd looked amused. And she was clenching her jaw in pain and forcing herself to walk normally so it wouldn't show. He would think...

What did it matter what he thought? It was only a game they were playing, one that couldn't go past the game. She could elevate it. Still, it would only be an elevated game.

Grabbing a chair just off stage, she didn't bother to go change. Only one act before Dio's. She'd pretend to watch the dark red woman and stay for his.

Cowboy had ditched his lasso and his costume and pulled a chair close beside her. "So what's up with that turning stuff?"

"Turning stuff?"

"You know what I mean. What's your story, Lina?" He was facing her and bent to prop his elbows on his knees, looking up at her. Her face, so far.

"Not worth telling."

He laughed. "I'd bet damned near anything that ain't true."

She shrugged and looked out at the red woman shaking her tired hips. Lina considered asking if he knew why she was still doing this at her age, but that was crossing a line she would not cross. They were coworkers. Nothing more. All of them.

"The old girl needs to retire. She's slipping." Cowboy shook his head and pulled them back from the stage. "If you don't want to talk, how about going with me to get a drink since we're both done for the night?"

"Thank you, but no."

A large hand slid to her leg. "Come on, Lina. Just a drink. We all hang out now and then. You're the only one who hasn't. Well, and Dio, but then he's an odd bird all around."

Lina picked up his hand and moved her legs farther away. "I guess I'm an odd bird, too, because I'm not interested in making friends."

"At work, you mean."

"I mean anywhere. But thanks for asking. Now if you don't mind, kindly keep your hands to yourself." She caught a stare in the short distance. Dio. Watching her talk with Cowboy. Or watching Cowboy. Until he gave up and left and Dio caught his eyes, also. A warning?

Something was definitely going on between them.

Caroline wasn't sure Dio wouldn't come over to talk, except that his music started. His jaw tightened and he started out to the stage, but he hesitated, turned back, and came straight to her.

Leaning so his mouth was close to her ear, his sword tip resting on the floor in front of her legs, he spoke barely over the music. "Be careful with him unless you like rough play." He caught her eyes briefly as he straightened and went back to the curtain leading to the stage.

When he glanced back, she gave him a nod of thanks.

His music. Caroline knew the voice, but not the song. Who was it? She thought back to singers she'd used recently, trying to match the voice, while she watched his act.

The coconut song singer. Harry Nilsson. Had to be. This one was something about fire and making "each other happy," with the same sensual-funky feel. She had half a thought of jumping on stage with him, adding funky dance moves to accent his sword work. Hayes might yell, but she didn't care a bit about that. Her foot hurt already, though. And she might throw him, Dio, and make him hurt himself with that heavy sword.

She could not risk that.

And she did not want to risk letting him talk to her when he was done. So she left.

Dio searched for her. She wasn't still on the chair just off stage. She wasn't in the hall back by the dressing rooms. Although he knew he shouldn't have, he asked one of the girls if she was in the dressing room. She wasn't. And not in the parking lot.

She'd left. Damn. He wanted to say more, to explain what he didn't have time to say earlier. She could be thinking a hundred different things about now. Most of all, he hoped like all hell she hadn't been sparked by what he told her and went to find the sadist.

Not likely, he supposed, after she'd given him that nod that looked like a thank you. But why did she leave after staying to watch his act? Dio had to assume it was his act that made her stay and not Greta who'd gone on after Lina and ahead of him. Unless she was trying to learn from the older girls. He hoped that wasn't the case. He liked Lina's own style.

By the time she got home, Lina wished she'd stayed. Too many questions. First in her mind was why he warned her about Cowboy. How did he know? Was it a test? Was he feeling as possessive about her as she was about him? Why?

Something about the guy with the massive chest and arms, in a black mask, carrying a large sword warning her about someone else being dangerous hit Caroline as rather absurd. Still, his act was an act. She knew very well that the inside was almost always different than the outside.

She should have stayed just long enough to ask why he'd warned her, just to see how he would answer. Maybe she would tomorrow. Maybe she'd even ask him if he wanted to go for a drink after work.

Stop right there, Lina. Too close. Too far. Flirt at work and leave it at that.

Well, and maybe on the beach, also.

Thirteen

Caroline knew he saw her. He looked her direction, and his movements paused as though he wanted to... But why would he? The way he was built, the talent he had, the amount of girls trying to get to him after each show at the club ... why would he want her? A washed up ballerina turned stripper.

And yet he watched her.

She had not waited after his show Saturday to talk to him. She'd chickened out. She had straight-forward chickened out and ran, just before he left stage. Then she regretted it. Caroline Corinth was not a chicken. Apparently, Lina from New York was, however, at least to an extent.

He had again used her music. Lita Ford. *Shot of Poison.* A message? Caroline knew it could be. And she wanted to talk to him. She hadn't seen him since then, Saturday night, five days ago. If he'd come out to the beach in his boat since then, she didn't know. By the time she got off work every night now, she was in too much pain to walk to the beach, or even from her car down to his part of the beach.

Today, she'd been off. After much of a day of lazing in the sun, she'd returned to shower and have a homemade buffalo chicken salad with a ton of veggies, and then made her way back to the beach via Lost Dog Café where she sat outside and enjoyed a soft pretzel and a couple of glasses of wine before ordering a coffee to go, with an espresso shot added.

She'd gone directly to the spot where she first saw him, propped herself in the sand, and watched dusk settle in. Now, it was dark and she watched Dio.

Slowly, he returned to his dangerous dance. Slow easy graceful gyrations. Large round sensual circles of flashing sword. She treaded closer, felt the water splash her ankles. It did nothing to cool the heat she felt as he quickened his pace, his face still directed her way, or she let herself think it was. She hadn't seen him in nearly a week and was amazed by how she'd missed just looking at him, being almost in his

　　　　　　　　　　Ella M. Kaye

presence.

She walked in farther. His thrusts softened.

Caroline pulled her sarong up away from her thighs where it barely covered her bikini, felt the wet chill on her knees. His sword made slow circles in front of his body. She waded farther until the water splashed her inner thighs. Undeterred by the cold soft waves, she continued, and pulled the sarong all the way off to drape around her neck.

He stopped.

She went farther.

He set the sword down and crouched to the bottom of the boat.

She was now waist deep and the water chilled her, contrasted with the warmth he'd brought out from her. He dipped his head, pulled something over it. His mask. From his costume. Why?

Edging in slowly, cautious of drop off points in the mossy slimy shifting sand below her feet, Caroline let the water circle her rib cage and stopped. Called check. She wasn't sure whether she wanted him to call check mate or retreat. He was beautiful. He was sensually exotically madly beautiful. She didn't want to lose that image.

He pulled up the anchor and picked up the oars.

She held still.

Slowly, he dipped the oars into the water.

Hers heart stilled as she waited to see whether he would ebb or flow, come or leave, accept her challenge or retreat.

He stroked lightly. The boat moved toward her.

Moonlight lit his shoulders as they surged with his movement. He was close enough now she would be able to see his face if it wasn't covered. She wished it wasn't. She wanted to see him. She wanted to see all of him.

He stopped.

The cold of the water sank into her flesh, deep down into her body. "So close and yet so far." She called out to him.

"Why do you keep leaving the club before I'm done?"

"Fear."

"I won't hurt you."

"Hurt? Or harm? Two different things."

"I don't want to do either."

"What is it you want?"

"Hard to say."

Caroline thought that might be the most honest answer she had ever heard in her life.

He held still. Studied her.

"I love boats." She added to the challenge.

"I love dancers."

"Strippers, you mean?"

"No. I mean dancers. What they do with it, I don't much care."

She grinned. "Come this way farther. My sarong will get wet if I come all the way to you."

"My boat will hit bottom if I come all the way to you."

She took a couple more steps until the water was just below her breasts, unwrapped the sarong, and held it over her head. With both hands. As though in surrender mode.

Maybe she was.

He rowed closer.

She took a couple more steps. The water splashed up onto her breasts.

He edged toward her, enough she could nearly reach the boat, but not quite. "I'll ground myself if I go in farther."

"I guess that's the end of our game then, isn't it?"

"Do you want it to be?"

"I don't want my sarong wet. I need it to wrap in for the walk home."

"You live close."

"Yes. Why did you put your mask on when I walked toward you?"

"Part of the game. Why do you keep coming out here?"

"Curiosity."

"About my sword."

"Yes. About your sword. And the way you use it. But my arms are getting tired so I'll have to call it a night." She stepped backward.

"Lina." He threw the anchor, moved to the front of his boat, and stuck his sword out, above the water, close enough she could touch it if she dared. "Wrap your sarong around it and I'll bring it into the boat."

Check mate. He'd called it.

She hesitated. How would she get it back out again dry? Did she want this risk? She knew nothing of him. She wanted to know nothing of him. And yet... "Why did you warn me about Cowboy?"

"Because I didn't figure you'd be interested in his kind of games."

"Am I the first one you've warned?"

"No."

"Did you bring the other girls into your boat after you warned them?"

"No. No one else has been invited into my boat, Lina."

"Why me?"

His chest rose and fell hard. "Curiosity."

Definite check mate. Fine. Lina stepped out close enough to his sword to wrap the sarong so it wouldn't fall off.

He pulled it in, unwrapped it carefully so he wouldn't cut the delicate fabric, and reached out a hand. "Coming in?"

"Sure you have room for me? It's a small boat."

"Not nearly as small as it seems from out there."

Lina figured if she was going to do it, she should do it all the way. She dove under the water and came up right beside him. Her hair was down and she had to brush it out of her face. He offered his arms. It was an awkward way to get on a boat, with the thing lilting deeply to one side, but they managed it without capsizing.

He handed her a towel as she sat on the wood plank seat facing him. So far he sat still and respected the distance. She supposed that was a good sign. She wrapped the towel around her hair and then unwrapped it to mop her body. Slowly. Seductively, she hoped. She pressed it against her breasts, lowered it to her stomach, ran it over her legs, and rested it on her lap. He followed every movement but he still held his distance.

The light she'd noticed reflecting off his sword was a small lantern. It gave his covered face an eerie look.

"Is Dio your real name or a stage name?"

"Is Lina your real name?"

"Right. Guess it doesn't matter and best to leave it alone."

He grinned. Damn, he had a beautiful grin. "You should know I never date coworkers."

Date?

"Or do anything else with them, either."

"Ah. Then why did you ask me to your boat?"

"To talk. Why are you stripping when you're more trained than that?"

Caroline faltered. She had started asking questions. It was her own fault. "I needed a different challenge?"

"Is that why?"

"No. I needed a job and mundane about kills me."

He grinned again. "That, I believe. I am in awe of you." He held her gaze. Still, he didn't move.

"Why?"

"I have no idea."

She laughed. "Well, I have to love the honesty."

"And you? Why are you here on the beach so often at night?"

"You mean why am I watching you here on the beach so often at night?"

"That, too."

"I am in awe of you. Of your skill."

"With the sword."

"Yes." She leaned forward. "And I enjoy looking at your body."

His chest expanded, his shoulders pulled back. "Mind if I row out again? I won't go farther than you want. Tell me to stop."

"Dio. I want you to go farther out. Away from sight of anyone on the beach. And I want like all hell for you to break your do nothing with coworkers rule. And no, I have no idea why I want that. I usually don't care too much about that whatsoever."

"Don't you? Why not?"

She shrugged. "It's just a thing, not that big a deal. So far that's been true, anyway."

"Is that so?" He watched her as he pulled the little boat back away from the beach, away from the lights of the pier, out into the ocean. "Just so you know, this mask always stays on when I'm with a woman. It's part of the act. Don't expect otherwise."

She grinned and reached back to untie the top of her bikini at her neck. "A man of mystery. That works fine for me. I don't want more than just this, anyway." She let it fall to her stomach. When he stopped, she untied the bottom and dropped the top half of her bikini to the side.

"You never go that far at work."

"No. Not yet."

"Yet?"

"I'm only paid as a beginner so far. That's all they get until Hayes wants to pony up better."

"Careful with him, too. Most of the girls only get as far as they do because..."

"I know. Not me."

"You haven't..."

"With Hayes? Not a chance in hell. Or the others, including patrons. It's not going to happen. Not this time."

Dio scanned her slowly. "They said you were new to performing. You're not."

"Never said I was. They can say what they want."

He pulled in the oars and lay them along the sides of the small boat which wasn't as small as it looked from the outside. "One condition."

"Okay."

"No one at work finds out."

"Of course not. I don't want that any more than you do."

"Why?"

"Easy. When you give yourself that reputation, you're taken less seriously. I expect to be taken seriously. And I don't want the jerk-wads who work there to expect I'll do it with them just because I did it with you."

"Understood."

She watched him throw the anchor overboard and return to her eyes. Waiting. "Why don't you do it with coworkers?"

"I don't want them to think I'm one of them."

"Aren't you?"

"No. Did you think I was?"

"No. I'm not either. But then, they all probably think the same thing about the rest of us. Don't you expect?"

"Maybe. Can you stand up in a boat without throwing us overboard?"

"I'm a dancer, Dio. I'm good at balance."

"Right. Come here." He stood. The boat swayed.

Lina made him wait. She would obey the order, but she would make him wait first. A show of power. When she stood, she stood slowly and ran fingers up from his calf to his thigh, over the thin small black shorts to his waist, stomach, up to his smooth chest and to his shoulder. Dio stood still, very still, and allowed it. His eyes followed her movement. The rest of him remained statue still, statuesque, powerful, controlled.

She was at nearly an arm's distance and could barely see him under the moon's glow assisted by the little lantern. Still, he was beautiful. Powerful. She loved the power of his body. She loved that she could stand in front of him almost naked and play with his skin as he waited.

"Dio."

"Hm."

She made an infinity symbol across his chest with her fingers. "You haven't touched me yet." Her voice came out a whisper. She hadn't meant it to.

"You're not ready for me to touch you yet."

She paused, met his eyes. "How do you know?"

He grinned. Stayed silent.

He was right. She wasn't. She wanted to explore him first. She wanted him fully naked before he touched her. Lina had tried it before. It never worked. They were never willing to wait that long.

She decided to push it further, see how far she would get before he released his control and took her. Slowly. She wanted to make him wait.

Continuing the infinity circle, she made it smaller each time around, closer to touching him more intimately. His body stirred. Barely. His chin raised slightly. His chest expanded and contracted faster, deeper. His stomach pulled in. Yet he remained still.

"You're still not touching me." She looked into his eyes this time. Daring him. It was too dark to tell the color.

"You're still not ready."

"Hm. How do you know?"

"I'll know."

Lina wondered if he would as she moved in to kiss his bulky strong magnificent shoulder and let her hands fall to his stomach, let her tongue continue the caress where her fingers had been. His chest expanded and contracted. "Dio."

"You're still not ready."

"Hm. Are you?"

"Yes."

"You're not going to ask for what?"

"I know for what. Yes."

She grinned and let her hands slide down from his stomach to explore what she couldn't see under his black thin silky shorts. His body pulled in. His head dropped back.

"Oh, Dio. You are magnificent, aren't you? All the way head to toe."

"Lina." His voice was breathy, constrained.

"Yes?"

"You realize you're torturing me."

"And you're holding still for me because you like it."

"I will stand right here not touching you until you tell me you want it." His voice was nearly a growl, a soft sexy sweet growl.

She met his eyes. "Yes?"

"Yes."

Her stomach twinged, a good twinge, a wonderful unbelievable tight twinge. It had been so long. And she ached to tell him she wanted it. Now. But this first time would be their only first time, maybe their only time, and she wanted to let herself enjoy it just as long as she could make herself hold off.

She liked the torture of it, as well, the exquisite, beautiful, maddening torture of it, of wanting him, of not allowing it. But she could allow more.

Lina released him, let her left hand drift behind to his curve, not much of a curve, but at least he had a curve. She hated men with flat butts. She seriously hated men with flat butts. Dio's soft curve was much more sensual.

He kissed her head.

"You moved." She looked up to see the very little bit of his face that showed under his mask.

"I'm sorry."

"You want me to release you now, to free you to touch me."

"Yes."

"No." She moved her face very close to his. "Not yet, Dio." There was a sparkle in his eyes. A slight grin on his face. He was adorable. On top of sexy. And talented. And controlled. He was adorable.

She kissed his neck. Rubbed her face along his and wished the mask wasn't in her way. "Dio."

"Now?"

"No. Tell me something." She stroked a hand through his dark, thick, shiny hair. "Before I release you." She teased his lips. "Tell me ... you want me to come back again. Before..."

"Yes."

"Yes? I'm still your coworker."

"I don't care. Lina, yes. I will be here on my nights off. Come when you wish."

She kissed him. She never kissed them, her conquests. Never. She also never asked them for more than the one night. Often they came back, sometimes they came back often. She never asked.

He kissed extraordinary. Her knees buckled.

"Dio."

"You're ready for me."

"Yes."

He wrapped his arms around her and locked her in a deep kiss, pressing his body hard against hers. He took over. Fully. Slowly. Demanding. But gentle.

And he was insatiable. She found her own release twice and still he continued.

"Dio."

"Not yet." He kissed her neck. "I don't work tomorrow."

"I know."

"Will you come?"

She groaned, felt her body answer for her, answer his demanding call, his need.

"Will you come?" His voice was strained. "Lina. Answer me."

"Dio, yes. Yes, I'll come tomorrow."

He let out a roar with his release and she felt her own. His body quaked. Trembled.

"Dio." Her voice was a whisper.

He met her lips. And her eyes.

"Take off your mask for me."

"No. Not until you take yours off."

"What?"

"You know." He kissed her again, harder, deeper, softer. "You'll be here tomorrow?"

"Yes."

"Let me take you home tonight. To your door."

"No. I…"

"Lina, I won't come to you. I'll wait for you to come to me. But I don't want you to walk home now, as late as it is. As … relaxed as you are. Let me take you to your door."

She nodded.

Dio wished he had something better than his old truck to drive her home. She didn't comment. She let him hold her door and slid over to the middle beside him, her head on his shoulder as she gave him directions.

They arrived too soon. He turned it off, but she didn't move to get out. "Lina?"

"I'm not ready."

He tilted her face up and met her lips and she shifted closer, holding him tight. "Walk me in."

Walk her in? And if he ran into someone in her building in his mask and the black shorts and T-shirt with Lina in nothing but her sarong? She hadn't put the bikini back on. She wrapped the sarong under one arm, tied it on the other shoulder, and climbed in his truck that way.

He stroked hair back from her face.

"Dio, walk me in. I'm not ready to let you leave."

"As you command. But I'm not responsible if I scare your neighbors."

"They're all long in bed by now."

He opened his door and she slid out behind him. "You left your suit." It was on the seat.

"Yes." She reached up to kiss him. "I'll get it back from you later."

He would have to hide it. Under the seat. Not that his mother was ever in his truck, but in case. This, he didn't want to explain to her. And he wouldn't be able to stay long. Dawn would arrive soon. He had to be home before then.

~ *Fourteen* ~

Dio paced in the hospital hallway and turned his head away whenever anyone drew near. Still, he got stares. He wished he could have taken his mother into Columbus instead of having to rush the fifteen minutes, or what should have been fifteen minutes and turned out closer to ten, to Charleston. He didn't want to be seen in Charleston, so close to where he worked.

When he got home this morning, too late this morning since he had trouble pulling himself away from Lina, he was concerned about what his mother would say. She wasn't naive. She knew he'd been with women. Hell, he was over thirty. Barely over thirty. That didn't mean he wanted to be obvious. And it didn't mean he wanted questions about whether she was a nice girl.

Yes. She was a nice girl. A naughty nice girl. A beautiful sexy intoxicating naughty nice girl. And she said she'd be there, on the beach, tonight. She didn't want him to pick her up. She wanted to walk as she always did and meet him as though she didn't know who he was and pretend she might or might not tread out to his boat again.

An amazing naughty nice girl. Dio wanted to see how long she would last, how long she would stay with him before she insisted on seeing his face. That was usually how it ended. They would insist. He wouldn't give in. They would leave.

Once he did. He did give in. Only once. He never wanted to see that reaction again. He'd rather let them go.

But Lina...

A clearing throat took his attention. His mother's doctor.

"How is she?"

"She has pneumonia. It's going to be touch and go for a while. You might as well go on home or to work or wherever you need to go. We'll have to keep her here."

"She won't stay. I'll take her home and take care of her. Just tell me what to do."

"I don't suggest that. It could be dangerous. As I said…"

"I want to see her."

"Yes, come in. We'll talk about it more."

Dio knew this guy expected his patient to give in to his advice, but he didn't know Cleo Troy.

She was still hooked to an IV and machines beeped her vitals from where they were attached to her finger. Still, her thick gray hair was neat and she was propped up in sitting position. "Well, there you are. Come here and tell this man I'm just fine."

"You're not just fine." Dio gripped her bony, age-spotted hand. "This is punishment, isn't it? Because I stayed out too late?"

"Late, my Diomedes? I would say you stayed out all night and well into the morning. Do I get to meet her?"

The doctor flashed him a look, a surprised look. Dio ignored it. "If she stays long enough. You know how that goes."

"One of them will. The right one will. I do wish you would hurry that along since I have such little time left to see you settled."

"Nonsense. And speaking of, the doctor thinks I should leave you here for a few days."

She frowned at the man. "I will not stay. I'll be perfectly fine. It's only a little cough and I told him this was a waste of money and his time. Diomedes, don't you dare leave me in this awful white smelly place with these strangers. If I keel over tonight, then so be it. I want to be home."

"You won't. But I'll take you home."

The doctor argued, emphasized in medical terms why she should stay. She flatly refused. Dio didn't dare cross her.

Caroline cringed with every step. She'd moved wrong, nearly fell when her foot buckled. It was all she could do to continue her routine carefully, with her weight off her foot as much as possible, then get backstage and out to her car without screaming at the pain. And then the awful drive to the pier using her left foot. Good thing it was so late at night, on a weekday, so the roads weren't jammed.

She'd have to find a different job. Before they fired her. She told them she just twisted her ankle and it would be fine, but it wasn't close to fine and she wouldn't be able to cover much longer.

Knowing she should have gone home to elevate it, and to keep driving to a minimum, Caroline told herself it would be worth it. She'd told Dio she would be there. And she wanted to see him.

At the beach, her only obstacle was to get down the shifting soft sand to the water, and then hide it well enough he wouldn't know. That might be the harder task. Hiding it from the drones at work who didn't care anything about her anyway was one thing. Hiding it from Dio would be another.

He cared about her. It couldn't have been that much of an act. He'd stayed far longer than he intended after taking her home and walking her in, long after they were both spent and simply lay next to each other, cuddled together. He fell asleep beside her, after he insisted he had to get up and go home. Instead, they talked. He actually listened to her when she talked. And they cuddled. And he fell asleep.

Lina didn't cuddle. Ever. But then she also didn't kiss. And she didn't take men to her apartment. And she didn't ask them to stay till morning.

It had been glorious, though.

She hoped for a repeat. It would make her forget about her stupid incompetent unforgiving foot.

Two different men asked if they could help when they noticed her limp. She thanked them and declined. It told her she wasn't hiding it well enough. She would have to be more careful.

She was late by the time she made it to the shore. And he was there. Sitting in his boat. Not twirling his sword. It gave her a bad, bad feeling and she considered turning right back around again, walking away before he could tell her to go away.

He saw her and stood.

She stayed at the edge of the water. She didn't want him to say it. Not yet. She remained still. He rowed nearer. Still, she couldn't make herself move to him. He got closer. And closer. Until he had to stop before he grounded his boat.

He called her name.

She shook her head. Backed away. No. She wanted him. She

didn't care about his sword. She wanted him. To kiss him. To cuddle with him in her bed, or his boat, or anywhere on earth.

"I can't stay, Lina." He called across the water.

She shivered, stepped back, nearly fell. Her stupid foot.

"Wait." He threw his anchor overboard and jumped into the water. His black thin sexy shorts stuck to him as he got close enough...

She turned and hurried away as fast as she could. Her foot throbbed. She told it to shut up and just keep working.

Dio caught her around the waist and encircled her in his arms. "No."

He turned her to him. The breeze hit the skirt she'd thrown over her costume. His wet shorts had plastered it against her. He smelled like ocean and animal and warm male. She shivered again.

"I can't stay tonight." He smoothed his large fingers into her hair.

"Let go. It's fine. Goodbye, then."

"No. Lina, I want to stay..."

"Don't lie to me. It's fine. Really. It was nothing. A fling. I had fun. So let it go at that. It's fine."

He pressed his mouth onto hers, pushed his tongue through her lips although she tried to keep it out. Pulled her body close. She felt his warmth mixed with the ocean's moisture. She felt him wanting her.

He breathed hard as he released her. "I want to stay, but I can't. I'll see you at work tomorrow. Let's meet somewhere afterward."

"Why can't you stay?"

"Something I have to do. I shouldn't even be here, and I have to go. I'm sorry. I am truly very sincerely sorry." He kissed her again. "Tomorrow. I'll see you tomorrow. Nap if you can and we'll do something after work. Okay? Tell me you don't think I'm brushing you off."

"Aren't you? It's fine. I expected it..."

"No. Lina, no. I would absolutely stay if I could. Tomorrow. Yes? Say yes. Please."

She nodded since it was the best she could do without letting him know she did not believe him.

With another brush of her lips, he hurried back to his boat.

He sure felt like he wanted to stay. And yet she was angry. It hurt so much to get there. Her foot felt like his sword was stabbing it over and over and over. Still, there was tomorrow. Maybe. It was possible he wasn't lying. Caroline would meet him somewhere if he asked. Damn near anywhere, truth be told.

She still thought he was brushing her off. He could see she did.

Dio shook his head as he tied the little boat to his dock and jumped up to get to his truck and back home to his mother. Maybe he should have told her his mother was sick, but it would sound like an excuse and he didn't want to tell her that much yet. *I live with my mother.* Yeah, that would be a big turn-on. Actually, his mother lived with him, but it would sound the same, he figured.

And she was skittish. She'd started to run only because he said he couldn't stay. Underneath that hard exterior was a hell of a lot of fear. Dio expected there was also a hell of a lot of pent up need. Could be he'd give her what she'd been lacking enough she wouldn't run as she got to know him. It was possible.

For now, he'd have to push her from his thoughts. It was bound to be a long night while he listened to his mother cough and did whatever he could to help. He wouldn't sleep. He'd listen.

If needed, he'd take her right back in to the hospital, no matter how mad she got, no matter how much she wanted to stay home. However often his mother said he should sell the farm and take the weight off his shoulders, Dio knew the farm was her last thread. His father had been her equilibrium. Since his father died a couple of years ago, it was the farm. Not him. Dio was a reminder of a past she didn't want to remember. The farm was her escape every bit as much as it was his.

He had no choice but to keep it running.

~ Fifteen ~

Slipping another pain pill after her act since her foot was killing her, Caroline washed off her stage makeup, pulled a long skirt and loose sweater over her shiny black and silver costume, a new one she'd found that featured a silky push-up bikini top with a diamond-shaped barely there lace piece between her neck and her cleavage. A thin silver collar attached to the top of the lace and ran around her neck.

The bottom was a shiny black flaring mini skirt with tan boy shorts underneath, accented by a silver garter on one leg. Under the stage lights, it would be hard to tell where the fabric of the shorts left off and her skin began.

An accidental-looking brush up against Dio as she left the stage and he was getting ready to go on was enough time for him to say he'd pick her up at her place and she didn't need to change first.

She didn't change. She did, in the time between getting home and when he knocked on her door, ice her foot. On stage, she'd worn supportive slip-ons, in black to match her costume, that only looked like lyrical dance shoes with her toes free and her toenails painted bright silver. After her act, she left them on and pulled black flats over top. Pulling the right one off to better ice the foot, she returned it at the soft knock on her door. Part of her costume. If he asked, that would work well enough.

Caroline let him in, closed the door, and kissed him. "Sorry I missed your act. I wanted to freshen up a bit before you came."

"I would have given you time, but it doesn't matter. Glad I caught yours. Very nice, Lina. You're getting the hang of this thing fast." He slid fingers alongside her head, behind her ear. "I'm not sure I'm glad you are, though."

"Why's that? Don't like me turning on all those men in the club?"

"I have no issue with you turning them on."

"No?"

"No. Just... I don't want you to fit in too well."

She kissed his neck. "It's just a job. A paycheck. And temporary until I can save some money and find something else."

"What else are you looking for?"

"Hm. I'm not yet." She ran a finger down his chest. "I didn't change." Lina undid the two buttons of her sweater she'd bothered with after her act to show more of her skimpy top.

"Willing to leave it on while we go out?"

"You like this one."

"I do."

"Then I'll gladly leave it... Out? We're going out?"

He grinned and redid the two buttons. "Ready?"

Lina expected his "do something after work" comment only meant coming back to her place. She hadn't expected to go out. "Um?"

"Trust me." He whispered it in her ear.

"Not something I do well."

"I know it's not. Will you? I don't like to be out during the day. So it's this or..."

"Okay." Caroline hoped whatever he had planned didn't involve a lot of walking, and she hoped she'd be able to hide the pain well enough.

Dio held the door of his truck and helped her in. He had something instrumental on the radio and the truck smelled like animal even more than it had last time, but Caroline said nothing about either and soon they were in the heart of Charleston. When he parked in a nearly empty lot and checked his watch, she got nervous. More so when he pulled something from the back seat. A bag. She considered jumping out, but how far would she get?

"We're early since I did plan to give you time to freshen up. But I brought you something."

She calmed at his friendly tone. "Should I have showered? I don't smell, do I?"

Leaning toward her, he sniffed at her neck and planted a soft kiss on it. "You smell incredible. Do you like raspberries?"

"I love them."

He grinned and pulled a little basket, the kind she saw at farm stands, out of a cloth bag. It was half full of gorgeous raspberries. "Fresh picked today."

"Oh, wow. I rarely let myself buy them because they're so expensive and often half of them are starting to go bad the day you buy them. These..." Caroline popped one in her mouth and closed her eyes a moment. "Luxury. Perfect. Where did you find them?"

"Out in the yard. They're expensive because of the thorns you can't escape while picking them, and they only stay fresh for about three days." Dio didn't hesitate to indulge as he watched her do the same.

"Mm. Absolute perfection. I'll be glad to help you pick more if you have more, thorns or no thorns."

"Careful, Lina. I may take you up on that." He looked across her out the window. "Our ride's here."

She looked over to find a horse-drawn carriage pull up next to the truck. "Really?"

"If you're interested. I have him booked for the next hour."

Caroline jumped out, said hello to the driver, and went to the horse. "Wow, he's beautiful." His head and shoulders were a pretty light brown that faded into a lighter whitish-brown with small dark spots fading into a pure white rump with larger dark spots. His front legs were light, his back legs dark. Amazing. She loved his coloring. "What breed is he?" She asked the driver.

"Appaloosa, and he's a she, not that she cares what you call her."

"She's gorgeous. Sure she doesn't mind doing this? Does she bite?"

Dio took her side and rubbed the horse's head when it nuzzled at him. "She doesn't mind. Appaloosas are sturdy work horses. This is light duty for her. And she's very friendly. Here, give her this." He handed Caroline an apple. "Her name is Degas, after the painter."

"The one who painted ballerinas." Caroline searched his eyes. What did he know?

"Right. That's why I chose her for tonight, and she just came back to work from two weeks out in the pasture resting, so she should be raring to go. Right, Cyril?" He looked at the driver.

"She is definitely ready to go. Had to rein her in a few times when we got started, but she should behave now." Cyril gave the horse's rear a pat with his hand. The horse paid no attention, too heavily involved in eating the apple from Caroline's hand.

"You ride horses?"

He gave her a grin. "At times. I take care of them more than I ride them, though." When Degas finished the apple, Dio accepted a towel from the driver, wet down with water from a thermos, and wiped the remnants from her hand. "Ready?"

"Oh, yes." She smiled and let him help her up into the small carriage.

Dio wasn't sure when he'd ever been more ... not content, he was far more than content. He was ... optimistic. It was the best way he could describe it. He loved Lina's fire and the fierce independent streak, the way she went after whatever she decided she wanted. Currently, she wanted him, but that kind of independence made him wary, as well. She hadn't answered his question about what other kind of job she'd have any interest in, but he was glad to know she didn't plan to make DanceOtica a career as some of the girls did. She had gumption to spare. She was smart, outgoing. She could easily do anything else. He also loved that she was concerned about the horse's welfare. That said something about her nature he needed to know.

Lina sipped at the wine he brought to go with the raspberries as Dio pointed out a few landmarks.

"Okay." She grasped his hand. "Admission time. I know Charleston well. I've been here often. So, I appreciate the information, but..."

"Through travel?"

"No." She looked out over the Atlantic from Waterfront Park. "I was raised nearby, close enough to hop on the bus and come into the city whenever I decided."

His head tilted. "You don't sound local."

"Voice training. I moved north for several years and didn't want to sound like an outsider."

"Several years? Three? Four?"

She swallowed more wine, obviously enjoying its deep fruity semisweet flavor. "Nine years. Never planned to come back, but sometimes, you have to ... restart from the beginning. Right?" She shrugged. "I needed comfortable, familiar, but different."

"Why did you leave?"

Silent, she looked out over the lit-up pier along the dark ocean.

Dio asked Cyril to find somewhere to park for a bit so the horse could rest. He got out and helped Lina down and she stumbled slightly. A good time to walk, he assumed, if the wine was affecting her. Giving Degas another apple, and leaving her watering to Cyril, Dio offered Lina his arm and headed to the pier.

She walked slowly and he looked at her a couple of times, asked if she was okay, and got a slight nod in return. He took her all the way to the end of the jutting part where there was little interference with the view, where lights weren't shining on them. Lina leaned against the wood railing and looked back at the water fountain glowing softly.

The girl was far too beautiful with barely a trace of light accenting her soft, pale skin. She was pale for a local beach girl, reflecting her years up north, he supposed. Nine years. He guessed she'd left home at eighteen, which would make her twenty-seven. He would have guessed a bit younger. He hoped she'd been at least eighteen. That was plenty young enough for kids to take off on their own, in his opinion. Not that he'd ever done it.

Dio touched her face and brought her eyes to his and she gave him a soft smile before moving into his lips. A short, sweet kiss. She was distracted.

"What are you thinking, Lina?"

"That you're not what I was expecting when I saw you on that boat."

"Is that good or bad?"

She smiled and wrapped her arms up around his shoulders. "Good. Very good. There's actual depth to you, which is nice, but then I wonder how fast that will make you get bored with me, since really, I don't have. I'm ... only what you see and nothing more."

"Not likely." He had to try not to laugh. "I mean, you are far more and I know it. You're a trained dancer, obviously, and yet..."

"How do you know I didn't teach myself those turns?"

"The technique is too professional. Can I ask?"

"Hm. You know, my plan when I treaded out to your boat was to not let myself know you, not let you know me. Just..."

"Just an intense sexual encounter or two?"

"Right."

"Should I take you home instead?"

She met his eyes, holding them, so serious when he'd tried to tease. "I've never been treated like this, so I'm not sure what to expect."

"Like what?"

"Like a lady. I mean, obviously you know you don't have to woo me or some such nonsense. You could have just come over and I would have been good with that. So, what's the deal here?"

"You've never been treated like a lady?"

"No. But then, I don't particularly act like one, either, and never did, so it's fair."

Dio pulled her in against his body and kissed her hard and deep. When he released her, her eyes stayed closed and he kissed each eye. "Lina, let me tell you a few things before this goes further. First, I expect nothing more than whatever you want to give. Second, you are a lady. I see it as well as I see an immense depth to your soul. Third, I acknowledge your physical need fully. I have plenty of it myself. But I know you need more than that, as well. As do I. The deal is I'm as wary of you as you are of me, and that's fine because neither of us are the easily scared type, right?" He caught a slight tilt of the head in acknowledgement.

"So, my end of the deal: I treat you as the lady you are whenever we're out and about, and when we're alone, in private, I do my best to give you what you need physically. In return, you don't ask to see anymore of me than you have until, and if, we get past that wariness at some point. Work for you?"

She stroked his head, through his hair, behind where the mask ended. "Okay. My end of the deal: I'll act like the lady you think you see when others are around, and I'll try to fulfill your needs when we're alone. But, one thing. If you ask something personal and I refuse to answer, don't get all offended. Until we're not so wary of each other."

"Deal."

She returned the kiss just as deeply and then ran fingers down his chest. "How about taking me home now?"

His body tightened, but he wanted to see more of her first, wanted to tease with the promise of what was to come. Unbuttoning the thin, soft sweater, he brushed it off her shoulders, leaving it to hang over her arms.

"We're going to do this here?" Her voice sounded amused. "I know it's dark, but..."

"No. I can't ask Cyril to wait for us that long. I want to see you first. Out here in the dark over the water. Before I take you home." He kissed her neck, her shoulder, wrapped her in his arm enough to dip her backward over the wood railing, encouraged that she didn't fight him, didn't act nervous. She allowed his support, wrapping her right leg up around his legs as though in a dance.

He reacted fast and gave into the ache for her enough to kiss her breast just above her bikini top, savoring the soft skin. Her leg tightened; her hips heaved up against his. Dio used his teeth to pull the silky fabric out of his way and took her into his mouth, saw her head fall back farther, felt her hips pressing in.

"Take me home, Dio." Her face pressed against his, against his mask, and he longed to feel the soft skin of her cheek. One day, maybe. He couldn't risk it yet.

She left the sweater down around her elbows as she took his arm and they ambled back toward their ride. Lina stopped in front of the large ground-level fountain with its short cement columns shooting water in toward the center and reached out to let the water sprinkle over her palm. Scanning the area and finding no one, since it was nearly two a.m., she pulled the sweater off, slipped out of her skirt, and walked in through the water. Her arms wide open, Lina went around the circle, positioning herself where the arching spray hit her shoulders and chest rather than her head, taking her time, and came back to him and out of the water with a huge smile.

"I have always wanted to do that."

"You could have. It's meant to play in."

"But there are always people in the way. I wanted to do it without interruption."

At that instant, she looked like a young child who had just gotten away with something that gave her an immense amount of pleasure. Also at that moment, Dio knew damn well he would have a hard time letting her walk away.

"I figure I'll dry well enough on the way back to the truck it won't get too wet." She took her skirt and stepped into it, nearly falling while trying to balance on her foot, her right one, the one she'd stumbled on before, and he caught her arm.

"So much for balance, right?" She laughed it off and took her sweater but didn't put it on.

He offered his arm and they headed back toward the carriage. Before they got too close to Cyril, she slipped the sweater back over her shoulders.

She was nursing that foot. Dio decided not to mention it since she was trying hard to hide it. If she'd twisted it and didn't want Hayes to know, she could say as much. He'd never betray her trust.

Not that she knew that yet.

~ Sixteen ~

Dio floated between the house, checking on his mother who told him each time to stop wasting work time *spying on* her, mowing the grass, feeding the animals, and brushing the horses' sleek coats before letting them out in the pasture to run.

Cyril had been impressed with his date. He did no more than give Dio a quick grin when he dropped them back off at his truck, but it was enough. Caroline had thanked Degas and patted her head. In return, the horse nuzzled her and she laughed. She was good with animals. Dio had to keep himself reined in more the more he learned about her. He couldn't afford to fall yet. If at all.

She'd agreed not to ask to see more of him. In some ways, he wished she hadn't; he wished she would insist and then tell him it was fine, she could deal with it well enough. But he understood why she didn't. It would be too easy for him to turn the tables and ask about whatever was in her past she didn't want to talk about. Only fair.

For now, they needed to let it be as it was.

Giving into a yawn and wiping sweat from his forehead onto his T-shirt sleeve, Dio sat on the old log bench on the top of the hill and surveyed his land while he caught his breath. So much work to do. Always. He could never keep up well enough. So often, he'd thought of giving in to his mother and selling the place. It would make a fortune. It had been in the family forever, passed down from his great grandfather who bought it as a young man with a new bride. His grandfather sold off part of it in his old age because it was far more than he needed. Too much work, is what he didn't say but likely meant. The man had seven kids, three of them boys who helped with the outdoor work, but it was still a lot of work.

Dio's father had him and his mother. They were all hard workers, his mother included until his father had a heart attack and left them and she turned old overnight, it seemed. He had no one to help anymore. He'd have to either hire a couple of people or sell. It was building up on him.

Maybe Lina could help him find the right people. She was a good judge of character from what he'd seen. She had the spunk and nerve to tell them what was expected and to tell them off if they didn't come through. She'd make a good business partner. Or wife.

With a jerk, Dio stood. *Don't go there. Don't go close to there.* He lectured himself as he went back to the horse's barn to call them back in for the night and threw out oats and carrots. As usual, a couple of them took their sweet time and Dio complained, which was pointless, then rubbed their heads, made sure the stalls were locked, and went to clean up so he could meet Lina without smelling like animals.

Inside, he found his mother making dinner. "You're supposed to be resting."

"I was resting. I got bored resting. Now I'm making you dinner. Go shower that smell off and come get your strength back. I'm making your favorite, that chicken, ham, and spinach dish with noodles, so don't dally about."

He frowned, both at her cough and the dish. It wasn't close to his favorite. He liked beef. Any other meat was fine, but a good steak was better than any other food in the world, and she knew he felt that way. She liked chicken. She was making her own favorite dish. But her cough said she shouldn't be standing there making anything. "Mom, go sit down. I'll finish it when I'm cleaned up."

"You're tired already, Diomedes, and I'm bored. Nothing fair about sitting around here doing nothing all the live-long day while you're out there working and then have you cook for me, too. I won't have it."

"You will have it until you recover." He set his hands on her arms and gently turned her from the counter, guiding her to the living room. "Better I run this place and do the cooking myself for the time being instead of permanently because you're too stubborn to sit and rest while you're ill."

"It's only a spring cold. I always do this in the spring. It's my allergies and that darned ragweed. It'll be fine in a week or two."

He crouched in front of her. "Mom, it's June. That spring cold was two months ago. This is pneumonia and the doctors say it's going to take some time to recover, that you need plenty of rest. That's what you're going to do." He stood and went to get her crossword puzzle book from the side table. "So you're not bored."

"I don't want this stupid thing." She threw it half way across the room. "You know I don't like those things."

"Mom, you've always done crosswords."

"Hogwash. I've always worked and I don't plan to stop now. Where are the account books? I'm a few days late taking care of them."

Account books? She hadn't taken care of the accounts at any time in the history of the farm that Dio ever knew.

"Ask your father where they are. He hides them from me because he thinks I'm incapable, the obnoxious man. You go find them and let me do my job."

Dio stared. She was serious.

"Go on now. You're as obnoxious as your father when you try to be. Stop disobeying and go after them."

"Mom. I'm... I'll be back in a minute." He listened to her complaints with several expletives thrown in as he considered whether to take her back to the hospital. He couldn't call the family doctor. It was Sunday. If he called the ER, they'd just tell him to bring her in; they never gave medical advice over the phone anymore, afraid of lawsuits. Her medications, maybe. She was old and sick. Chances were good the drugs were messing with her head.

Convincing himself that's all it was, Dio stalled, considering how to handle it and wondering if he should cancel his plans with Caroline. She didn't have a phone hooked up yet and she didn't carry a cell phone since she said she had no one she needed to call, anyway. He'd have to at least drive over and tell her.

Except he didn't want to cancel. They were both off so they could start out earlier, and he had plans.

Warming a cup of tea in the microwave, Dio added a chamomile tea bag, let it steep a couple of minutes, stirred honey in it, and took it out to his mother with a muffin he'd picked up from the little store where he bought local-made items, where they knew him and were used to him, and hoped he could stall her on the account book issue.

"How's this? They were baked fresh today. Peppermint and white chocolate." He set it on the TV tray table and moved it in front of her. "I'll grab the account books later, okay? Treat yourself first."

"What a sweet boy you are, and why on earth would I want the account books? You know I'm no good with numbers."

"You said..." At her look, Dio changed tracks. "Nothing. I'll finish dinner as soon as I'm cleaned up."

Since Dio thought she was a lady, at least somewhere within, Caroline decided to dress the part. Donning a long rust-colored sundress with a halter top that fit snug around her bust and waist and flowed gently down to her ankles, she debated about her shoes. Generally, she would wear sandals with a dress, but she wanted to wear her supports and that would leave them showing. He would surely ask if he saw them. It was getting dark, so her black flats would work fine.

She topped the dress with a deep yellow crocheted wrap with wide arm holes and wrapped her hair into a loose bun at her nape. Her bangs fell down around her face. Satisfied that she at least appeared lady-like, Caroline grabbed the ice pack and held it against her foot as she swallowed two pain pills. She'd managed to do without the pills all day by using her crutches to keep her foot rested.

All day was a bit of a misnomer, since he stayed until nearly five a.m. and she slept from about ten minutes after he left until one o'clock. She hoped he'd been able to go home and sleep a few hours at least.

At the knock, she put away the ice pack and hid her crutches and gave herself a few seconds to stretch her toes and put easy weight on the foot to be sure it would hold. He was in jeans and a tight V-neck gray tee, and he looked incredible.

He grinned and scanned her outfit. "You look nice."

"Overdressed?"

"Not at all." He raised his fingers and kissed them. "Ready?"

"We are actually going out again?"

"Unless you'd rather not."

"Oh, I'm good with going out. I love to be out at night and not alone so I have to worry about ... well..."

"That's one thing you shouldn't have to worry about while you're with me. I do tend to keep people away."

Caroline ran fingers through his hair and brushed his lips. "Not me. And it is nice. I love being out in the dark when it's so quiet and private. And not nearly as hot, either." She grabbed her little handbag. "So where to tonight?"

"Picnic on the beach?"

She smiled. "Perfect."

"Sure? You're dressed nice for that."

"The sand won't hurt it."

With a light nod, he offered his arm.

They went out to the county park and luckily he pulled up right next to the water so they wouldn't have to walk far. She had to chuckle about him being as prepared as any good Boy Scout would be when he set out a lantern and two citronella candles and spread a large blanket, then starting pulling plates and covered containers out of a large cooler. He had everything. Fruit, including more raspberries hand-picked that day, and cheese in an assortment which he admitted getting from the store rather than doing it himself, rolled up cold cuts of different kinds, celery and carrot sticks, and a different bottle of wine, less sweet, he said, since she commented on the sweetness of the last one.

"Careful, Dio." She tossed a sly smile as she bit into a strawberry. "You keep doing this, you'll never get rid of me. I'll follow you around like a puppy."

"Is that right?"

"Hm." She put the other half of it into his mouth.

"Careful about letting me know what might keep you around."

"Oh." She slid closer to him, around the smorgasbord. "Keeping me won't be the issue."

"And what will be the issue?"

"Putting up with me, because I'm not easy."

A chuckle rumbled up from deep in his chest. "I've never liked easy."

She kissed him, congratulating herself on her control, being that it was the first time she'd kissed him since he'd picked her up.

"Mm, wondered when you might get around to that." His eyes sparked humor.

"Well, since you think I'm a lady and all, I thought I might try to act like it tonight."

"Lina." He breathed her name against her neck. "I want you exactly the way you are. No pretenses. Just be you." Kisses fell from her neck to her chest and he lay her back on the blanket, planting kisses between her breasts. "I have been thinking of you all day." His nose ran along the top edge of her bodice, the tip of his nose, the only part uncovered.

"Me too." She slid an arm around his neck.

"Do you swim?"

"Very well and as often as I can. I meant to go today, but I was a bit worn out from last night."

"Come on." Sitting up, he pulled out a thin towel and threw it over the food, then helped her up. "You might leave your shoes here."

Leave her shoes? It was dark. She could pull off her supports with her shoes. He shouldn't see them if she faced away from the lantern. She sat back down to do it so she wouldn't have to try to balance on her right foot again and she saw the question in his eyes, but he said nothing.

Grasping her fingers in one hand, carrying the lantern in the other with two towels over his shoulder, he led her down the beach to the tree that extended out into the water, walked around behind it, and removed his shirt and jeans. He was wearing the black shorts he'd worn in his boat.

"Your turn."

"I'm ... not wearing a bra."

"It's dark." He lowered the light on the lantern and set it up just out of the water, then came back to her and raised her dress, up over her head, revealing her rust-colored lacy panties that matched her dress. She always had underwear to match her clothes, a silly obsession. Not that he could see the color of them in the near black of night. As he directed, she went into the water, next to the branches that would hide her silhouette if anyone came near.

Dio turned the lantern up higher and joined her.

They swam for some time and Caroline enjoyed the fact that he was every bit as good a swimmer as she was. When she tired, he took her back to the beach beside the tree, where they could sit in the water and be part covered. And he lay her back, her head on his arm to keep it above the water, teasing her body until she gripped his back and pulled at him. He slipped into her almost before she realized he had the remaining fabric out of the way.

Dio wanted to stay since she asked him to stay. If his mother hadn't been so erratic earlier, he would have. Instead, he apologized, left the picnic remnants with her, gave her a long kiss, and asked her to please think about getting a phone hooked up so he could call her.

It felt like a very long drive home. He didn't want to leave her. He didn't want to go face having to listen to his mother's cough and wonder constantly if he should take her back in, just to have to listen to her bitching at him the whole way there and forcing him to take her home again. He didn't want to deal with the stares from the hospital staff.

He'd left the phone beside her bed with orders to call 911 if she had any issues, and her records said if they couldn't reach him at home, to call Harry and Nelda. Dio supposed he would have to get a mobile phone, as much as he hated the idea. People lived without them forever until recently; he figured he could, too.

Pulling into his drive, his first thought was that everything looked fine. The house was standing, not on fire. No emergency vehicles. So far, so good. Maybe he could just look in on her and go to bed.

A glow from the living room caught his eye as soon as he walked in. The television. Silent but on. Going over to turn it off, he startled at a cough, a deep, heavy cough from the couch.

"Mom? Why are you up?"

"Where else would I be at eleven o'clock in the morning?"

"It's eleven at night." He glanced at the television. Some girl was silently screaming while running through the woods. "Why are you watching this?"

"It came on. Why would they put this on at this time of the

morning? I turned it down so I wouldn't hear that awful screaming. Why do they always have the young girls screaming? Wouldn't a man scream at that, too? They never show the men screaming, but I bet they would."

"Yeah." Dio turned it off. "You could have changed the channel."

"Couldn't find the remote."

"It's right beside you."

"We never used to use those things. We used to have to get off our asses and change the thing ourselves, one of three channels, maybe four if the weather was just right, and none of that screaming chasing crap, least ways not in the morning."

"Mom." Dio scratched his head and pulled the mask off. "Come on. You need to be in bed."

"I don't nap first thing in the morning. You know as much."

"It's nearly midnight. *Night*, Mom, not morning. You need to sleep so you can get better."

"I'm fit as a fiddle." When she stood with his help, her cough doubled her over.

Dio half carried her to her room and told her to lie down while he went after tea to soothe her cough. How long had she been watching that thing? She never watched anything harsher than Gunsmoke reruns and often couldn't stand that. Her confusion was alarming. He'd checked her prescription and it had a warning with it, so he expected it was that along with her age, but he didn't dare not give it to her. He did keep it up where she wouldn't find it to be sure she didn't take extra.

What was he going to do with her if she didn't get better soon? The question nagged at his brain while he showered and lay in bed thinking about Lina, about her foot since he knew something wasn't right with either the foot or the ankle, about what kind of dance training she'd had and why she turned to DanceOtica.

They were both working the following night. But depending on how his mother was, Dio would likely have to leave it at that, at least until she was feeling better and in her right mind again, or as right as it had ever been.

~ Seventeen ~

She was in pain. Dio could see it on her face, even during her act while she smiled and teased.

Lina was using her foot okay, but she was still favoring it. Would she tell him if he asked? As she came off stage, he caught her eyes. Sauntering over as though she was flirting, she touched his arm and whispered in his ear. "Coming over tonight?"

"You're in pain. What's going on?"

She hesitated but recovered fast. "Bad timing." She set a hand on her stomach, only for a second. "But you know, we can still find a pretty place to enjoy the view. I'll bring dessert this time."

"I can't. Tomorrow?"

Her teasing smile faded and she shrugged again. "Okay." Her fingers slid away from his arm as she headed back to the dressing room.

It wasn't the *bad timing* causing the pain, at least not all of it. And she didn't want to tell him. A bad night to brush her off. He hoped she wouldn't think he was bowing out only because she couldn't be with him. His mother...

He couldn't think about that at the moment. He had to go perform.

Caroline didn't stay for his act. Her cramps were annoying but not a big deal. Her foot, on the other hand... No amount of resting it during the day helped anymore. Just as well he couldn't come over. She'd go put it up and maybe use the double excuse to stay in bed all the next day.

A couple of the girls tried to talk to her as she washed her face and put her street clothes on, but she wasn't in the mood. Caroline cringed all the way to her car, cursed when it wasn't sure it wanted to start, grabbed a breath of relief when it did, and drove stiltingly, with her left foot, back to Folly from the edge of Charleston. She was lucky she hadn't been pulled over and tested for a DUI since she drove so slow and started stopping so soon at lights and signs. All she needed was to try to explain that she had to drive with the wrong foot to get to the strip club for work because she couldn't afford a taxi every night. That would go over well.

Unlocking her door with a sigh, she plopped onto her couch and pulled her shoes off. Swollen. The stupid thing was swollen by now. As Caroline debated whether to bother with ice or just shower and go to bed, a soft knock on her door made her frown. He'd said he wasn't coming.

With a quick check of the peephole, she opened the door just a smidge. "Hey. I thought…"

"I can't stay. Can I come in for just a minute?"

"Of course." She tried not to cringe as she put weight on her foot without the support of her shoes.

Dio slid a hand alongside her face, resting his palm on her cheek, fingers entwined with her hair. "I didn't want you to think I wasn't coming only because…"

"Because you're not getting any?"

"If you want to put it that way. That's not the case. I want to stay, but … family duty calls."

"At this time of night? I didn't even know you had family."

"Not much and maybe not for long. But Lina, if I cancel on you this week, it's only that." He gave her a soft kiss. "I have to go. Feel better." With a kiss to her forehead, Dio let himself out.

Family duty. Not for long? What did he mean..? Her stomach twinged. She should have asked. Was she supposed to ask? Weren't they still keeping things casual?

After a quick run through the shower, Caroline pulled into her old comfy pajamas, grabbed an ice pack and a wrap to keep it on her foot, and settled in bed with a dance magazine she hadn't read yet. The longer she looked at it, the more frustrated she got until she flung it across the small room and out the door. She needed different reading material, anything that did not have anything to do with dance. With no television and no smart phone to entertain herself, her magazines had worked well enough, but now they were only a reminder of what she couldn't do.

With a sigh, she unwrapped the ice, tossed it on the floor, and curled up under her blankets.

Family duty. Not for much longer. What was he dealing with? Who was helping him deal with it? Siblings? Cousins? From what she could tell, including his soft southern accent, he'd been in the area a long time, so he would have family, she supposed. *Not for much longer.*

Stretching her tired muscles across the bed, Caroline reached over to where he'd slept beside her. Her bed felt terribly empty. An odd feeling. She liked to sleep alone and unbothered. She slept well that way. And yet she missed the feel of Dio curled up around her, making her feel so secure, so wanted. It didn't feel right without him.

What the hell was wrong with her?

He'd kissed her forehead. Caroline didn't think she'd ever in her life been kissed on the forehead. It was sweet.

When her eyes watered, she cursed herself for being emotional, blamed it on her hormones, and forced her thoughts to the beach, to swimming, with the sensual brush of ocean water against her skin...

~ Eighteen ~

Caroline slipped her phone number into the hem of his tight black pants as she headed onto stage. To cover the way she'd been flirting with Dio at work as an excuse to talk to him enough to set up times to meet, she made herself do the same with the other guys and some of the regular customers that didn't worry her.

She could stop with the flirting now that she'd picked up the cheapest no contract phone available and the smallest card for it. He wanted to be able to call her, and she got tired of the attitude she got whenever she used the phone in the rental office, even though it was only twice and only local calls for work. Now she didn't have to bother.

Every night she worked, she relied more and more on the stage props that kept weight off her foot. She also added more and more ballet moves into the mix. Hayes still bitched now and then, but she blew him off. The audience liked it, especially with as flexible as she was. They loved when she grabbed her ankle, the right one, and extended her leg all the way up against her body and then leaned her body backward away from it. Most dancers pulled their stomachs in when they did the full extension. Lina had worked up to over-extension, which she had plenty of warning against, but it did get a good reaction. And it was something she could still do that took away from what she couldn't do.

Using her own music, favorites from Lita Ford's *Dancin' on the Edge* album, she added in small jetés and piquè turns, mixing them with more sensual moves, always with her right foot favored.

Still, Dio was noticing. Caroline had averted his questions a few times already. She'd have to be more careful. At this point, letting him know she had a bad foot would probably be okay, but how she got it … that was a different story.

His own act lacked spirit, or it seemed to lack spirit. Of course it was ridiculously hot, even now after the sun had gone down, and the humidity had everyone dragging, so she supposed it was only that, although it was plenty cool inside the club. Caroline let herself watch him before she went to change and realized she wasn't the only one watching from backstage. Catching Sandy's eyes, they gave each other a *why are you watching him* glare and then turned away, back to Dio. He was off. A couple of times, she worried that he might be too far off and hurt himself.

At the end of his act, though, when he was still unmarred, she slipped away before he came offstage. It was too hard to control her expression around him and Sandy was watching.

She changed quickly, skipped washing her face, and made her way out back to the somewhat lit parking area, holding her pepper spray in her hand and trying not to curse at the pain in her foot. Her new phone beeped where she'd left it in the center column. A message. Already?

Dio. He'd used the club's phone; she recognized the number. He couldn't come over, but he'd call the next day. Fine. There was no point in him coming over this week, anyway. Why would he?

Her stupid emotions tried to overwhelm her. Too tired. Too much pain. She was fine. Everything was fine. Except for her foot. Time to find a new job, something sitting. They saw each other too much, and not enough, in their separate acts, and after work in the late, dark nights.

Not otherwise.

He didn't like to go out during the day.

She was a creature of the sun, the beach. Outside. Whatever the humidity, whatever the temperature. At least part of the day. Now that she didn't have to live inside the studio practicing early morning and preparing for shows all afternoon, dancing at night, Lina fast became as obsessed with the sunshine and fresh air as she was before. And Dio didn't like to be out during the day.

Just as well he wasn't coming over. She needed to sleep. She needed to keep her foot up. She needed...

Something else. Not darkness and hiding and ... and... But Dio. She wanted Dio.

He called her for the third time. Had she given him the wrong number? Was he reading it wrong? Maybe he'd read it wrong. When he left a message, the voice was mechanical, the one that comes with the phone. Could be anyone's phone.

With that thought, Dio left his mother's bedside, telling her he'd be right back and getting a scowl in return, to go find the scrap of paper she'd tucked into his pants.

Where was it? He'd stuck it in his wallet. He was sure he had stuck it in his wallet after his act, after he'd put it in his memory while he called her from the club office...

The office. He'd set it on the desk in the office.

Cursing, Dio was glad she at least hadn't put her name on it.

Nineteen

Lina swallowed far too many pain pills.

The pain in her foot made her breathe hard, trying to conquer it, and she hadn't even performed yet. She hadn't seen Dio yet. He would be there, since it was his work night, but she would have to leave as soon as she was done and go put her foot up. He could come over if he wanted to see her.

If she could just get through this performance.

"Hey, you okay?" Sandy leaned over her shoulder as Lina finished her stage makeup.

"Yeah. Why?"

As the redhead shrugged, her breasts nearly lunged out of her sparkling orange bikini. "You just seem not okay. Thought I'd ask is all."

"I'm fine." Lina knew why she asked. Sandy wanted her out. Lina was already later in the lineup than Sandy. Some nights. Some nights Hayes threw Sandy a bone in return for the one she gave him and put her in the spotlight. Not as a closer, and never on a Saturday night when the place was at its busiest. Lina was nearly a closer, but never on a Saturday night. Yet.

Although she expected she might not make it there since she was so damned incapacitated.

Why? Caroline had been so close to a principal dancer spot before her foot, before the stupid ignorant ridiculous decision that destroyed her foot, and now she was so close again. Just once, she wanted to be on top of something. Damn near anything. She was always almost there when something screwed her out of it.

Okay, sometimes it was her own fault. Often it wasn't, and not only her fault. It did take two to tango, and there was always a tango of some sort involved.

She would keep going until she got the Saturday night closer spot. Just once. She only needed it once. Then Sandy or any of the other girls could sleep with Hayes as often as it took to get there. She would do it without that.

"*Lina.*"

She jumped and half turned to Hayes. She never gave him the courtesy he didn't deserve of turning all the way to meet his face. She didn't want to look at that soft manipulative square face more than she absolutely had to. "What?"

"Of course you mean: *Yes, Mr. Hayes?*"

She rolled her eyes. "I'm about to go on. What do you want?"

A hush came over the dressing room.

"No, you're not." He propped himself in the doorway.

She forced herself not to look fully at him. He couldn't fire her. She would not accept that. She'd done nothing wrong. She also wouldn't let him shake her as he was trying to do. It was all over his smug face when she glanced at it through the mirror. "Why aren't I?"

"The sword called off. We're rearranging. Sandy, get your cute little ass out there now to fill Lina's spot. Lina, you fill the sword's spot. And jazz it up more tonight. Last night you looked like you didn't want to be there. His shoes are hard to fill. Kick it in gear."

As he left, Lina stared at the doorway. He called off? Dio called off. No. He couldn't. She had to tell him she traded out her phone already due to some idiot leaving nasty messages. She reported it, said someone must have had that number recently and she was sick of dealing with the messages and strange numbers, so they traded it and she had to tell him. Caroline didn't have his number and had no idea where he lived. He had to show up.

Or he'd brush her off the rest of the week since it wasn't doing him any good. He'd said it was family issues, but Lina had heard plenty of excuses, good ones.

She heard the snide remarks about how she must be doing Hayes good to get Dio's spot, but she didn't answer. She wouldn't do Hayes if his face was the most scrumptious she ever saw. Or if his body was, as Dio's. Why did he call off?

Kick it in gear? She cringed inwardly. Her foot... The hell with her foot. The hell with Dio. This was her chance. If she shined enough tonight, she could move into the closer spot easy. She wanted that more than anything else, more than she wanted him. Maybe.

When she stood, her foot tried to give, and she held her breath and gripped the chair. They were staring. She had to pull it together. He could have just told her to take a flying leap. Really.

It was going so great, too.

Lina pinched her lips tight to keep from cursing a blue streak. She'd had them in the palm of her hands, or at least in the palm of something. The reaction spurred her on as she kicked it into high gear. That and the song she chose. Pink. *Try*. It was written for her. Or so it seemed. She wasn't a give up type. She was a keep trying no matter what type. So she had. She'd pushed. Too far. She wasn't careful enough. Or smart enough. She'd done a simple stylized tour jeté and they loved it, until her foot gave out. She got up. Lina did get up. She did continue. But she had to pull back, had to resort to hip swerving and shoulder shaking, mostly while balanced on her left foot, the right barely on the floor.

Cowboy, wearing hardly more than his hat and spurs, asked if he could help when she limped off stage. She tried hard to refuse, but by the time she got that far, Lina could barely hold herself up. She let the fake cowboy with the big arms and skinny waist put an arm around her. It wasn't good enough. She couldn't stand the pain. Lina did well with pain. She was well used to it. But she couldn't. Not without screaming out and she wouldn't do that. So she let cowboy pick her up.

Maybe she would let him drive her home as he'd offered a few times. She couldn't imagine getting there by herself and Dio had called off after he brushed her off for "family issues" in the middle of the night. Probably had a wife and kids, maybe a whole bucketful of kids. Who else would need him in the middle of the night? Maybe that's why he hid his face at work and while he was out with her, so the little wife wouldn't find out. Of course. He was married. Why else would he be hiding?

The hell with him. Why not let the Cowboy take her home? Not that it would do him any good, since if Dio was right, Caroline would never let him inside her apartment, but she supposed it could be hard to keep him out if she let him take her that far.

He set her on a chair in the dressing room and Lina pulled her right foot over her left leg. She tried to make herself massage it. Massage would help, she'd been told. Never mind it already stabbed bolts of pain from one side of her foot to the other.

"What in the hell happened out there?" Hayes barreled in.

Cowboy said it looked like she hurt something.

"I'm fine. It's fine." She spoke through gritted teeth. "Just twisted my ankle. I'll ice it tonight. It's fine."

"Quit showboating out there and you won't hurt yourself."

She looked up at Hayes. "You told me to take it up a notch."

"I *meant* sexy. Show more. Shake your ass more. Shake your small tits more if you can. Take more off. I didn't say to jump around like a kangaroo."

Kangaroo. If she had the strength, Lina would grab something heavy to smash over the arrogant mushy condescending face.

As he left, Cowboy squatted in front of her. "It looks like it hurts bad. Sure it's okay?"

Okay? Not close, but she wouldn't tell him as much. Lina strangled the edges of the chair to keep from yelling out.

"Need help getting home?"

She nearly said yes, but she didn't want him there. She didn't want him to know where she lived.

And she didn't want him. She wanted Dio.

Something had to be wrong. That kiss he gave her, on the forehead, and the way he reacted to her kisses, the way he listened when she talked, actually listened, told her something was wrong. And she didn't know how to contact him to find out. If she asked anyone at work, they would want to know why she asked. Lina couldn't do it to him. She'd promised. "Don't suppose you'd want to help me to a taxi?"

"Thought you had a car."

"Didn't bring it tonight." She wasn't about to tell him she was having a hard time driving.

"Okay, so how 'bout I drive you home and help you in?"

"No."

"Wouldn't be so bad, would it? I could help you forget about that foot." He ran a finger down the middle of her chest.

She grabbed his hand and turned it back until he winced. "Forget it. I'll get myself home. Don't touch me again."

One of the girls came to him, said she'd gladly take a ride if he was offering, and looked at Lina like she was insane. She watched them walk away together, the girl's hand on his back, his on her ass. Putty and bluster. She was putty. He was bluster. A perfect pair. For a moment, Caroline wondered if she should pull the girl aside and warn her, but Dio would have done it already, she supposed, and honestly, she knew nothing about it herself. Could be he made it up only because Cowboy was hitting on her.

Forcing herself to change and make her way to the bar, using chairs along the way as support, she asked the bartender to call her a cab, sat and nursed a cola since she didn't dare add alcohol to as many pain pills as she'd swallowed, then made her way to the street to wait, cursing under her breath, and at times, not so much under her breath.

When the driver asked where she was headed, she said the pier. She knew she was insane, but maybe Dio would be there. Maybe he would tell her what happened, if he needed help.

When she stepped out of the cab, she nearly fell. Her foot wouldn't hold her.

"You alright, Miss?" He asked through the open window.

Biting back tears, she shook her head. He got out and came around. "Meeting someone?"

"I don't know." She tried again to put her foot down. It wouldn't happen. She'd never make it as far as the pier, much less the beach. "No. I can't. I'm sorry. I have to go home instead."

"Good idea, I'd say." He helped her back in and closed her door.

Lina bit her lip hard as she watched the pier lights fade with distance. It was over. All of it.

At her building, the man was nice enough to help her to the front door, but Caroline wouldn't let him go farther. She offered a bit extra for his help, but he wouldn't take it. Instead, he asked if she had someone up there or around the area who could help her until she healed.

"No, but I'm well used to caring for myself."

He shook his head in a wide slow motion. "A pretty girl like you. Shame you don't let someone stand with you. Lots of you don't. I get it. My wife, she tells me why it is, but it's a shame. Anyway, take care of yourself. Here." He handed her a business card. "Most drivers'd take advantage of your offer to pay for a bit of help and a lot of them won't come out this way from the city. Call me instead. And don't worry, my wife would whack me over the head with an iron skillet if I as much as thought about looking at a woman wrong. It's safe enough. Night."

His kindness nearly made her cry, but of course she would not. It helped nothing. She had to get up to her apartment.

And then, in the morning when she could think again, she'd have to decide what to do next.

~ Twenty ~

She hated her crutches. Lina hated them with a passion, especially in sand. Hayes had yelled when she called off for the night, although she gave him plenty of warning. She had to wonder if he'd yelled at Dio like that. And she wondered if he'd be there.

Lina nearly made herself go in just to see if he would be there, but her foot had to rest. She said she needed two days to let her ankle heal. By Tuesday when Dio was at work, maybe she'd be able to face him knowing it was over and be okay with it.

The rubber pads on the bottom of her crutches sank too far into the sand. It was too hard, the sand too soft. Instead, she made her way back up to the sidewalk and hobbled out onto the pier. She had to stop to rest now and then. Her arm muscles were only somewhat still used to the things. She hadn't used them more than around her apartment in ... four months. She wasn't used to them enough, and yet she was too used to them. She hated them. But if she was going to get back to the club, to get that closing spot, Lina had to stay off the foot for a couple of days or so. Completely off.

To make herself feel better, she would spend the day at the beach, all day lying in the sun, after she made her way down to the end of the pier to look out as far into the ocean as she could. She had to stop several times on the way, but she got to the square-ceilinged gazebo, to the farthest point where several men of different ages were fishing and a little girl was playing at fishing with her little pink pole. Cute, Lina supposed, but rather pointless since her line didn't even go down to the water.

Would he be there later? Would he sword play if he was there, or would he only be there to look for her, to tell her he couldn't stay, to give her a toe-curling, heart-racing, mind-numbing kiss? If that was the only thing he was willing to offer, Lina would take it as often as he offered it, or as often as she could take it from him.

Her underarms ached from leaning against the banana-like cushions of the wood crutches and she lowered onto one of the picnic tables, her bad foot outstretched.

"Are you all right, Miss? Do you need a hand?"

She looked at the man. The boy. He was no more than a boy, about twenty, if that. A kid who worked there, she guessed. "No. What I need is a good foot. You can't help me with that."

"Sorry, I…"

"No. I'm sorry. Just a bad day. Thank you, I'm fine."

"Okay. Let me know if you do." With a forced grin, he left to talk to someone else. Definitely someone paid to care if she was okay. Just as the horn dogs in the club paid to act like she was worth attention. Paid to get a thrill off a stranger.

But then it was no different than ballet. They did the same. They only dressed better and stayed quieter while they did. They were paying to watch beauty, only a different kind of beauty.

With a sigh, Caroline pulled herself up to her left foot and the wooden sticks. She hobbled slowly back down the pier, not sure whether to be grateful or annoyed that everyone moved out of her way as though she couldn't go around them. It was Sunday. The pier was crowded. So was the beach. But she'd promised herself a relaxing day of sun and sand.

By two, she decided it was time to eat. She knew where she wanted to go but wasn't sure she could get there, and if she got there, could she get up to the top deck where she liked to be?

Caroline decided to give it a try. She had all day. She could stop as she needed.

People swerved around her again. She supposed they thought she was deformed since her foot wasn't wrapped and didn't look bad unless you looked close to see the swelling. Let them think so; what did it matter? In her long shorts and baggy T-shirt, she didn't get the looks she got in her bikini and sarong, but the crutches more than made up for it.

It took Lina nearly forty minutes to get inside Snapper Jack's and she still had the stairs to reckon with. Unless she stayed on the bottom level. But she wanted to be on top. Looking over the Atlantic. Over the spot where Dio came to meet her and where she hoped he would again.

Dio pounded on her door. He had to explain why he wasn't at work, or to at least tell her he was sorry that he wasn't. He had to see her. And he had only a few minutes.

"Come on, Lina, open your door."

"She's not home."

He turned to the apartment across the hall. The woman jumped when she saw him and closed her door. "Come on, lady. Where is she?" He went to knock on her door. "It's just a costume. For work." Except he wasn't headed to work. And he was wearing regular street clothes. "Please, can you just give her a message?" No answer. She wasn't about to open the door.

Jogging back down to his truck, he shuffled through the glove box in search of something to write on. He could leave a note under the door. Nothing. Not even a pencil. He shoved his hand under the seat in hopes of a receipt. And what would he write on it, or how, with nothing to write with? Under the driver's seat, he found her bikini. He'd forgotten about it in all of the mess with his mother. He could use it as a message.

Dio pushed the bottoms back under his seat and hurried up to her door, tied a bow in the top string, and hung it from the handle. She would at least know he was there, that he wanted to see her.

Caroline sat at the top of the beach close to the sidewalk and wished she had the energy to hobble down through the sand to the water's edge. If he did come, she'd never get there in time for him to see her. But she was exhausted. Frustrated. And he wouldn't come.

She studied the long row of lights along the pier against the dusky sky and thought of her first night back in town, back on the beach, when she'd done an arabesque at water's edge. Only a few weeks ago. It felt so much longer.

As dusk fell into dark, the row of lights brightened, becoming the focal point of Folly Beach.

Folly Beach.

Maybe it was in the name. Officially, it got its name from the dense foliage way back when, and later it was known as a dumping point for the sick and dying people on ships trying to dock at Charleston Harbor so they wouldn't be turned back. Maybe it was folly for Caroline to try to make a new start in such a place.

Maybe she should move on.

She could let Dio and his sword haunt her future, let it feel like a quick summer romance that could have been more, let it serve as a reminder of why she had decided not to try again. Caroline could find a regular guy, a construction worker or store manager, and settle contentedly enough. She'd had her thrills. They left her sunk and sore and defeated.

Not defeated. She didn't believe in defeat. She believed that when one course failed, you started anew and tried again. Maybe she did. She used to. Before she'd been kicked in the teeth too often.

Oh Dio. Why did I meet you just for you to be another kick?

Before he kicked her even harder, she would pull back.

Caroline pulled herself up from the sand, using the crutch handle to do part of the work, keeping her foot fully off the ground. No weight. She'd been told to put no weight on it when it acted up, which they told her it would with overuse. Let it rest. As long as it needed.

She considered calling a taxi, the friendly taxi that had given her a card, but she wanted to walk. She wanted to walk on her own two feet, feel the stride in her leg muscles, the increased air in her lungs, the relaxation in her brain. If she was going to have to use the stupid crutches for very long, they would have to adapt, become part of her stride, not an annoyance.

She could do this. She'd done so many things she would never have thought herself capable of doing. She'd been told too often she wasn't capable. Some would have believed it, and failed. Caroline was far too stubborn in her belief of herself. It was all she had. That, she would keep. The hell with Dio. She could write anyone off. Him, included.

No matter how much she adored his body, his hands, his ... his sword. Damn he was talented with his sword. And gentle. And sweet. He actually talked to her while he made love to her. Sweet encouraging appreciative words, next to her ear, soft, strong, beautiful. No one on earth had ever made her feel that way, physically or mentally. Her Dio.

Lina had no right to think of him as hers, but she had, from the moment he pulled her into his boat, she thought of him as hers. The way he touched her skin, admiringly, lovingly, skillfully told her she was not just another lay. The way he teased, the way he grinned, the way he kissed her told Lina it meant something to him.

Unless he was always that way in bed. She supposed he could be. She doubted it, but anything was possible.

Shaking herself from the thought, since she didn't want to think of him with anyone else in the world, Lina realized she was nearly a third of the way home. Her arms ached but she'd covered ground well. Thank goodness for good street lights. With a deep breath, she continued on. A couple stepped out of a bar, arms around each other, laughing, pausing for a kiss, and heading off together. She wanted that. She couldn't just write men off, because she wanted that.

Before she could let herself have that, she had to have the Saturday night closer position. She needed it. No one would distract her from it.

Lina needed to rest her arms and hands so she could still use them in the morning, so she went into the bar. The place was crowded and noisy. A local band sounded decent enough. Lina made her way through twenty or more *excuse me*'s. People gave her a leave-me-the-hell-alone look until they saw her crutches, then they moved aside and helped push others aside, as well. She guessed there was some benefit to the things. All in all, she'd rather push through on her own.

A tall, blond guy with highlights that had to be from spending plenty of time out in the sun, based on his healthy-looking tan, looked over at her, away, then back. He glanced at her crutches, looked around at the stools and tables, all occupied, and tapped his friend on the shoulder, beckoning Lina over.

When she hesitated, he came to her. "My friend is saving the chair for you. Looks like you wouldn't mind being off your feet a while."

"Does it show that much?"

He grinned. "I'm afraid it does. Please." He held her crutches while she finagled her way up onto the tall bar stool and he propped them where she could reach. She'd half expected him to put them out of her reach.

"I'm James. What's your name?"

"Lina." Damn. Why had she said that? She only used that at work. Everywhere else she was Caroline.

"Lina. Beautiful name. Can I buy you a drink?"

"If you'd like, and if you realize it won't get you anything in return."

He laughed. "I appreciate the warning." His friend took off to hit on some girl nearby as Lina asked for a strawberry margarita. James relayed the order to the bartender and studied her face. "You're a tourist?"

"Why do you ask?"

"Your accent, or lack of." He also lacked an accent, at least a local accent.

She brushed hair behind her ear. He was cute. He had a sweet smile. He emitted a nice cologne, rugged but not harsh, somewhat sensual, not overpowering. It would be fine to talk to him for a bit. "And you're from up north but not northeast."

"Right. Lake Erie area."

"And yet you vacation on the water?"

"Almost always. It's in my soul. I have a quest to spend time on every body of water I can and in the most beautiful spots on the water."

"Nice. Good luck with that."

"And you? Do you have a quest?"

Lina pondered his question. To be on top just once. But she didn't particularly want to tell him that. It would be too easy to turn sexual, too easy to become an offer. Did she have a quest otherwise? "Yes."

He grinned. "Can I ask what it is?"

To find what that laughing couple had. "No."

"Okay. You're a secretive girl."

"I'm a careful girl."

He nodded and watched as she accepted the margarita from the bartender and sipped at it. Lina waited for him to ask about the crutches and wondered what she would tell him. Not the truth. She told no one the truth. It was a dirty secret no one needed to know. She'd even lied to the doctors and physical therapists.

"So. You often come to bars alone?"

He was fishing. "If I'm alone and I need a drink and a place to get off my feet." She nodded toward the band. "These guys are good."

"They're okay, but I wouldn't pay to hear them. So, no friends to hang out with? Boyfriend?"

"My boyfriend's working tonight." Why had she told him that? Maybe he was. Or maybe he was in his boat hoping to find her.

"Ah. Should have known."

"What?"

"That you'd be attached. Shame."

"Is it? If you're looking for a vacation fling, you've got the wrong girl, boyfriend or no."

"Nah, I'm looking for someone who doesn't think my quest is crazy who might want to go on it with me."

"Uh huh. And you don't think these crutches would be in the way?"

He looked over at them like he'd forgotten she had them. "Ah well, I figured they were temporary. You don't look comfortable on them. Aren't they?"

She took a too large sip, through the tiny straw, which she knew she shouldn't do. It made her head spin for a second. "No."

"Ah. I'm sorry."

"Just as well I have a boyfriend now, right?"

"I'm not sure it would have mattered to me. Honestly. I could work around that." He pulled his eyes away and returned them. "And I mean, we could have ... well, no matter. My guess is your boyfriend is a very lucky man."

"My guess is he's not."

"What?"

She shook it off. "Nothing. Thanks for the drink. I should be going. It's late and..."

"And you've barely started on your drink. Stay. Finish and I'll keep you company if you don't mind."

"Why would you? Won't it be hard to find your travel companion that way?"

"I'm not in a big hurry. Sometimes the quest is more important than the victory, you know. If I don't hit every beautiful body of water on earth, I'll be glad for the ones I did hit, and if I don't find someone to do it with me but I love her anyway and settle for what she will do with me, I'll be happy with that. I at least had the quest. Right?"

Lina swallowed more of her margarita. Maybe he was right.

She talked with James and listened to the band she thought he wasn't giving enough credit, not that she was a big music buff, and although she intended to drink only half the huge drink, before she knew it, it was empty and he asked if she wanted another. She refused, insisted she had to get home, that it would be hard enough to walk on the stupid crutches with the buzz she already had.

"Let me drive you." He leaned close. His cologne was too strong when he was so close. It nearly suffocated her.

"No. Thank you." She grabbed her crutches.

"Please. I would feel better since I kept you here longer than you wanted and I'd worry otherwise about if you made it all right."

It made sense to her, at least with the buzz it did, and she answered him when he held his door and helped her in and put the crutches in the back seat and got in beside her that her boyfriend worked very late and he didn't live with her and ... and she smacked herself for telling him that. She knew better than to drink strawberry margaritas. They always made her do stupid things.

She guided him to the front of her building and he turned off the engine.

"Well, thank you. For the drink and the ride."

"Lina. Wait." He gripped her hand and leaned in to kiss her.

She kissed him back. A water quest. Around the world. He could work around the crutches. And Dio wouldn't come back. Why in the hell not?

He slid his hand up to her breast and she let him. She let him caress her as her body tightened. And she let him kiss her deeper. Margaritas always made her do stupid things. But it felt nice.

Dio had lit her fire too high again. She'd had it down to a dull roar, but now … she realized how she'd missed a man's touch. Especially a stranger's touch. A cute fit stranger's touch. He lowered the hand down her stomach, down…

"Oh. No." She pushed him away. "You can't…"

"Let me walk you in."

"No."

"Are you sure? Because I'm kind of getting a lot of yes vibes." He kissed her neck and returned the hand to her thigh, moving it slowly to her softest strongest warmest spot over her thin shorts. "Let me walk you in. At least to the door. You can decide from there."

She nodded. She yelled at herself silently for nodding, but she nodded. He grinned and got out of the car.

What was she doing? She wanted Dio. But he wouldn't come back. And she was so on fire for him and she was so damned pissed off at him for doing it so incredibly lusciously crazy well and then walking away, or at least not telling her why he hadn't shown up, had called in to work. He could have let her know.

The door on her side opened and James held her crutches but offered his arm to help her out. It was muscular enough for his size, and warm, and sturdy. And she was so on fire. For Dio.

But Dio left her. Like they all did.

She was unsteady on the stupid things and his arm assisted, made sure she didn't fall. When she got to the steps and dreaded having to hop up the things with him watching, he slid an arm around her waist, took her crutches with his other hand, and told her to think of his body as her right leg. It was far easier than hopping. She let her fingers slide down into his jeans as she held his belt for support. As soon as she was inside, she'd pull them right off of him and … and wish he was Dio.

Damn. Damn, damn, *damn*. She didn't want this guy. But she wanted it tonight. Stupid margarita. Stupid Lina. Stupid, *stupid* Lina.

He got her to the second floor – she was glad it wasn't a top floor apartment that had been available – and laughed. "What is this? A sign? You have a roommate warning you to stay out for an hour or so?"

"What?" She looked at her door. Her stomach lurched. Her swim top, the one she'd left for Dio. He'd been there. Why? Was this supposed to be funny? Was it a break up message? Was he still there? It was only half her suit. He still had the other half. If he was breaking it off, wouldn't he leave both? Maybe he'd talked the landlady into letting him in, and he was...

"I'm going to be sick." Lina tried to dig out her keys fast. "Please go. Now."

"You okay?"

"No, numb nuts. I just said I was gonna be sick." And in about three seconds. She struggled to get her key out of her little bag and into...

Too late. He jumped back as she let it go in the corner beside her door. As it forced itself out. Damn, she hoped Dio wasn't in there. She wouldn't want to explain this. But she also hoped he was.

"Yeah, I gotta go. You gonna be okay?" Mr. Travel the World backed down the stairs.

"Get *out* of here. *Go.*" She wiped her mouth and forced the damned key into the hole and worked herself around the mess so her stupid crutches wouldn't slip in it and she wouldn't break something else. Lina made her way to the bathroom with her stomach still lurching, barely in time. She shoved the damned crutches away and dropped to her knees, leaned over the bowl.

He'd been there. Dio had been there.

He wasn't still there or he would be checking on her by now. Wouldn't he?

Tears fell down her cheeks to mix with the nasty assortment of junk food she'd eaten during the day along with pain pills and topped by a stupid strawberry margarita, the thought of which made her sick all over again, or it was the thought that she'd let that stranger touch her, almost let him in her room to take her, when Dio had been there.

Stupid, stupid, *stupid* Lina.

As Dio sat at his mother's side and listened to her strangled breathing, he thought of Lina. Had she gone home before work to find his message? Or did she go straight to work from wherever she'd been during the day? She told him she liked to walk, so he'd driven a quick pass around her neighborhood after going by her place, although he shouldn't have taken the time.

He so badly wanted to go back to her apartment tonight, now, to see if she was home and if she was all right. He couldn't. He couldn't leave his mother that long. He shouldn't have gone to work. Her cough was bad, worse than before he left just a couple of hours earlier. It doubled her over. Dio was afraid she'd crack a rib or two coughing like that, afraid of the pneumonia shutting down her lungs.

He was afraid of being alone in that big house on the big farm and that he would give in and sell it if she left him. What else would he do? He couldn't get a regular job without the stares, the wariness. The rent he received from the beach house at the edge of the property, the ridiculously expensive property, supported the place well. His mother dealt with the tenants. She advertised it. She talked with them. She kept it rented nearly all year and enjoyed meeting the variety of vacationers from everywhere who came to enjoy the warmth and serenity of Folly and its easy jaunts to Charleston, Fort Sumter, and wherever else they day-tripped between beach bumming.

Who would manage that if she left him? Who would be around at night to treat him like who he was, not how he looked?

Not that Lina would treat him the same after she saw him.

With realization setting in that she was very unlikely to treat him the same once she saw him unmasked, Dio sighed, pulled a blanket over himself, and tried to get comfortable in the big chair in the room his mother had claimed on the main floor in order to avoid the stairs.

~ Twenty-one ~

Dio grabbed the phone, listened for the caller, and told Hayes he didn't have time to talk.

"You have to come in. Sandy's out with ... whatever her newest excuse is. Lina called off again. And Cowboy has hives or herpes or some disgusting thing. We have to have you. I want you to close tonight. I'd have Lina do it but she wouldn't even come in for that."

"Why'd she call off?"

"Not your concern. Fact is, she's not here and I have to have you tonight."

"Can't do it." He heard his mother cough. Rough. Faint.

"You'll do it if you want your job. I'm out of options and you're not sick."

"My mother is."

"Get someone else to take care of her. I expect you here by ten, no later." The phone clicked.

Someone else. As though there was anyone else. Dio mentally told Hayes to go screw himself as he went back in to her and tried to avoid the question when she asked who was on the phone. She asked again.

"Doesn't matter." Except he'd lose the one job that got him safely off the farm and around other people.

"Diomedes, I asked you a question."

"It was work. Drink your tea. It'll soothe your throat."

"What did they want?"

"They asked me to work tonight. I told them I couldn't. Here." He helped her hold the cup.

She took a couple of sips and shook her head. "Go on to work. No sense in you sitting around here watching me sleep. That's all I'm going to do. Go on."

"Mom, you're very ill."

"Oh poppycock. It's a summer cold. Go on to work now. All I'm going to do is sleep." She leaned back and closed her eyes.

The only job he could get. And she was sleeping most of the time. Her breathing seemed better than the night before and she'd come through fine, had been up and around making lunch, against his orders. He could run in just for his set and run back out again.

They wanted him to close. Actually, they wanted Lina to close. She'd refused a closing spot. How sick was she? That's why she hadn't been there? She was sick? Had she been sick in bed when he stopped? Maybe he didn't give her enough time to get to the door. He could stop on the way to work and check on her. She could need help.

Caroline heard the knock but she didn't want to get out of bed. Just after ten in the morning. Who on earth would be there?

Dio. Maybe he'd come back. For him, she would get up.

Using her crutches with a twisted stomach was torture and she was nearly sick again by the time she got there. It wasn't Dio.

The landlady gave her a glare. "I'm vacating you from the premises. Pack your stuff and be out by tonight."

"What?" She needed to sit.

"It's not bad enough you bring two different men here, but hanging your private things on your door and making a mess in my hallway and…"

"I cleaned it. I even disinfected it. It's cleaner now than it was." And she'd nearly gotten sick again as she did it.

"No matter. I can't have that behavior here. And your *friend* scared Mrs. Tennan half to death yesterday in that black mask pounding on the door, yours and then hers. She should have called the cops and she will if he comes around again…"

"Wait. Dio?" Lina looked past the landlady to Mrs. Tennan. "Did you talk to him? What did he say?"

"Well no, I didn't speak to the beast. Why would I? I'm a decent lady, thank you. He near scared the life out of me."

"Why?" Lina saw the two biddies exchange glances. "He's not scary. He's…"

"He's not welcome here. And neither are you. Leave by tonight."

"I can't. I can hardly stand up and my lease is for a year. You can't just tell me to go."

"Not my fault your lechery is making things difficult for you. And your lease has fine print that says you have to be respectable and quiet and not a bother to anyone else. You and your male *friend* broke that."

"No, it's not what you think." Caroline opened the door enough they could see her crutches. "My foot is acting up. I can't pack like this, or if I could I can't carry boxes."

"Then hire someone."

Caroline shoved a hand through her hair. Get out? She hadn't done anything except the mess and she cleaned it up.

"Fine. I'll give you till tomorrow night, considering your injury. That's all I can do." The landlady walked away, down the stairs.

Caroline tried again to stop Mrs. Tennan, to ask if Dio said anything. The old bitty turned up her nose and nearly slammed the door behind her. Caroline imagined the woman had never been lucky enough to have a Dio of her own, even for a night. Sad. Damn sad. It would do her good. Or maybe she had one and lost him.

Evicted. By tomorrow night. She guessed it was a good thing she didn't have much to pack and it was a furnished apartment. But that meant she had to go out today, to find somewhere to take her few things. And her stomach was still upset. She had to talk to him. She had to know if it was over so she'd know whether to find something else local or to just leave and go far away.

She would stop by the club tonight, but it was Monday. He didn't work Mondays. It would be near torture to wait until Tuesday. By then, she likely wouldn't have a job and she could pick up her final paycheck at the same time.

Dio, don't give up. Come talk to me.

He stopped by Lina's and knocked on her door. No answer. If she was sick, why wasn't she home? He tried again, gave her time.

The door opened across the hall. "She's not here and if you don't leave, I'm calling the cops."

"I'm not doing anything."

"You can't just wear a mask like that to run around scaring people. Get on out of here."

"Where is Lina?"

"Who? I don't know anyone by that name."

A stage name. Of course. "The girl who lives here. Do you know where she is?"

"If I did, I wouldn't tell you. Go on outta here now."

"Look lady, I'm a friend of hers and I heard she was sick. I just want to check on her."

"Sick. Right. Drunk more likely. And it doesn't matter after today. She's leaving. Now get on outta here. We don't want you and your black mask in our building scaring the heck outta people. I don't scare easy. You just gave me a start yesterday, that's all, so go on now."

"I'm not trying to scare anyone. What do you mean she's leaving?"

"Leaving, as I said. Now *get*. Before I call the cops."

Dio clenched his jaw. "Fine. I'm going. If you see her, tell her I need to speak to her and I'll be at work tonight. Would you do that?"

"Why should I?"

"Because you're a human being?"

"Hmph. Get out now."

With a shake of the head, Dio left before she could make good on calling the police. He didn't need that kind of trouble.

Lina was leaving? And it wasn't her real name. How would he find her? Work records. Hayes would never tell him, but he could get someone to find out for him. Drunk? The old lady said she was probably drunk? No. He couldn't see it. At least not enough to make herself sick. Not his Lina.

But what did he really know about her?

Not even her name.

Caroline pulled her car in front of her mother's house and sat looking at it. She shouldn't have driven out there, not with her right foot unusable and her left foot not used to driving. But she made it well enough.

Did she dare go in? Maybe she could at least crash there for a while, just long enough to pull her head together and find another job. She laughed at herself. Pull her head together at her mother's place with whatever boyfriend she currently had? Wishful thinking.

With a sigh, she pulled away from the curb and made the slow trek back to Folly Beach, with a stop through Charleston to pause at the Riverfront to ponder Dio and their time together, to try to figure out whether or not he was real. No answer came to her and she set her mind on finding a way to move by herself as she headed out of the city, stopping again at a bright red box in front of a church. A Little Free Library. She'd heard of them. She needed better reading material. And free was what she could afford right now until she got resettled. A quick perusal led to two that looked interesting, but Caroline would have felt bad taking two, and so chose one, hobbled back into her car, and headed back to her place to face what she had to do.

Passing the old Folly Boat, she looked over as she always did to catch whatever was newly painted on the hurricane-stranded vessel. Usually it was horribly uninteresting. Birthday announcements were dominant, as though everyone else cared. The recent camouflage paint to wish someone well was nice. Now and then there was actual artwork on the boat, such as whales in water.

More writing this time. *Lina...* She slowed to look better:

Lina, work Tues. Please. D.

D. Dio. Work Tuesday night? She couldn't work. She couldn't even put pressure on her foot. But she would go.

Oh Dio, don't play games with me. Please.

~ Twenty-two ~

She was packed. Everything Lina could carry with a backpack or by pushing down the stairs was in her car. The rest she couldn't do. Her childhood books and treasures that she'd carted from home, her mother's home, were in three small boxes, with her Starfish collection on top, wrapped well, but not well enough to shove down the stairs as she had with her clothes boxes and bags. A few pots and pans filled one. A few mismatched dishes another.

Her landlady had checked to make sure she knew to be out by nightfall. Caroline assured her she remembered but asked if she could get some help carrying the boxes to her car. With a disparaging frown, the woman told her it wasn't her problem, but if they were in the apartment after nightfall, they would be locked inside and would belong to her.

It was getting far too close to nightfall. Lina had spent the first half of the day again looking for a place. No luck. Nothing she could afford or feel safe in had surfaced within twenty miles. Soon she would not only be homeless and jobless, she also wouldn't have her starfish, her pans, her dishes. No, she would have her keepsakes. Even if she had to shove the box with her crutches and sit down on the stairs and lower it one step at a time, she would have her starfish and other keepsakes, karma be damned. She supposed she could do them all that way.

Except she was exhausted and she was almost out of time.

Oh Dio, come find me. I could use a black knight about now.

With a deep breath, she got a grip on herself and decided to use her brain, to get out of her fantasy world. She was smart. She could do this.

The taxi driver.

Caroline dove for her handbag and dug through to find his card. He'd said to call if she needed help. She had to hope he was as safe as he said. At this point, she had few options.

A woman answered. Lina hesitated, then asked if he was there, reading the name. The woman corrected her pronunciation.

"I'm sorry. I ... I'm trying to move out of my place and ... I'm packed but I can't get my things downstairs although it's only a few boxes, heavy boxes, and he said I should call if I needed help, that it would be safe because his wife would ... would...

"Hit him over the head with an iron skillet?"

"Yes. That's what he said. If he even thought of looking at another woman, which he didn't. I have a bad foot. He helped me get home the other day when it refused to work. I just ... I have to be out before nightfall and I don't have anyone else to ask."

"Give me your address." The woman took it, or at least Lina hoped she really did. "We'll be there in a few."

"We?"

"Sounds like you need more than brute strength. Hang tight." The phone clicked.

Lina nearly cried, but she wouldn't. She hoped she hadn't just set herself up for another trap. She could open the door, leave it open, and...

Hell, let the damned Fates do as they would. She was too tired to fight it.

Leaning back on the stripped bed against the headboard that she'd cleaned with disinfectant before she used it, Lina let her eyes close. She hadn't been so tired since ... since her early days of dance school.

The knock jolted her awake. She looked out the door with the chain still latched. The taxi driver. He said his wife was there, also, and gave someone a nod. The woman stuck her face where Caroline could see it and offered a hand through the door.

"Need help, child?"

Caroline nearly cried again. Instead, she nodded.

"Well, open the door then."

Obeying as though she was the woman's child, Lina closed it enough to unlatch and open it. She explained again why she'd called for help.

The woman shook her head. "You're not the first it's happened to. Don't worry about her and her kind." Her strong hand clasped one of Lina's. "Things have a way of working out, they do. Is that all you have?" She looked at the five boxes.

"The rest is in my car. I know. I should have been able to…"

"On those things?" The woman rolled her eyes. "Nonsense. Harry, grab those and bring them down. I'll walk with … what did you say your name was?"

"Caroline."

"Caroline. What a beautiful name. That's Harry who you already met. I'm Nelda. We'll get you where you're going. I do spose you're not going too far?"

"I … hopefully within ten miles or so but right now just to my car. I'll … have to find a hotel or…"

"No hotels available tonight, child. Big meeting of some kind in town. Everything's full. You mean you have no place in mind to go?"

"I … no. I've been looking since yesterday. It wasn't enough time."

"Nasty old biddy, doing such a thing to a girl, a girl with a lame foot, no less. She'll pay her due when it's time. You'll stay with us tonight. All we've got's an old couch if that'll work…"

"Oh, I can't ask you…"

"No askin' involved. Come. Harry, move it along."

Since she had no other option in the world, Caroline let Nelda take the lead. She pointed out her car and Nelda asked how she drove that way without the right foot. She shook her head when Caroline answered. "Nonsense. I'll take you in the taxi. Harry can follow in your car. I don't drive a lot but I can drive that old thing no farther than we're going. Harry, he's a good driver. No worries about the car."

"I'm not worried about it, only my things that are in it. It's ancient, anyway. Not that I would doubt his ability. I only mean…"

Nelda grinned, a beautiful grin, and patted her hand. "Don't worry. We're not touchy. Come get in the taxi now and get off your feet. We'll take care of things tonight. Tomorrow you can start sorting it all out."

"I … I have to be somewhere tonight. By nine. It's important."

"Harry'll get you there and back, then. Don't you worry. Time don't matter at all to him. He can sleep for ten minutes and jump up and go whatever the time day or night. Don't you worry."

Dio drove like hell. She was barely breathing, gasping for air. He'd carried his mother to the truck and jumped in and gunned it. He hadn't even grabbed his mask.

He hadn't called in to work, either. He would do that from the hospital as soon as they took care of her. They would take care of her, and this time, like it or not, she would damn well stay there until he didn't have to worry every minute.

"Still okay?" He glanced over.

She gave him a slight grin. Very slight. She didn't answer.

He whipped around a car that poked along trying to read the damned boat where he hoped Lina saw his message... And he wouldn't be there. If she saw it and he wasn't there... Dio would have to worry about that later. First things first. Ten more minutes to the hospital. Or less if he could make it less. His mom hated when he drove even the speed limit which she said was too fast, but she'd have to understand this time.

Only a couple of minutes left, and red and blue lights pulled in behind him. He wasn't stopping. They were nearly there. He'd explain later. And he could just see that going well.

Dio nearly laughed at the irony. Two days ago, the threat of cops only because he knocked on Lina's door and today he would have to explain his speed without his mask. He'd wind up in jail yet. Wouldn't that be the topping on the stripper's cake? Not bad enough he had to live with hiding his face and having to run a farm by himself and that he'd probably just lost the one girl who might have had the spunk to stay with him when she saw him, but a jail record for evading arrest on top of it?

He did slow down as he pulled into the hospital parking lot. He wouldn't risk some other poor soul's life to save his mother's. Whisking around to the emergency room, he stopped right at the doors, threw it in park, and jumped out to hurry to her door. Orderlies came.

"She's having trouble breathing."

They looked at him and drew back at the same time the officer stepped out of his patrol car and came at him.

"My mother." He reached in to pick her up and turned to where they could see her. "She has pneumonia. She's barely breathing."

At the look of her, the orderlies hurried forward again, with glances at him, and helped her into the chair.

"Take her in. I'll be right there." Dio turned to the officer. "I'm sorry. I don't drive like that, but she..." He pointed.

"Yeah, okay." The man eyed him. "You have a license?"

Dio pulled it out and handed it over. It looked just like he did now, full face scar and all.

"You're Dominick Troy's kid."

"Yes."

"I was sorry to hear of his loss. Alright. Just move your car to a parking space. Hope Cleo's okay." With a nod, the officer left.

One right thing.

Sometimes all it took was for one right thing to happen. That's what his father always told him.

Twenty-three

Caroline thanked Harry for driving her to DanceOtica. He looked at it, then looked at her. "Sure you want to go in there? Know what it is, right?"

"Yes, I know what it is."

"If you're meeting someone, I can walk you just inside the door and make sure you find him."

Caroline knew she could act like she was only meeting someone, but she wouldn't lie to this nice man who'd been a true life saver. "I work here. The bouncers know me. Anyway I did. Can't now. I have to ... pick up my final check and tell them I won't be back. If you want to change your mind about letting me stay with you, I understand."

"You're not the first I've known who works here, and not the first from here who's stayed with us a night or two. They're good folks, overall. Still, I can't say I'm not glad you're moving on to something else. Hold on." Harry turned off the car and got out to come around. He held her crutches and gave her a hand. "I'll walk you as far as the door. Just in case. Can't go farther than that unless you need. Wife would have a hissy fit for sure."

"No, it's okay. I should be only a few minutes. If I need to be longer, I'll come tell you."

"Go on and take care of your business. I'll be here." Harry greeted the doorman like they knew each other and Caroline heard something about another rescue as she disappeared inside.

It was more crowded than normal for a Tuesday night. She pressed through and passed some of the employees who didn't even give her a glance. No wonder, since she was in her loose jeans and an old sweatshirt. If Dio was interested, he needed to be interested in more than her sarong, her bikini, and her stripper costumes. He needed to see her as she was, bad foot and all.

She did catch attention when she went through the employees only door and people turned to stare.

"Lina?" Sandy tilted her head with a stupid look on her face.

"Wow, it is you. You look different."

"Yeah, I have four legs now instead of two."

"What?" The girl glanced at the crutches. "Oh. No, I meant... Wow, you really twisted that ankle good, right? Hayes has been fuming, I mean absolutely fuming."

"I really can't care. Is Dio in tonight?"

"Why?"

"Because I asked, that's why. Is he in?" Screw that he didn't want people to know. He got her kicked out of her apartment. She really couldn't care if he didn't want people to know, especially since she no longer worked there.

"He's not here." Sandy eyed her. "Why do you want Dio?"

"Not your concern, Sandy. You're sure? Or are you trying to hide him as though he'll ever give in to you?"

The girl pushed her chin up. "What do I want with him, anyway? Not like I don't have options."

"*Lina.*" A loud gruff voice came from behind her. Hayes. "What in the hell is this?" He nodded at the crutches.

"This ... is why I have to quit. I just came to let you know and to get my paycheck for last week. You can't mail it. I moved."

"You quit? You can't just quit. I need two week's notice."

"Two weeks for what?" Unwilling to air her personal issues in front of her ex-coworkers, Lina hobbled out into the hallway and turned back to Hayes as he followed like a puppy dog. "I can't dance, Hayes. I can't even walk without these things. What do you want me to do? Book work? I can do that, if you want. I've never done it, but I'm a fast learner, so I can. Any other sitting job you have? I'll take damned near anything about now. Yes, I'm that desperate. Is that what you want to hear?" Lina noticed the dressing room guard staring, but she didn't care. Dio didn't show. He asked her to come and he didn't show. "Please, just give me my last check and I'll be outta here."

"It's not ready. You know they aren't cut until Thursday. We'll mail it to you. Leave your new address."

"I don't have a new address. I have no address. I have nothing. I depleted my account on that damned beachside apartment so I could walk to the pier which I can't do anymore and the old bitty wouldn't even give my security deposit back though I left it better than I found it. I have nothing." She shoved a hand through her hair. Of course he didn't care. Why would he? "Fine. I'll be back Thursday night if I can get here." She started to leave, but she had to ask. "Was Dio supposed to be here tonight?"

"Yeah, he was *supposed* to be. Just called in. Why?"

"Why did he call in?"

"That's…"

"Confidential. I *know*. I don't give a shit if it's *confidential*. Tell me." She grabbed his shirt collar. "*Tell me*."

"He's at the hospital. His mother's in bad shape. No one else to take care of her. Only reason I haven't fired his ass yet."

Sandy chuckled from behind Lina. "You haven't fired him 'cause you'd lose most all your female customers if you did."

Hayes told Ms. Orange to go on back to work and lowered his voice. "I'll find something around here for you to do, a sitting job. It won't pay as well, but come back in the morning, and I'll see what I can do."

He was being human? Lina almost preferred he wasn't. It would be easier to take than to have three people in one day jump in to help, to be kind. She wasn't used to it.

Dio's mom was in the hospital. No one else. It meant he wasn't married, no siblings. No one? Did he really have no one else? "What hospital?"

"Can't tell you that. Come back in the morning." He walked away.

"You and Dio have something going?"

She looked over at the door guard who was staring. "Not your business, and that was a private conversation."

"Yeah, well, I know where you can find him. Have you seen him out of costume?"

Caroline straightened. She wasn't going that far.

"I mean without his mask."

"No. And I don't care. Whatever it is, I don't care."

"How'd you get here like that?" He glanced at her foot.

"Cab. Where is he?"

"Whose cab?"

"Why?"

"Harry, by chance?"

"What? Does everyone know everyone around here?"

He grinned. "Most of us know Harry. Tell him you're looking for Dio and he'll get you where you need to go."

"Why should I trust you?"

"What choice do you have?" He shrugged. "Okay, so I've noticed him talking to you. He looks at you different than he looks at the other girls. Figured something was going on, especially when he told me to keep an eye on Cowboy around you. Hey, don't worry. I'm good at minding my own business."

"Yeah. Sounds like it." Still, he was right. She didn't have much choice. Hurrying out as well as she could, she sighed in relief that Harry was still there and asked if he might know what hospital Dio might have gone to with his mother.

He grinned. "Get in, hon. I'll get you there."

Dio wanted to pace up and down the hall, just to stretch his legs and relieve tension. His mother was asleep. Dangerous stage, the doctor said. She would go home healthy or not go home.

He tried to imagine the large house without her, alone, with his heavy footsteps echoing through the rooms and up the stairs. He could rent out the second floor, he supposed. Maybe turn the smallest room into a little kitchenette/dining space so he wouldn't have to share his.

He couldn't think of it now. It was morbid. He'd deal with it as it happened.

Or he would go find Lina and move her in. Would she? Lina on a farm? Dio couldn't see it, even if she did like animals. Lots of people liked animals but wouldn't like the work of a farm that came along with the animals. He also couldn't see her with him. She was beautiful, smart, witty. Why would she want him once she saw him? Without his mask, he looked like that Maul guy from *Star Wars*.

The doctors and nurses who came in were getting used to him. They were wary still but they no longer jumped or startled if he moved. He was hungry, near starving. He'd been there since before dinner and it was after ten, but he didn't dare go out in the hall and down to find the cafeteria. No sense scaring people who were already worrying about their loved ones.

Shoving his hands through his hair, Dio collapsed back onto the edge of the chair and propped his elbows on his knees. Maybe he could find a weary prostitute who was tired of living on the streets and tired of different strange men every night who could deal with his face in return for a safe home and an occasional romp in the sack as they both felt the need. If his mom didn't go home again, he would consider that direction. And maybe sell the farm. His dad had told him not to sell, that land was precious and not something to let slip out of your fingers, but what good would it do him alone, with no children to pass it down to, no woman to share it with, at least not a woman he cared about enough to make it part hers eventually?

The door opened. Another nurse, he supposed. They were in and out constantly. He appreciated that they were taking such good care of his mother, but he was tired of the in and out. Dio didn't even bother to look up. He was tired, exhausted, from worry, about both his mother and about the woman at Lina's apartment saying she was leaving, from trying to keep up with the farm work and his job and Lina, and he was hungry as hell. All he needed was for his stomach to growl. Wouldn't that add to his character bit? A growling monster. Yes, he could see that go over just great.

"Dio?"

He nearly barked at whoever was bothering him until he realized he knew the voice. Lina. It was Lina's voice. Why was she there?

"Are you awake? I snuck in. They said you were here. I just ... I had to see you."

It was Lina. His hands still covered his face. His face was still dipped where she couldn't see him. His whole body clenched in order to keep himself from running to her and holding her tight.

"Dio, it's Lina. Can I come in?" She was still at the door, her voice soft. Afraid of waking his mother, maybe? How did she know?

"Why are you here?" He spoke through his hands.

"I ... I got your message. On the boat. And I nearly strangled

Hayes until he told me where you were. Dio, please, look at me."

"You can't be here." Not until he warned her. He couldn't startle her the way he did everyone else. He had to warn her, tell her about it first, give her time...

"Will your mom be all right?"

"Go." He stood and turned his back to her. "Just go, Lina. Go find someone ... someone you can walk down the street with, during the daylight, someone who'll go with you for your long walks, someone who can..."

"I doubt there will be any more long walks. Please, look at me."

"Why?"

"It's all right. I don't care, Dio. I don't care. Just look at me."

He snickered. "It's easy to say you don't when you don't know."

"Yeah? What do you know about me? Nothing. Do you still want me? Do you think you might? A dancer turned stripper who can't even do that anymore, who has no future whatsoever, who will never get to the top of anything now? Who doesn't even care anymore if she does? Think I can't deal with whatever you're hiding if you can deal with that? Or can you? Because I won't be back at the club, other than Thursday to get my check."

He started to turn, but stopped himself. "Where are you going?"

Silence. Had she gone? He didn't hear her leave. His hearing was good. He would have heard the door. A ploy to get him to turn, to look at her. He was in no mood to play games. "It doesn't matter. Just go, Lina. Wherever you're going, just go." His stomach growled. Wonderful.

"Caroline. My name's Caroline. Goodbye, Dio."

Caroline shoved out the door and nearly fell on her face when her crutch caught the bottom corner. *Just go.* Fine. She'd gone out of her way to get there, to see if he needed help, to let him know who she was and how to reach her. And he wanted her to go.

She hoped he starved to death sitting in that room alone.

"What are you doing here?" An orderly stepped in front of her.

"Leaving."

"It's after visiting hours."

"Nice to know. Thanks. Move, would you? I don't have the energy left to swerve around you. My palms are bruised and my foot is killing me and ... my heart is about to burst. So just get the hell out of my way."

The young man stepped back, then he hurried around her to open the next set of double doors. She didn't bother to thank him or to apologize. She had to *just go*.

Dio kicked himself. Damned pride. His mother warned him it would do him in if he wasn't careful. She'd come to see him, to check on him, and he told her to leave. And she was leaving. He would have no idea how to find her.

Thursday. She said she would pick up her check at the club on Thursday. He could meet her there, see if she would still talk to him.

Two days away. He didn't want to wait that long.

Why would there be no more long walks? She loved to walk. Why couldn't she strip any longer? Not that he thought she should. She was too talented. She should use it better. She was beautiful. Perfect.

And he let her go.

No. He would go Thursday, if his mother's health allowed. If not, he'd send a note.

Pacing, Dio tried to decide if he should catch up with her, but he could just see it. After he'd acted like an ass, a monster, he would run up behind her, she would turn, and she would jump twenty feet at the sight of him. Why bother? She wouldn't want to touch him again.

He'd paced long enough she would be long gone. He'd never catch up to her now. When the door opened, he hid his face with a hand in case she'd come back.

"Hey, don't worry, I've seen you already." An orderly he recognized came forward and didn't jump when Dio lowered his hand. "Here." He shoved a paper bag at him. "That girl who just left sent this up for you. You're nuts, man. She's really hot, crutches or no. I'd sure be willing to put up with a lame foot for that."

"What?"

"The beautiful girl with wavy hair and ocean green eyes and about the best build I've ever seen? I'm not into big-busted girls, so to me it was pretty much perfect, right? Her build, I mean. Wasn't she just in here?"

"Yes. Li... Caroline. You know her?"

"Nah, but I sure wish I was old enough. Sweet girl, and still plenty sassy. I like that combo, you know. She a friend of yours? Does she like younger men?"

"Crutches?"

"Yeah, she's good on 'em but I held the doors anyway, just, you know, as part of the job. And delivering food isn't part of my job, but I couldn't resist doing it for her. Gonna take this?"

Dio accepted the bag and looked in. His stomach growled louder at the smell. A hamburger. Maybe two hamburgers, and a ton of fries. Damn he loved her about now. Crutches. The foot he'd been asking about.

No more long walks.

"Where did she go?"

The orderly shrugged. "Got into a waiting cab, though it had its light off like it was off duty, and took off."

An off duty cab? "See the driver?"

"Barely. Short stocky guy with a wide smile, at least wide for the lady. Can't imagine they were together though, you know? He had to be a good twenty years older than she is. Had a funny hat. Can't tell you what it's called."

Dio grinned. Maybe he could find her before Tuesday. "Thanks." He dug out his wallet and tipped the guy a $20. As he left, Dio sat and devoured the two hamburgers, every last fry, and the cheesecake at the bottom. Even warm, the thing was wonderful.

If she was with Harry, Lina ... Caroline ... would be fine tonight. Leave it to Harry to find those who most needed help.

Caroline settled onto the couch and wrapped tightly into the soft worn blanket. Funny that she felt more secure in Harry and Nelda's small house than she did in her apartment on her own.

Just leave. His words rang through her head. Why had she taken the time and trouble to send food? Because she put up with too much. Because her heart was too soft. It wasn't. She'd made it not too soft over the years. She'd had enough of that.

But the orderly said Dio hadn't been out of his mom's room since he got there early evening. And his stomach had growled. He needed to eat. Caroline couldn't stand the thought of him not eating. The orderly also said he was kind of a scary sight, but it didn't scare him none. He'd even told some of the nurses who talked about the 'monster' in room 369 to shut the hell up 'cause you shouldn't talk about patients or visitors that way. He figured he wouldn't get reported since he'd turn the cards and tell their supervisor what they were saying.

Scary looking. Dio? He was afraid she would think he was.

Oh Dio. You should have just turned around to talk to me, to let me prove it to you.

Maybe she'd go back in the morning and try again. Except she had to search for a place to live. And a job. First things first. From what she overheard, the poor woman would be there for several days, if all went well. She had time.

Twenty-four

As Caroline made her way through the row of columns under the pier, she thought of a wedding she had seen there before she moved away. She could nearly see herself in a long white gown and a soft veil treading down the long stretch of wooden planks with Dio at the end, under the gazebo, as her prize. Or they could do it in the sand under the pier. Weddings were generally on the pier, not under it, but for her and Dio, under would be more appropriate.

Stupid. Stop thinking such stupid things, Lina.

With a sigh, she paused to rest. Her palms throbbed. They would get over it eventually and just behave again. They needed to behave soon. She was too irritable to have to deal with aching palms on top of an aching foot and her aching heart.

Just leave, Lina.

With another sigh, she made her way farther down, nearly two thirds of the way by now, and stopped to rest her palms. Luckily, the sand was fairly well packed beneath the pier. It wasn't too hard to manipulate on her crutches, or she was getting used to them again.

Caroline shoved her hands against her face. She didn't want to be used to them. She was nearly a principal dancer. All those years, those hard soul-tiring, excruciating years of working her way up: the pain, exhaustion, the mental fight of it … gone. Useless. So she'd stepped on a few people on her way up. Everyone on top did. That's how it worked. Everything worked that way. You were nice and you got stepped on and got nowhere, or you did the stepping and got to the top. She wanted to be on the top. Just once.

As she looked out over the water, at the seagulls drifting along the breeze over the water waiting for any opportunity for a meal, Caroline realized that wasn't what she wanted. Not now. Now she only wanted to dance. And she'd screwed herself out of it.

To try to get to the top.

Stupid, stupid, *stupid* Caroline.

No sense dwelling in bygones, she supposed. With a stretch of her fingers and a rub of her palms, she continued on. To the end. As far as she could go without getting wet. She should have worn her suit under her clothes. She could try to swim.

Caroline should be out looking for work, for shelter. Harry dropped her off at the pier on his way to look for paying passengers. He'd found one as soon as he turned his sign on. Lina grinned. She was glad he found a fare. It was fair. He helped her for free. It was only fair that it helped him in return. Someday she would return the favor. Somehow.

She would. Caroline would pull herself right back together, Dio or no Dio, and she would still come out on top in something. Maybe Karma was a bitch, but she could be one, too, and she would win.

Dio just missed her. Nelda said they'd gone to the pier. Harry was dropping her off and heading out to work.

The pier. Even with his mask, since he'd stopped at home for a shower and change of clothes, and to grab the thing he was sick of wearing, Dio did not want to be on the pier during the day. He didn't want the stares.

He hated to leave his mom alone at the hospital, but he'd finally broken down and told her about Caroline, only the main points, not the details. The wicked old woman, sweet as she was inside, asked how good the girl was in bed. After Dio got over the shock, after his mother said she was young once, also, and no fairy tale princess herself, he admitted he could spend a lot of years to come with Caroline, and with her alone.

She then asked if Caroline had seen his face yet, which led to her calling him a vain arrogant exasperating fool. When she was done ranting, his mother told him to find her, to bring her back to the hospital since she'd been "rude enough" to be asleep last time the girl visited.

Dio didn't dare drive too fast, in case he ran into the same officer since he didn't have a sick mother with him this time. He headed to the pier, although he wasn't sure he'd have the guts to get out and walk around to look for her. She wouldn't go too far too fast on crutches in the sand. Or maybe she hadn't gone into the sand. Maybe she'd be on the sidewalk, or had gone into town, or... She could go anywhere from there.

Dio parked as close as possible, turned off the engine, and drummed his fingers against the steering wheel. Someone looked in at him then away again. So what if they did? So what if they all veered as far around him as they could get? There was only one person, at this point, whose reaction mattered. Harry said to give it a shot. She was a tough girl, he said. He wouldn't say anything about the crutches except she was on them and managed well with them, even packed her own stuff and got most it down her stairs and to her car with them.

Dio wished he'd been there to help. He thanked Harry greatly for being there to help, for letting her stay with them overnight.

Gritting his teeth against the possible furor, Dio shoved a hand through his hair and got out of the car. He saw the reactions range from fear to annoyance. He figured the mask itself wouldn't be so bad if he was a small scraggly guy. With his build, though, his weight lifter build as it had been called more than once, most of what he saw was fear.

So be it. He had to find her.

Taking his chances, Dio headed underneath the pier. Yes, that was likely to go well. A monster hiding under the pier. That would be good. He could see it now. At least it wasn't dusk. The sun was bright. He was in jeans and a T-shirt, as innocent looking as he possibly could be.

"Hey."

He looked over at the voice. A young kid. Someone who worked there. "Yeah?"

"You can't... How about you take that off? You're kinda freaking people out."

"And why is that? I'm only walking."

"Yeah but man, come on. People are kinda freaked out about ski masks, you know. So unless there's a reason, I have to ask you to take it off so we can all go about our business." He stayed a good distance away. Other people around stared.

"It's not a ski mask. It only covers part of my face, none of my hair."

"Whatever, man. It's freaking people out."

"You want me to take it off so I don't freak people out?" Dio chuckled. "You've got that backward. I have it on so I don't freak people out. Have a nice day."

"Come on, man, don't make me call my supervisor. Just humor me, all right? You seem like a decent enough guy. Let's keep this easy and civil and all. Yes?" He was scared. As much as the kid tried to hide it, his voice gave him away.

"Fine. Don't say I didn't warn you." He eyed the small crowd waiting for some note-worthy event, Dio supposed. And he supposed this would be one. He lifted the thing off his face.

A few people gasped. Others backed away. The kid's jaw dropped.

"Happy?"

"Uh..."

Dio pulled it back on. "Yeah, that's what I thought. Want to mind your own business now?" He saw the whispers, saw a woman with her hand to her stomach like she would be sick.

He continued on his quest.

Would Lina do the same? Caroline. Would she? Dio was nearly sick at the thought of it. Still, he kept going. He had to at least talk to her, see if he could do anything to help.

He saw her from a distance, barely outside the water's touch, between the middle and left pillars. So beautiful, even from this distance. As he walked, he admired her dancer's frame, her strong but delicate shoulders leading to her ribcage leading to her concave waistline leading to her nicely rounded feminine hips.

He wanted to set his hands on those hips, to nuzzle into her neck, around that silky hair, to kiss her jaw, her ear, her cheek, and ... and her lips. He wanted to run his hands along from her hips up her stomach, up to her perfect breasts she thought were too small. They weren't too small. They were perfect, pert, beautiful, just the right size to cup in his hands as he teased with his tongue.

With a light groan, Dio told himself to stop seeing it, to stop focusing on the glorious nights with her. Maybe, though, she would be willing again, before she saw him. Maybe she didn't need to see him, would be content with what he could offer. As much as he hated to wear the stretchy fabric over his face, he could wear it at home, also. With the promise of her touch, of her body, he would.

Oh Lina, please be as tough as Harry thinks you are. I'll offer you everything I have to offer. Just be tough for me.

There was someone behind her. Lina felt the approach. It was much like electricity, the charge just before the shock from a metal appliance in the winter. Her skin tightened. Her body tensed. Yet she wasn't afraid. She'd rarely been afraid of anyone. She always figured she could hold her own, or even if she couldn't, there was no sense being afraid. She could or she couldn't. Worrying about it wouldn't change that.

This wasn't fear. This...

"Caroline."

Her eyes clenched. She held her breath. "Dio." It came out a whisper.

"Yes."

He was close but not too close. Her crutches were at her side. She could brush it off, say it was only a turned ankle. But she wouldn't. If he asked, she would tell him the truth.

"I'm sorry." His voice was nearly as much a whisper as her own. "I shouldn't have told you to go. I didn't want you to go. I was..."

"Afraid." She grabbed a deep breath but kept her gaze out at the ocean.

"Yes."

"You don't have to be."

"You don't understand."

"Dio, I may never dance again. At all. I may only be able to walk now and then without these crutches, until I push it too hard and ... and it's permanent. This is a permanent thing. It can't be fixed. If you can't deal with that, say so, or walk away. If you can, then come to me. But don't come to me unless you're willing to come all the way to me."

Her body trembled as she tried not to shake, tried not to turn to him and crawl up to his legs and hold on, tell him not to go. He was silent. She focused on the seagulls, on the waves, the wakes made from passing motor boats and jet skis. She'd always wanted to try a jet ski but she couldn't now. Her foot would never hold her well enough.

She closed her eyes in the silence and hoped he was still there. Seagulls cried out. She felt like joining them, leaping into the water and just going as far as she could out over the ocean. "Dio?"

"I'm here."

Her eyes clenched. Her heart nearly stopped. "Please. Come to me."

"Lina..."

"I'm not Lina. Lina is fake. I'm Caroline. My mask is off, as you asked. I'm just Caroline, an ex ballerina, ex stripper. Nothing more. I have no job, no home, no more pretenses. Nothing. I have nothing much to offer you, or anyone."

"That's not true. Your company matters more to me than anything has in a lot of years. And I love your real name. It's beautiful, as you are, and you..."

"So are you."

He snickered. "What you've seen?"

"You. I see you, inside of you. And you are. Dio, please. Come to me. Come all the way to me."

"I can't stand the thought of ... if I let you see me. Caroline..."

"Please. Just come to me now. We'll deal with that later. I won't ask you to do it now." She listened to silence. Except the birds. The waves. A few voices in the distance. She would not turn to him. He had to come to her. He *had* to come to her.

The electricity sparked in her body. Her skin tingled. Her heart rate accelerated as she felt his legs close to her back, as she felt him crouch behind her. His fingers sent a shock through her soul as they reached up to smooth her hair from the side of her face.

"Caroline." His lips barely touched her just below her ear. "You have so very much to offer. I love talking with you." They touched her neck. "I love watching your excitement for life, your energy." Her body drew in, her head fell back, closer to him, her eyes closed. "I am so sorry. About your foot. It has to be extremely painful, at least mentally. You're such a beautiful dancer, I know it's in your soul. I'm sorry you've lost that." He kissed lower on her neck. And he lowered to the sand behind her, close against her body.

"It is extremely painful. Mentally. And physically. Sometimes I wake up in so much pain I can't help but cry out. I try not to. I do try." She had never told anyone. She didn't acknowledge pain. She was a ballerina. It was part of who she was.

But she wasn't anymore. Truth was, she didn't have any idea who she was anymore.

Dio slid a hand around her face and tilted it to his own. He was in his mask, but his dark brown eyes drew her in, along with his full lips, the ones that gave her so much pleasure in so many ways. "How can I help you?"

She laughed. It started out a small sarcastic laugh and turned into a deep wild crazy laugh. He looked at her like she was crazy. Maybe she was. How could he help?

As her body wore itself out with the heavy thick hard laughter, Lina grabbed deep breaths. Her eyes watered. She shook her head.

"Oh Lina." He drew her face to his with both hands and kissed her. Softly. Tenderly. Lovingly.

And it broke all of her control. She grabbed him, his shoulders, her arms against his arms, pulling herself to him, using one leg, her left leg to turn and face him better. She threw her body at him, pressed into him.

His strong thick talented hands wandered her body, down her hips, up again to slide under her shirt to hold her waist and up farther to her rib cage where his thumbs scissored out to touch the bottom of her breasts. Lina wouldn't care if he stripped her right there in the daylight under the pier next to the water and took her as the tide rose, meshing his body with hers, excruciating her with pleasure, with longing, with need.

"Oh Dio. I've missed you. I've missed your touch. Your eyes. Your ... all of you."

He nuzzled his lips against her neck. His hands moved to hold her breasts, still under her shirt.

"Oh yes. Go ahead."

He pulled back enough to catch her eyes. "They'll throw us in jail."

"I don't care."

"Mm, but I do. They'll put us in separate cells." He teased her lips.

"Oh. No, that... No."

"Come home with me, Caroline."

Home. With him. "Your mother... How is she?"

"Not good." He slid his hands back down to her waist, to her hips. "I'll have to get back to the hospital soon, but she wanted me to come find you before I was stupid enough to lose you."

"Find me? She knows about me?"

"Yes." His chest rose hard and fell fast. "Caroline, I'm sorry I told you to go."

"You said that already."

"Yes, but I..."

"No, don't. I've done some really stupid things in the past few days. Dio, I ... I nearly took someone home, some guy in a bar, a tourist. I thought you were blowing me off. And yet, at the door, the thought made me so sick..." She settled in half turned away, leaned against his body, sitting between his legs.

"You didn't let him past the door."

"No. It was the day you put my bikini top on my doorknob. I got kicked out for that, partly for that. But I..." She grabbed a breath and drew in the sand with her finger. "I didn't want him. I wanted you. Tell me your name. Is it really Dio?"

He caressed her face. "My name is Diomedes, but I only use Dio. Yes, my mother has a strange sense of humor and an obsession with Greek mythology, possibly one reason she married a man named Dominick Troy, grandchild of Greek immigrants, when he was everything she didn't seem to want. They were constantly at war over every little thing and she apparently thrived on that since she so often said after he was gone that she didn't know what she would do without him.

"She always wanted me to be different, to stand out. I guess she got her wish."

Dio's chest rose and fell hard. "I'm Diomedes Troy, a farmer who's obsessed with boats and water and unable to do much with either because I'm all my mother has and she's all I have and she gets very sea sick very fast and when... She had me very late in life and she's up there in age so she'll leave me soon and her greatest fear is that I'll be alone. I don't disagree with her. I figure she's probably right. I do my shopping at a little place on the other side of Charleston where no one knows me and I stay on the farm during daylight hours and work at the club at night because it's something I can do in a mask and people think it's just the costume. My mother says I'm too vain. She says the right girl won't care about my face. I have trouble believing anyone would be willing to ... walk down the sidewalk with me the way normal couples do and not be embarrassed by the stares, by the way people go out of their way to avoid me. I don't know that I can let myself allow someone I care about to go through that."

"Oh Dio." Caroline stroked the hair above his mask. "What happened? Were you born with it?"

"No. I seared it all to hell when I was young. Lucky I still have my sight, that it didn't destroy my lips, my eyebrows. They kept telling me how lucky I was that I walked away with only a scar. But it's not just a burn scar, Caroline. It's ... worse. Far worse. They kept saying it would heal and become normal-colored scar tissue, but that didn't happen. Something called post-inflammatory hyperpigmentation set in. It's dark-colored, patchy and raised, with some dark red thrown in for irony, I guess. I tried tanning my face to make it contrast less with my normal skin, but it only made the scar darker. It's... I was young at the time. If it hasn't healed by now, it won't."

"I don't care, Dio. I mean I'm sorry, for you, but I will absolutely walk down the sidewalk with you. I don't give a flying fuck what anyone thinks. Really, I don't. I learned not to years ago. And you can let me prove it whenever you decide. Until you feel safe enough with me, I'll understand. Just tell me you'll give me that chance. Because I want a real chance with you, Diomedes Troy, even with that name. I do. And I don't want you to be alone forever any more than your mother does."

"Would you be willing to meet her?"

"Will she want anything to do with me, or for you to have anything to do with me, when she knows I'm a stripper, an ex-stripper, with a bum foot and limited options for the future?"

"She knows how we met. She knows we were together the night we formally met. She knows where you work, or worked. She finds it all terribly romantic and yes, she wants to meet you. I told you, she has a strange sense of humor."

"Okay." Caroline ran a finger down his huge chest. "Dio."

"Hm?"

"Take me somewhere you can be with me. And then we can go tell your mother I don't plan to let you be alone forever so she can rest better."

"Caroline, until you see me, until you know..."

"I don't care. I told you I don't care. Wait to tell her if you want, but I don't care. Yes, I'll go home with you. No, not just because I'm desperate to find a place to live. Because I want to be with you. I'll do anything I can to help, you or your mom. Just tell me she'll let me share your room at night because I..."

He closed his mouth over hers, rolled her down onto her back and lowered on top of her. A beautiful deep sexy kiss. Yes, it was good that the searing didn't ruin his lips, his wonderful, passionate, full lips. They moved to her neck.

Lina gripped his back. "Take me. Here. Right here. I want you now."

He groaned.

Someone yelled from a distance, something about public display. Dio pushed himself up off her and said they were leaving. "Let's find somewhere else to be. It'll have to be quick. I need to get back..."

"Of course. Quick is okay. This time. Sometimes it is." She winked and reached for her crutches.

Dio helped her get up. He didn't ask about her foot. Caroline was glad he didn't ask yet. Enough was enough at the moment. He was taking her home. The rest would come.

She stopped a third of the way up the path.

"Are you all right?"

"My palms get sore. Give me a few seconds. They'll eventually get used to it again so I won't have to stop so much. The sand makes it harder."

"Come here." He took the crutches, handed them to her, and swept her up in his arms. She wrapped her right arm over his shoulders and threaded her left in the crutches to move them out of the way.

Caroline had never let anyone help her because of the foot, other than the cowboy only for a minute, and the cab driver, and never like this. She was determined to do it on her own, not to let it slow her down or need special attention. But it was different with Dio. She rested her head against him and gave into his concern, his care giving. It felt ... excruciatingly wonderful.

Twenty-five

"Where are we going?"

Dio maneuvered the car down the gravel path as he watched for wildlife that often jumped in front of him. "You said you would go home with me."

"You live way out here?"

"I love privacy. So did my father. My mother always wanted to be in town around people and she would have when we lost him if not for me, because I refuse to be around people more than I have to be. Sad that she never got what she most wanted, but I can only give in so much." He turned off onto his own drive, still gravel, but smooth gravel, since he kept it filled in. "I feel guilty about that when she complains about being out here away from civilization. She doesn't drive, never has, and I have to work."

"I'm sure she understands."

"No, she says I'm too vain. Still, I promised my father I wouldn't sell the place, so it makes more sense to live in it than to rent it, I guess."

"A farmer who doesn't want to be constantly tied to farm work." Caroline's voice was nearly a whisper. "What do you want, Dio? What is it you would do if..."

"If not for this face? You can say it."

"If you weren't so vain. That's what I started to say."

"Great, now I'll have two of you telling me I am."

"Oh well, I can't say much. I'm easily every bit as vain as you could be. Enough I don't know when to say when. Vain isn't only about looks, you know."

"It's not all bad, either. I think a lot of people could stand to be a touch more vain and do the rest of us a favor."

She chuckled. "Right? We have no need to see underwear and bra straps. Seems kind of like discussing your paycheck, you know, showing off what you have behind the scenes to people with no need to know. Hell, I'm not finicky, obviously, but I don't even want to see it."

"Nice metaphor. You just came up with that?"

"No. It's something I blurted out once when some dude caught me shaking my head at his girl wearing a skinny low-cut white tank over a black bra in the grocery store."

"You'll get yourself in trouble that way."

"Wouldn't be the first time, but he was too confused to know whether to be insulted. By the time he understood, if he ever did, I was long gone."

Dio shook his head with a chuckle.

"So? What else would you do if there was nothing keeping you from it?"

"Head out to the sea. Fishing boat or something. Like I said, I love boats and water." He took the curve around the clump of trees and watched her reaction as the house came into view.

"Wow. Now that... Wait, you live down another path here?"

"No. That's my house."

She stared. "Your mom's house."

"Mine, technically. My mother is ridiculously bad at figures, at business, at real-life decisions, so he left it to me. And she never wanted to live out here. He figured it would be gone the day after he was if he left it to her. I call it hers because it should be hers as long as she's still around. Not bragging, just want to be straight with you."

Caroline stared up at the two and a half story white Colonial farm house with its wide southern porch, as his mother called it since it was meant to have people over to gossip in the evenings, and the white wooden railing he repainted every two years, adorned with four oak rocking chairs he re-varnished on opposite years of painting the railing.

"I bet there are a lot of stairs in that thing."

"There are a lot of stairs, but there are two guest rooms on the main floor. Mom's in one of them right now and the other's been turned into a library, but it has a nice big daybed, so if you want that, it's yours. Or..."

"Dio." She rubbed his leg. "If I stay, it'll only be to share your bed. So if that's not okay with your mom, I'll find somewhere else."

He felt his chest heave as he relaxed at the thought of being able to wake up to her every morning. "In all truth, I think she'd rather you have me and keep her library. It was only an offer. I didn't want to assume." He pulled in and turned off the engine. "It is a lot of stairs, though. My room's up top. The second floor isn't used much, other than the small bedroom I use as an office. We can move down into one of those rooms, though, if you need."

"No. I can do the stairs. I don't want you rearranging your house for me."

"I will, though, if it gets too much for you. Not that big a deal." He took her hand and kissed it. Then he went around to open her door.

"I need my crutches."

"Not right now, you don't." He scooped her into his arms. "Right now, you are at my mercy, and I think I like it that way."

"Do you?" She gripped his neck with both arms and kissed him hard. "Well go ahead, then. Take me wherever it is you want to take me."

"Oh Lina, watch what you offer. This grass looks good to me about now."

"Are there sticker bushes in that grass?"

"Absolutely not. I don't allow it. They get yanked by the roots before they get far."

"You put a lot of love into this place you don't like."

"No, I love the place. It's the everyday farming I don't like, just because there's so much of it."

She looked around him at the grass. "Put me down."

"You want your crutches?"

"No. I want to feel that soft grass on my bare back."

"Your back isn't bare."

"Hm. Not yet. Put me down. There's no one around, right? It's private property?"

"No one comes here without notice. I don't allow that, either. The *no trespassing and no soliciting* sign out front isn't meant to be a joke, and most people don't tend to see me as the joking type, once they see me." He carried her over to a soft grassy spot away from the parking area and kneeled. "My bed is nice, too."

She grinned. "Guess we'll have to try that later. Put me down, Dio."

It wasn't what he intended when he asked her to go home with him, but it was a gorgeous day, warm, sunny, breezy, and taking her outside in the midst of nature, on the land he tended was too much temptation. He set her down gently and kissed her, moved over top of her, still on his knees, laid her back on the grass and leaned down over her body.

She reached between them to unbuckle his belt.

"In a hurry, are we?" He kissed her neck.

"You said it had to be quick. You have to get back..."

He'd nearly forgotten. Hell. He didn't want it quick. Maybe... "Hold on. Let me check. I'll be right back." He got up but she grasped his leg, still on her back looking up at him. He bent enough to take her hand away with a grin. "Don't go anywhere."

"Oh, funny. Don't be long." She unsnapped her own jeans.

Dio hustled into the house, called the hospital's number, and waited impatiently through the automated garbage he hated until he found a voice. He asked about his mother, if she was all right, if he should get back immediately.

"Oh, she's awake and spunky today. Our food is bad. We disturb her too much. She talks the ear off anyone who walks in, either like they're an old friend she hasn't seen in near forever or like they're the pure devil incarnate and nothing's right. I'd say she's doing well, given that's normal enough. Did you want me to put you through to her room?"

Dio hesitated. Spunky. Talking ears off. He didn't want her to talk his off right now. "Sounds normal to me. You're sure she's doing well, then?"

"Very much, I'd say. She's a tough ole bird. She should be able to leave by tomorrow if all stays as it is."

Home tomorrow. Dio grabbed a deep breath. "Thank you. I'll be in to see her soon." After he took care of more pressing business. His mother told him to go find Caroline. He was obeying orders.

He stalled only long enough to grab the small thermos he always carried when he worked and filled it with ice water. He didn't know how long Caroline had been on the beach, but he was thirsty already. She likely was, too.

On the front porch, he looked over at her and stopped. She'd stripped. Completely naked. And she sat with her hands behind her propped up to watch him approach. With a grin, he forced himself to walk slow, to tease her as though he might change his mind. She had one leg, her left leg, propped up, her right extended. Her hair was now out of the elastic that held it up at the beach. It flowed just over her shoulders.

"Thirsty?"

"Come here. You're wasting time."

He moved closer. "You didn't answer me."

"Come here, Dio."

He got to within a couple of inches of her outstretched leg and opened the spout to take a large swallow. "Want some?"

"Yes."

He moved to her side but refused to let her take it. "Huh uh. Open your mouth." When she obeyed, Dio tilted it slowly to let the water dribble onto her tongue. She closed her eyes and swallowed. Teasing, he moved it, still trickling, to her bare shoulder and her body pulled in slightly at the coldness of it, but she kept her eyes closed and her head back, encouraging him. She groaned softly as he moved it to her breasts and down her stomach, down to the hair she kept trim and neat. Her body clenched. He moved it back up her stomach, up to her mouth, then took another swallow himself.

Dio lowered beside her and helped her take another swallow, a deeper swallow, then put it aside and took her in his arms, kissed her hard and deep, and lay her back, her bare back, against the grass. She said nothing. She surrendered to him.

Moving down to kneel between her legs, he told her to keep her eyes closed until he said otherwise. With her promise, he kissed her stomach, and her thighs. And he pulled the mask half way up, out of his way as he spread her legs farther and kissed the soft skin of her inner thighs.

Dio had to know. One way or another. He took the mask off so he could feel her skin against his face. Quickly he pulled his jeans off, and his shirt, and gave her only the slightest warning before he entered her.

Her eyes remained closed as she pressed up into him, her fingers now gripping his hips, pulling him close. She obeyed well. At least when she agreed to obey.

He couldn't control it any longer, but he wanted to know first. "Caroline." He whispered beside her ear.

"Yes. Dio, yes."

"I want you to see me for all that I am."

"Yes."

He started by rubbing his face against hers and it nearly made him finish far too soon. He'd never felt a woman's face touch his face, or her fingers. He should let her see him first, he supposed, in case she didn't want it, but just once, he had to feel a woman's face against his.

"Oh my Lina. Be tough for me. Please. Be tough for me."

"Dio." She raised a hand behind his head. "I don't care. I told you, I don't care."

"Open your eyes, then. Before I come into you, I want you to see me." He'd never let himself go all the way inside a woman. He'd always pulled out. But he didn't want to pull out. And he couldn't control it any longer. "Caroline."

"My eyes are open, Dio. Raise your face, baby. Let me see your eyes..." Her breath quickened. Her body tightened. She was there again. At that point.

He raised his head, gritted his jaw, prepared himself for her to push him away.

Her eyes watered. The hand behind his head caressed his hair. "Oh Dio. Yes, baby. Let yourself go with me."

He found only passion in her expression, and she slid the hand around to touch his face. She touched every part of his face.

He let himself go, and felt her let herself go. Dio pulled her as close as possible until he was nearly afraid he would break her, but she pulled just as tight. He felt moisture in his eyes. "Caroline."

"Yes."

"Now tell me. Would you walk down a sidewalk with me, like I am now?"

"Naked? Well, I might but..."

He caught her eyes. He still saw no fear, no disgust.

"Yes, Dio." She touched his face again. "Absolutely. Or at least I'd hobble down the sidewalk with you. What a pair we'll make, right?"

He rubbed a hand over the top of her head. "Is Mom right? Am I being too vain?"

Her eyes wandered his face. "Well, no, people will..."

"Veer around me like I'm infectious or something."

"Probably. But so what?"

"You don't care? You won't be embarrassed?"

"I'll only care if you let it hurt you. I don't want you hurt. If you want to lock yourself away in this house and behind that mask forever and only take me out at night, away from people, I can live with that, but if you want to ... just be you and not let the idiots bother you, I'll be at your side. Just don't be surprised if I say something to let them know they're idiots. I might. I do it for myself. I'll damn sure do it for you."

"Funny. I'd never thought I'd be the one with a bodyguard."

"I will be, though. Fair warning."

He kissed her. "Interested in seeing the inside of the house now?"

"Hm. Thought you were in a hurry."

"She's doing well today. I may bring her home tomorrow. Figured you might want to shower and maybe dress again before we go see her."

"Dio?"

He stroked her face, her beautiful, perfect face. "Yes."

"Are you keeping me? Did I pass well enough?"

"Oh Lina, I am absolutely keeping you. And as lame as you are, you'd have a hard time getting away from me. I'm faster than this build looks like I would be."

"So I'm your prisoner now?"

"At least until that foot heals and you can dance away from me. Then I guess it's up to you."

She dropped her gaze. "It might not heal."

He set his hand aside her face. Her face was so small in his hand, her expression one of ... giving up. She looked like she was giving up. "We'll see."

"If it doesn't?"

"I guess you're stuck with me."

"Hm." She wrapped into him. "Guess that would be the good to go with the bad, then." She kissed him softly. "I do need a shower. Want to hand me the crutches?"

"No." Dio scooped her into his arms and stood.

"Um, forgetting something? Our clothes?"

"I'll get them later." He admired her body as he carried her to the front porch and into the house. In turn she studied his face, stroked it with her fingers, ran the tip of her pointer finger along the ridge that started on one cheek, ran across his nose, and to the other cheek where it widened.

"How did you manage to do this?"

"I'll tell you later. Right now I want to let it sink in that you didn't jump away from me."

"You're beautiful."

He snickered. "You say that because I have you naked and in my arms, away from your crutches."

"No." She pulled his face down for a kiss. "I say it because you are. And you are as unique as your name. And I don't want any other woman to ever touch you the way I do. Promise me." It was nearly a whisper, a panicked insistent emotional whisper.

"I promise you." He started up the stairs. She hadn't even looked at the downstairs. She was fully focused on him. He took her to his room and stopped in the middle of it.

Finally, she looked around. "Wow. This is one room? I've had apartments smaller than this."

"Dad built the house. Everything is big except the kitchen, at Mom's insistence. She didn't want that much to take care of. She wanted small and easy care. He liked big and space. He was a big man..."

"Like you?"

"More."

"Wow."

"Thinking you got jipped now?"

"Not at all." She ran a hand over his shoulder. "I think even bigger than you would be scary to me. Is your mom a big woman?"

"You were at the hospital."

"Right, but I was only paying attention to you. Is that bad?"

He kissed her nose. "She's smaller than you. But damn is she feisty. That's a warning."

"I think I can deal with it. Because, you know, if she rattles me I'm going to find you and make you unrattle me."

"Careful, Lina. I'll have her rattle you on purpose."

She gave him another kiss. "Tired of carrying me around yet?"

"I could carry you around all day long and feel like I was on vacation. But on to the shower, so I can take you to see if you can put up with my mother well enough to live here."

Caroline marveled that he had his own private bath, and not just a bath but a spa compared to those she'd always had and had to share. It wasn't extravagant looking. The fixtures and countertops were all normal Formica and silver plate. The tile was just vinyl bathroom tile in a green and blue swirl. But it was big. The shower was bathtub size, large bathtub size with large shower heads and frosted glass doors and just enough of a side to be able to bathe instead of shower.

Dio set her down carefully and reached in to lower a fold-out bench. "How's that?"

"I think I've died and gone to heaven."

He ran a hand through her hair. "I like this place about a million times better right now, even knowing I'll have to work longer hours farming it for a few days to catch up with what I've missed recently."

"Dio, hire someone. Can't you?"

"I'm bad with people. I've tried. Between the mask and my ineptitude, I can't keep them or I find fast that I don't want to keep them. Mom used to be good at it, but she's ... well, until recently, it was just easier to do it myself and keep away from people."

"Yeah, I understand that one. But if I'm staying here, I'll find ways to help you enough to earn my keep. You better know that."

"Your company, someone my age to talk to after the long work day, will be enough, along with helping to keep an eye on my mother, if you would." He ran his hands down her hips. "Of course, knowing I can look forward to this at least some nights won't be bad, either."

Caroline moved in against him, hopping slightly to be close enough, and slid her arms around his shoulders. "Most nights, if you're up to it. Maybe at lunch time, too?"

"Mm, depending on thc day."

"Good enough. And of course I'll help watch over your mom, but I do mean more than that. I am good with people when I want to be. I can't say I like people much, but I'm good with them, which might make me a bit psychotic or something, but whatever I can do to help with that, tell me. Maybe once this foot is better than it is, enough to drive, I can take your mom into town now and then to keep her from being too bored out here in the boonies."

"Or to keep yourself from being bored out here? Will you be?"

"Absolutely not. With all of this beautiful outdoor space? This is heaven, Dio. I bet I can learn how to help you outside, too. I'm ridiculously high energy and I love being outside, so you might as well take advantage of that."

He chuckled. "I think I have been already, and damn, I wish we didn't have to leave the house today." He backed away enough to let his eyes roam her body. "But you better shower. I'll go gather our clothes. Will you be okay in here by yourself?"

"Are you kidding? Alone is what I know."

"I understand that one. But not anymore, Caroline. Not if I can help it."

~ Twenty-six ~

Dio was nervous as hell.

Caroline was fine about meeting his mother, but he was nervous as hell. Not that it would change anything. The house belonged to him. He had the right to move anyone in he wanted. Still, he paused outside her room and took a deep breath.

"It'll be fine." Caroline rubbed a hand over his back. "I'll make this work for you."

Unable to resist, he set his mouth over hers. He wanted to take her back home, to let this wait another day, to hide her away from the world with him only for twenty-four hours.

"This must be Caroline." His mother was at her door, in her robe, holding the rolling metal thing that held her IV. A nurse at her side turned to hide a grin.

Dio couldn't answer.

"Yes. I'm Caroline Corinth." Lina offered her hand. "You have to be Mrs. Troy. It's a pleasure to meet you."

"I am not Mrs. Troy. I'm Cleo. The rest of it doesn't matter at this point."

"Mom, she was being polite."

"For heaven's sake, Diomedes, you think I don't know that? I'm not that old yet. Corinth? What kind of name is that?"

Caroline gave his hand a light squeeze. "To tell you the truth, I have no idea. I know when I was in school, kids saw it funny to call me CiCi, no matter how I hated that."

"Yes, most will do whatever they can to annoy you if they see they can get away with it. And how did you handle it, if I can ask?"

"Mom, you should sit, shouldn't you?"

"Diomedes, I'm talking to the young lady. Mind your manners. Besides, I'm on my way to take a walk." She looked at Caroline again.

"Mostly I ignored them. I'm good at that."

"Mostly?"

"Sometimes they wouldn't let it go and got too much in my face."

"And then you … whined for a teacher?"

"No, then I knocked them down and reminded them of my name. I got suspended for it twice and caught hell at home, but it stopped after that."

"That's what I woulda done the first time. Guess you have better sense than I did. So, you were out here enjoying my son, it looked like."

Dio groaned, but Caroline laughed. "Yes, I was enjoying him. I enjoy him a lot, really." She rubbed Dio's arm.

"So I heard."

"Mom…"

Lina laughed again. "Well good, then we both know where this stands, right? So to speak, since it looks like right now neither of us are terribly good at standing. Can I walk with you?"

His mother looked up at him. "I think she just might be able to handle you. Go on now and fetch me some real food. Caroline and I are going to walk up and down this hall a couple of times." She excused the nurse, said she would be fine in Caroline's hands.

Dio agreed, with no choice but to agree. He asked what real food she wanted, and when she chose a restaurant a few blocks away without a pickup window, he did argue. He didn't want to go inside a restaurant close to home, and she knew he didn't.

"Oh for heaven's sake, Diomedes, just knock 'em down like Caroline would if they get too fresh with you. Don't let your girl show you up. Look at you, you big brute. I think you can handle it, and it's time I stopped coddling you."

He started to fume until Caroline set her crutches against the wall and clung to him, her arms around his neck. "She's right, baby. Just ignore them and think of…" She reached up to talk into his ear, quietly. "Of the way I look at you, of the way I adore you. And tonight, I'll do it again. Any of it you want. I think it'll be my turn to be in charge, right?"

Dio cleared his throat and tried his best not to let her effect show on his face, in his eyes, anyway, since nothing else showed on his face under the stupid mask. "Right." He patted her rear and reached for her crutches. "Be careful. Don't let her trip you. Mom, be nice to her."

He retreated down the hall, then turned to watch a moment. The old woman liked her. So far. The being alone bit was a test.

Lina hit the stupid elevator button repeatedly to get the door to close already. "Close. Just *close*." Her yelling at the machine made some woman change her mind about getting in with her and the stupid door finally closed. It lurched. Started down. To the ground floor where she could get out. Fast. As fast as she could on the stupid crutches.

She was tempted to just drop the things and make her foot work. Even if it hurt like hell, it would be faster. She had to get out of there before Dio came back. She'd go somewhere close and call Harry. No, Harry might tell Dio where she went if he took her anywhere. But her car was still at Harry's, with everything she owned inside it. She'd have to get back there somehow.

Dusk was starting to fall as she finally got off the damned elevator and over the too-polished hospital floors, carefully, the rubber of her crutches squeaking on the polish, and outside. Lina took a huge breath of fresh air. Not fresh enough. Not ocean fresh. She wanted to be on the ocean, somewhere Dio wouldn't look for her. Maybe she'd just sleep out there for a while, a few nights. She had a $20 she'd stuck in her pocket before she left Harry and Nelda's to job hunt, her ID, and her phone. Her phone. She rubbed the left jeans pocket where she'd put her phone. It wasn't there. She knew she'd... At Dio's. It probably fell out during her romp in Dio's yard. He'd retrieved her clothes. Hadn't he seen it?

She'd said one thing too much. Only one thing. But she'd trusted the old woman. They were getting along fine.

Stupid, stupid Lina. Trusting again. She knew better.

At least she had the $20 and she figured it would be enough for a taxi from Charleston to the edge of Folly Beach, plus some food for the night. Maybe he would take pity on her and get her all the way to the pier. She could hope.

Lina flagged the first one she saw, told him where she was headed and asked how much. More than she could afford. She said it was more than she had. She wasn't stupid, not completely. She had to keep some cash on her.

"Sorry, lady, I can only take you to Oak Island Drive for that. Take it or leave it."

That would still give her more than a mile to walk. She was far too tired and too sore. "I have to leave it."

He shrugged and pulled away.

Lina hobbled the direction she wanted to go. If she walked part of it first, then hailed a cab, she might be able to do it. Then a thought struck. It was the way Dio would return from the restaurant, and it was about time for him to be back. It wasn't like she could look away and hope he wouldn't recognize her in the dusk. The crutches would pull his attention. She should have paid the extra. Frantically, she watched for another. As she did, she moved close to the buildings. She would also watch for Dio's truck and duck inside one of the stores if she saw him. With any luck, she wouldn't be too far between stores to be able to get to a door.

A block down the sidewalk, she spotted another cab. Lina moved back to the outer edge and flagged him. This time she didn't ask how much. She got in, told him where she was headed and how much she had and he could just stop when he got to that amount on his meter.

"That don't include the tip, right?"

"What?" Lina barely glanced up at him as she watched for Dio's truck.

"That amount, that with or without tip?"

"Are you kidding me?"

"Hey, a man's gotta make a living."

"Yeah, and a girl's gotta eat. Just take me as far as that'll get me. In the straightest direction possible. I'm not a tourist. I know the roads."

The man rolled his eyes.

She kept an eye on him and on the meter. He stopped just after Little Oak Drive and pulled over, in the middle of nowhere. "Come on, at least cross over to the town for me. You have to turn around anyway. You can't do that here. Besides, there's a few cents left."

"Yeah, I go all the way across the intersection and it'll go a dollar or two over your limit."

"You have to turn, anyway."

"Not with you in the cab."

"Oh for fuck's sake."

"Hey, no cursing in my cab." He pointed at the crucifix hanging from his mirror.

"Right. Go on just into town. I'll pay it."

"So much for all you have, huh?"

"It means I don't eat tonight."

"Not my problem, lady." He shifted back into drive and sped down to the bare edge of town. She gave him the twenty.

"Gonna get out?"

"I want my change."

"You're kidding me, right?"

"Hey, a girl's gotta eat. At least a bag of chips." Lina sat right there until he handed her the dollar thirty-nine. "Thanks for doing the job you're getting paid to do." She got safely away from the door. *"Jerk."*

On the sidewalk, she sighed. At least Dio wouldn't find her outside the hospital. And when his mother repeated what Lina said that made her so angry, he wouldn't look for her, either. Maybe she could call Harry. But she didn't want to call Harry. She didn't want to see anyone she knew or kind of knew. She wanted to get to the beach.

Maybe she would take Hayes up on his offer and accept some sit down job at the club. But she didn't trust him. He would turn into the same as that other one, the one who caused her all this trouble in the first place. It wasn't worth the risk.

So now what, Lina? You can't leave well enough alone, can you?

With another sigh, she plodded her way down Center Street. Her palms burned. Her underarms were chafed. Her upper arm muscles tried to cramp.

Oh Dio, I'm so sorry. I'm really so sorry. Please move on. Find someone tough enough without a sordid history. Please.

She paused only long enough to brush her eyes with her sleeve. Making her way across Huron road in the dark, she jumped when a car turned in front of her and got far too close. The guy yelled a *sorry* out the window.

"Watch where you're going, jackass!" He wouldn't hear. His music thumped too loud.

On the other side of the road, barely on the sidewalk, Lina started to laugh. She moved farther away from the road, laughing harder, and harder still until she couldn't hobble at the same time. What there was to laugh about, she didn't know. Nothing. And yet she couldn't stop.

She was too tired to get to the beach. It was too far away. She was hungry. Dio was bringing her food, to the hospital. She'd let him choose.

Oh Dio, I'm so sorry.

Her laughter turned to tears and she stood propped on her crutches, her right knee bent to keep pressure off her foot, her left leg burning with the extra strain, her face cupped in her hands.

She sniffed the mucous back that tried to run out her nose. She didn't even have tissue. She had to stop. She had to reserve what strength she had in order to get ... somewhere. To the beach. Even if it took all night. What else did she have to do, where else did she have to go? She'd sit on the sidewalk and rest as she needed.

As she needed now.

Lina made her way to a building and carefully lowered to the cement, let her back rest against the wall. She breathed heavy and wiped her hands on her jeans and her face on her shirt sleeves. She sniffed the rest back. Maybe she would just sit right there until morning. Or until she rested well. She let her eyes close.

"Hey."

She opened them to a rough female voice.

"You cain't sleep here. Go on now and go on home. Move along."

"I just need..."

"I don't care what you need, hear? You'll chase my customers away looking like a vagabond sleeping at my store front. Go on now or I'll call the cops."

Lina wondered if she should let the woman call the cops. If she said she had no home and no money for a hotel – not quite true but her credit card limit wouldn't take much more – they'd put her in a cell for the night, wouldn't they? And they'd feed her. It might not be any better than the hospital food the old lady bitched about, but it would be food.

"*Go on.*"

"Fine. I'm going." With a sigh, Lina pulled herself up with her crutches, nearly fell, but made it okay enough.

"Wait." The woman disappeared into her store and came back again. "I'll call my son-in-law to give you a lift to wherever you're going. He does local only, anywhere on Folly." She handed her ten dollars and a plastic bag. "There's some fruit in there, for strength. Don't tell him I gave you the money. It's a bright blue car with a magnet sign on the door. Wish I could do more, but I gotta run my business, you know."

"Thank you. I'll repay it as soon as I can."

"Never you mind. Just you be careful out here in the dark, a girl as pretty as you. Don't you have no one to call?"

"No."

"And that means no one you're willing to call, my guess. Pride is a powerful bad thing, missy. Just you wait and see. Don't let it destroy you. Ain't worth it. Go on and give them a call, whose-ever it is you ain't willing to call. Make it right. You'll be glad in the end."

"Thanks." It was all Caroline could say. She understood her point, she did, but the woman had no idea.

Hobbling farther down the sidewalk in order to lessen the distance she'd have to pay for, Lina was nearly at the end of her strength's limit when she saw the blue car. She moved to the edge of the sidewalk and waved one arm. He slowed, did a u-turn, and came back. A big magnet on the side advertised Folly Beach runs and she guessed he mainly picked up partiers to get them back to their hotels.

She got in before she told him she only had ten dollars so if he could just take her as close to the pier as he could on that, she'd make do.

Lina didn't watch this one. He seemed okay. He didn't ask if tip was included. She closed her eyes and let herself rest before she'd have to get out and hobble the rest of the distance.

"Miss?"

She opened them to his voice.

"We're here. Sure this is where you want to get out? Someone meeting you?"

They were there. All the way there. At the west end of the beach, a short distance from the pier. "Oh, but I only have…"

"Don't worry about it. Took the long way to let you rest your eyes a bit longer. Sure you're okay here?"

"Yes." No. But she'd have to be. "Thank you…"

"Forget it. Got a real good tip tonight I felt guilty about accepting. It'll more than cover your ride. Have a nice night. Enjoy the pier. They have music tonight. Some of these days, I'll not be working on a night they have music and I'll enjoy it myself."

"Yes. You should. Thank you again." She pulled herself out of the cab and closed the door with a nod. Her arm muscles tried to cramp when she put them back around her crutches, so she stretched a bit before moving.

Music on the pier. Like the night she came home. Or the night she started searching for home. At least the air smelled like the Atlantic, not like the city. Caroline knew people who detested the smell of the fish and seaweed and whatever else gave the ocean and surrounding air its unique scent, or they stopped noticing it, but to her, it was home, even if it wasn't.

Making her way barely into the sand, she sat down and remembered the bag of fruit. No. Damn. Damn. *Damn.* She'd left it in the cab. And she was starving.

When she could find strength enough again, Carline would go find something cheap to hold her until morning with the ten the driver refused to take. Then she'd find somewhere more remote to curl up and sleep.

Twenty-seven

"Sorry it took so long..." Dio cast his eyes around his mom's room and set the bag on her tray. "Where is she?"

"Left." The old woman pushed herself up to sitting and propped her pillows behind her. "Push that over here. I'm starving by now. What took you so long?"

"What do you mean, she left?"

She patted the bed to motion for him to sit.

"Why did she leave? What did you say?"

"Diomedes, my son, she is not the girl for you. A nice girl, I said. Find a nice girl. You can't have that one, not for more than a playmate and I think you've had enough of those. Now don't get me wrong, I know how it is for young men, but the time comes..."

Dio sucked in a deep breath to control his fast growing temper. "What did you say to her?"

"She won't stay, you know. The girl is more vain than you are. Arrogant. She'll take one look at you and run. I know the type."

"*What* did you say to her?"

"The truth, Diomedes. That you fell for her looks and her talent and it'll be no more than that, that she's hardly the first stripper you've brought home but it's always temporary, and when she finds the truth, she won't like it. And that when she looks inside far enough to find the truth about herself, she won't like that, either, and she'll realize she's not right for you, and that you deserve better. She's all cockiness and false vanity, Diomedes. Nothing but that. That's what I told her. And it only hit her so hard because she knows I'm right."

Dio put a hand over his chest and forced himself to breathe. "Not the first stripper I brought home? She sure as hell is; she's the first *any* woman I've brought home. Why did you tell her that?"

"She would have left you when you showed yourself. I saved you the heartache."

"No." It came out a whisper.

"Son..."

"No. She didn't. And you're wrong." He felt his knees try to buckle. "I took it off for her. She didn't even flinch. She ... she caressed my face, and still looked at me like ... like I was her prince or something. Like I *was* someone, like I *am* someone. She sees me, Mom. *Me*. As I am. How could you do this?"

"She saw you?"

"Yes. She saw me. All of me. As I am."

"Then it's just because of the house, the land. She'll get her hands on it and then walk away and want half of everything. It's just for what you have, Diomedes."

"Like hell it is. She agreed before she knew any of that. I told her I was a farmer, nothing more, and she still said yes, even after seeing my face, she wanted to stay, wants to help however she can. With a lame foot, she wants to help around the place. For *me*, Mom."

"She saw your face. And she still..."

Dio headed back out the door as his mother called to him. He had to find her. She couldn't have gone far. Unless she got a ride. A cab. Dio skipped the elevator and jogged down the stairs and out the door. He looked both ways down the sidewalk. Which direction would she head? Toward ... the beach. She would go to the beach. But it was eight miles or more.

She would have called Harry.

Dio went back inside and asked for a phone. The registration attendant pointed him toward a hallway. Why hadn't he bought himself a cell as his mom kept saying he should? He didn't like the things, but now it would be convenient. Finding a payphone these days was about like finding a dragon.

Finally, he grabbed the receiver and paced a few steps each direction back and forth until Nelda answered. "Nelda, did she call Harry? Did he pick her up? Where'd they go?"

"Whoa Dio, what are you talking about? A little slower."

"Caroline. Lina. Whichever name she gave you. Did she call Harry for a ride?"

"When, honey?"

"Now. Half hour ago maybe."

"I haven't heard from her today. Figured she was with you."

"She was. I have to go find her." As he started to hang up, he heard Nelda call his name. She asked where he was and what happened. He told her briefly and said he was starting at the beach.

She wouldn't like what she saw when she looked inside herself. What a vicious thing to say. Especially since Lina ... since she would believe it. She was covering much of who she was. Dio knew she was. He didn't care. Her inside truth might well be deep and dark, but he didn't care. He wanted her.

He loved her.

He swallowed hard at the thought and kept his eyes peeled on the sidewalks on both sides of the road. If she was trying to avoid him, she might have gone down a side road instead. She would know he'd go the most direct route to their spot first. She would know.

Dio hoped she would make it easy for him to find her. She'd asked if he was keeping her. She acted as though she wanted to stay. She... She didn't turn away when she saw him. She looked at him like ... like she loved him, or could.

Maybe she could.

But why did she run? She could have got away from the old woman and just waited in the lounge, at the entrance, somewhere he would see her. Why would she run? Or hobble, as she called it. All of her things were at Harry's she said, except her handbag that was in his truck so she wouldn't have to carry it. He'd assured her he wouldn't need it in the hospital, so she only had her ID and a bill of some amount tucked into her pocket. She couldn't have gone far.

Lina made her way down the beach, just off the sand where it was still grassy. She'd head to the tall grasses beside the palm trees. It would be a good hiding spot to lie down and rest a while. He wouldn't look there.

She could hear music drift along on the breeze from the pier. She wanted to go closer, to hear better, to sit up on the pier and look out over the water and ... and eat. Something. Anything. They hadn't even thought about lunch until well after lunch time as they were headed to the hospital and she'd barely eaten breakfast at Harry and Nelda's because she didn't want to impose. She was so hungry. So exhausted.

Too exhausted to get far enough to find food. Her hands burned. She just had to sit.

A group of kids came her direction. Boys. Early twenties, she guessed. They laughed and pushed at each other, stumbled over nothing. Lina veered away from them, but then she was in the sand and it was harder going and she was too fucking tired to take the harder path just because the three bombed stooges were perilously close.

"Hey, need a lift?" One of them looked over at her and laughed.

"Yeah, piggy-back ride. What do you think, sweetheart?" A different one. They headed toward her.

She veered farther away.

"Aw come on, we're just offering a ride, you know, on our backs. 'Course if you wanna be on your back, we can do that for you, too." More laughter. They moved in.

"Come any closer, gentleman, and I'll use these crutches to take away your interest in me or any other woman for days to come. Got it?" Lina did her best to sound not tired and not starving and not scared.

"Ohh, big talk from a little girl." More laughter.

"Don't think I can? Trust me, I can. Won't be the first time I've broken a guy's balls and I don't mind doing it. So get the hell away from me and go jump in the ocean to cool yourselves off." She set her right foot down just enough for stability and wielded her crutch the way Dio wielded his sword, in warning.

One of them pulled at the other two. "Leave her alone, she's not in the mood to play."

"Yeah, not worth it. Let's find some who are."

Lina took a deep shaky breath as they left, watched them long enough to be sure they were leaving, and lifted her foot. It throbbed. She should have whacked at least one of them for scaring her, for making her use her energy that way, for making her foot throb again.

Putty and bluster. All of them. Assholes.

With the strength that came from a battle won, Lina maneuvered back up to easier ground and sped her pace. By the time she got to the tall grass, she nearly fell into it, into a small cleared spot, curled into a ball, her crutches in her hand, and closed her eyes.

Dio couldn't care any less if he scared everyone on the beach. He stopped anyone he saw and asked about her. Some tried to back away before he could ask but he yelled behind them, said she needed help and he needed to find her. He only got empty stares and shakes of the head.

Oh Lina, come on baby. Come find me.

"Hey Dio, slow down for an old man."

He turned to the dark figure hidden by the sinking sun's glare. Only the voice gave Harry away and Dio went to meet him.

"Nelda says you lost your girl already. Just imagine that, would you? Funny that I happened to run into the girl you happen to be seeing, and not just seeing, from what I figure, with the way you look right now."

"I asked her to move in with me. She said yes, and then she talked to Mom and ran. Not that I blame her after what was said, but she has nowhere to go. I've got to find her."

"Not entirely true, son. We invited her to stay as long as she needs. Figured she'd call us."

"I told her you know me well, so she's not going to call you if she's avoiding me."

"Yeah, guess that'd be true. Think she's here somewhere?"

"No idea." Dio shoved a hand through his hair. "She could have left town for all I know."

"With all her stuff at my place, and her car? Calm down now. We'll find the girl and then it'd be best to keep her away from crazy Cleo until she's more hooked on you."

"Harry..."

"Dio, you gotta face facts. That woman is crazy. Yes, she can be sweet as pie but she can also be one of the nastiest witches you ever did see, and whatever she admitted to saying, my guess is it was 'bout a hundred times worse. You know it's true. I've done sure heard her be nasty enough to you, and you're her own blood. Your old man knew it just as well, bless his soul for putting up with her. You did warn the girl first, didn't you?"

"To an extent."

Harry's head shook. "All right, we'll fix it, but let's get on to finding her. When this dark hits, it's gonna get cold. Here." He pushed a large flashlight into Dio's hand. Where've you already been?"

Dio couldn't even say. He'd wandered, jogged, up and down and back and forth, starting with their spot and he couldn't say from there. Harry shook his head again and laid out a search pattern and shoved Dio out on it. "Oh." He handed Dio a whistle on a string. "Give it three short blasts if you find her and I'll do the same so we can find each other again. Wife and I use this method to hunt for a pup when one goes astray. Your girl, she loves that batch of pups we have. I'm half a mind to give her one or two of 'em."

"Let's wait on that thought, if you don't mind." Grateful for the help, and that Nelda was home by the phone in case Caroline called there, Dio took off on his given route. And he listened carefully for the whistle.

He slowed some time later, aware of fatigue in his muscles, and checked his watch. Nearly ten. He'd been searching for ... more than three hours. And he wished he'd brought some of the food with him. At least he'd given himself a head start and ate the extra biscuits he ordered as he drove back to the hospital. He'd been starving. Caroline had plain worn him out and ... and she hadn't eaten. But she would have stopped somewhere, grabbed something. He hoped.

Come on, Lina. Answer me.

Dio pressed on and became aware that the path Harry gave him included the pier. He couldn't go up on the pier. Too many people. They had music tonight. It was crowded. But maybe she would be there. In the crowd. Hiding. And not hiding. She had to know it was about the last place he'd want to be. Damn Harry. He could have gone this path himself. He had no issue with being in public. He had no problem chatting to strangers or interrupting conversation to ask questions.

Would she be there?

An hour left before he was to meet Harry at the agreed spot to make a new plan, if needed. Dio gritted his teeth and headed to the pier.

The music grew louder, voices started to float across to him. He stopped. The pier. A crowd. *Hell, Caroline. Why? I didn't do it.*

Dio reclined onto the sand, his legs in front of him and his arms behind. The way she sat in the grass, at his house. Naked. Waiting. The image filled his thoughts and he replayed the moment, his pulse racing as he approached her, his palms sweating. His groin trying to reach her through his jeans, the aching. The incredible luscious inviting ache for her. *Lina, come on baby. Come.* He lowered over her in his thoughts, took full control as she let him take full control. She'd said it was her turn tonight.

With a snicker, Dio realized she'd sure done that. She'd taken control. Every fiber of his being was wrapped up in finding her, of taking her home, of letting her take full control of him in a much more pleasant way. Not only for the sex. That was, by now, a nice side benefit. It was her: her energy, her vitality, her optimism, her gentleness and her strength. Her companionship. He wanted her to be part of the farm, belonging there with him, working alongside him.

He turned his head toward the music, the crowd. The row of bright lights stretched out along the long dark pier like a marquee. Like an invitation, a silent scream to pull lone dwellers in. Come. Come. Come and find me, it said. *Come and find her* screamed in his thoughts.

Dio stood again and brushed off the sand.

Fine. He would go to the pier. Let the sea foam land where it may.

He saw the heads turn as he went through the building that housed the shops and the restaurant, saw people veer away. He only looked at the faces long enough to know they weren't the one he wanted. A few more feet and he would be out on the pier. He slowed. Nearly stopped. But he couldn't stop. He needed to find her. Breeze off the ocean picked up, a chilly breeze. She was in only a skimpy T-shirt and jeans and her sandals. He hadn't even asked her yet what happened to her foot. He should have asked. He should have finished the story of his face, then maybe she wouldn't have taken the old woman so seriously. Harry was right. She was crazy. As often as he tried not to admit it to himself, Dio couldn't deny it anymore. She was crazy. And all he'd done the past few years was to feed into it, let it go, to placate her.

It was his fault. Caroline left because he'd refused to admit it.

Time to stop hiding.

"Hey." Some uniformed guy with a nightstick at his side, his hand clenched over it, stared at him. "You can't go on the pier like that."

Dio sighed. And he nearly argued.

Time to stop hiding.

Fine. "If you say so." He clenched the mask in his hand and pulled the thing off. The guard stepped back a half a foot or so. "Better?"

"Uh... I..."

"I'm looking for someone. A woman. About five-six, light brown hair, medium length, incredible build, on crutches. Have you seen her?"

"Uh..."

"Yes? No? You would remember if you had."

The guy was still staring at him, as were several people around.

"Anyone see her? She's my girlfriend." They exchanged glances. "Yeah, I know. Surprises me, too. My mother chased her off and she's upset. I need to find her. Have you seen her?"

They relaxed enough to at least answer that they hadn't.

"If you do, tell her ... tell her Dio is here on the beach and we need to talk. She'll be tired, her hands are sore, so if you'd have her sit and rest and come get me, I'd be grateful. After the pier, I'm headed toward the marshland. I'm easy to see ... with my flashlight."

A couple of girls chuckled as he ran it up and down his body. Then he moved on, toward the gazebo, out over the Atlantic. The stares at least broke conversation so it was easy for him to ask about her. Most shook their heads as they stared. Some just stared. He asked all the way up and it took forever to get to the end of the thing. He asked there, also, on each corner and in the middle.

A girl approached slowly, studying his face. "You're Dio from DanceOtica. So that's why you wear a mask." She kept some distance.

"How about you don't spread that around?"

"Yeah. No. I won't. You're my favorite performer. It's why I'm always there. You're really hot with those swords."

"Thank you." He started away.

"Guess I'll see you tomorrow."

He looked back. "Not if I don't find Lina by then, you won't."

"Lina. The stripper Lina? Wait. She's who you're looking for?"

"Yeah."

"Your girlfriend? Whoa. No wonder my friend said you always turn her down when she hits on you. Lina's hot. Haven't seen her dancing recently."

"She injured her foot. You haven't seen a girl out here on crutches anywhere?"

"No, but I'll help look. We all will." She motioned to her friends and told them of the quest, told them who he was, never mind he'd asked her not to spread it around. But it turned out to be helpful. Soon a whole group had volunteered to help look. They even talked to him like he was human.

A couple of the girls stayed by his side, to help him talk to idiots who would be scared of him otherwise, they said. One, the friend of the one who recognized him, was too handsy for his liking, but in return for her help, he'd ignored the way she so often touched him. Usually his arm. Sometimes his shoulder as though testing to see if it was real. Once his ass, although she apologized like it was an accident. It wasn't, but he'd let her touch damned near anything if she and her group helped him find Caroline.

Harry had seen no sign of her, either. He was surprised that Dio met him at their agreed spot with a small group in tow. And he looked as tired as Dio felt.

"Go on home." Dio set a hand on his friend's shoulder. "I'll call you if I need. Thank you for..."

"You headed home?"

"No. I'm staying right here."

"You've gotta sleep, too."

"I have to find her."

"She might not be here."

"If she's not yet, she will be." Dio told Harry again to go home. The group of kids told him they'd stay and help, that they were always up till all hours of the night. Harry agreed muttering something about young people and lack of work ethic. Dio couldn't care less at the moment. At least they were willing to help.

"You do look wiped out." The touchy-feely girl rubbed his arm. "Sit and rest a while. We'll keep looking."

Giving in, he lowered onto a wooden bench, slumped down, and let his eyes close. Only a few minutes. He heard the girl tell her friends she would stay and look after him and they should go ahead. But she left, too. Dio was glad she did. The girl was entirely too friendly.

He felt his body give in to the fatigue and frustration. He could sleep sitting up. It would hardly be the first time.

"Here."

He opened his eyes to her voice. Lina. No. Not Lina. The girl. She shoved a bag at him. Food. He could smell it.

"Heard your stomach growl. I love these. Hope you like sausages. They're my favorite. I love sausage, any kind. The bigger the better." She winked.

He nearly devoured the things. She rested a hand on his leg as she sat close and ate her sausage suggestively, eyeing him. As he finished, she slid the hand up toward his crotch.

Dio grasped it. "Not going to happen."

"I just wanted to ... you know, see if your size is all-over. I've heard big men aren't all-over big but I figure you are. You look like you are at the club, unless you add size with a sock or something."

"I don't add anything. And no, I'm not proving it. Like I said, Lina's my ... she's mine. I'm hers." He crumpled up the bag and got up, using the flashlight to check his watch. After midnight.

She stood next to him. "So I'm not trying to steal you from her. I just ... you know it can be nice to just ... play around with someone else now and then, right? I have a boyfriend, too, but we're kinda open and..."

"My face doesn't turn you off?"

She hesitated. "No. It's not your face I want."

Dio grabbed her hand and raised it toward the scar. She yanked it away. "Right. Look, despite my job, I'm not a toy at your disposal. If that's the only reason you're helping, gather your friends and go on."

"No, I'm sorry. It just..."

"Forget it. Don't follow me. I can't deal with this tonight." He pulled his wallet out and handed her a ten. "For the food." Then he turned and stormed away from her, away from the direction her friends had gone.

An hour later, he had to give in to his body and rest a while. Dio made his way back to the sidewalk where Harry could find him if he tried and reclined on the grassy edge of the sand. He was chilled, but not like she would be if she was on the beach. He didn't chill easily. His mom said it was all the bulk, the muscle, that stirred his blood fast enough ... and who knows but she made that up. Harry was right. She was crazy.

And she'd chased Caroline off. Dio supposed he should call the hospital to check in, but he was still far too angry.

He gazed up at the star-spattered black sky and the half moon ... and gave in to slumber.

~ Twenty-eight ~

"Dio. Wake up."

He opened his eyes to ... the girl again. What in the fuck did she want now? It was daylight. Barely. A brief bit of light crept over the horizon.

Not only the girl. Three girls. And three guys.

He sat up as the guys stared open-jawed.

"Hey, I'm sorry about last night." The girl crouched next to him and spoke into his ear. "I was ... not myself. Don't say anything to him. The tall one is my boyfriend. I found him on the pier after I left you. I thought he'd taken off with someone else and I was... It doesn't matter. I'm sorry."

"Forget it." He pushed to his feet and stretched as high as he could.

The boys stepped backward. Dio would have laughed at any other time.

"They saw her last night. Lina. At least I figure it was her."

"Saw her where? When?"

"Close to here, actually. We were headed to the pier coming from that way." The boyfriend pointed down the beach into the grassy area. "Stopped to talk to her."

"Sexy thing for her age." Another one snickered. "No wonder she's a stripper. But she's uppity as hell."

"Vicious, I'd say. A little flirting and she..."

Dio grabbed the collars of the two shorter ones. "If you touched her, I swear I'll drag your asses up to the end of that pier and dump you over the side."

"Hey. No. We didn't dare. The bitch threatened to take off our family jewels with her crutches. Looked like she meant it, too. Didn't get close enough to find out."

Dio shoved them away. "Don't call her that again." Definitely had to be Caroline. "What direction was she headed?"

"That way." The boyfriend nodded toward the tall grass not far from him. "And I wouldn't have let them bother her. They were just out of it. They didn't mean any harm."

The girl stepped beside the boyfriend and took his arm. "He pulled them away. He's a really good guy. Those two are royal jerks."

The other two girls objected. Dio ignored them and headed off the direction they pointed him. The girl told her group to scatter and head the same way.

"Hey *look*." One of the guys called over to him.

Dio ran over. A footprint with what looked like sticks being dragged on either side. Caroline. Her crutches. The sand was damp enough from evening and morning dew to hold her tracks. Dio jogged along and followed them into higher grass, under a palm tree.

She was there. He spit out a huge sigh of relief, knelt beside her, and touched her arm. She was cold, covered in goose bumps, shivering. With a start, she grabbed a crutch and swung it up at him. He caught it just before it bashed him in the face. "Lina. It's me."

With wide eyes, she took him in, then dropped the crutch and reached up to him.

He cuddled her shivering body against his and kissed her head, her face, her mouth. Her arms slid from around his neck to his chest as though she had trouble keeping them up. Her stomach growled.

"Let's get you home and warm."

"Dio..."

"We'll talk later."

"No. Your mom..."

"My mother is a crazy woman. I should have warned you better. I shouldn't have left you alone with her. I'm sorry."

"But she's right." A tear trickled from one eye.

"Lina..."

"Dio, she's right. I ... I have done things..."

"I don't care." He adjusted her so he could use one hand to wipe the moisture away, to caress her face. "Caroline, I don't care about your past any more than you cared about my scar. I don't care. I love you. And you're coming home with me. If I have to keep you by my side twenty-four hours a day to be sure you don't run again, I'll do that. But I'm keeping you. I told you I was. I told you I could outrun you. So don't try again."

More tears fell. He wiped them away and glanced out over the water. "Look."

She turned toward the sunrise. A bright yellow beautiful sunrise over the Atlantic with the pier standing at attention over the sand and ocean.

"I think I should marry you on the pier at sunrise. And I think I won't let you argue."

"Oh Dio. There's so much..."

"You can tell me when you're home, warm, and fed, and I'll tell you the rest. But it won't matter, Caroline. I'm keeping you."

Caroline melted into his arms, his body, his warmth. She heard him ask if one of them had a phone he could borrow and heard him talk to Harry, tell him he found her and they'd be there soon for her things. She felt him move as he handed it back, thanked whoever it was, and cuddled her in closer.

"Let's go, baby."

She shook her head. "I can't. My hands..." She turned them palm up. Blisters were scattered here and there. Some had popped and were red and oozing.

Dio wrapped her arm over his shoulder and lifted her. "Looks like you go nowhere without me for a while, my little captive." He asked someone to carry her crutches to his car.

Caroline didn't even look to see who they were. She didn't care. She shivered and scrunched closer to him. He kissed her head as he walked. He didn't have his mask on. It suddenly dawned on her he was with others, talking to them, without his mask. "Dio." She raised a hand to his face. "You're..."

"Not in hiding. No, and it's okay."

"Is it? Is it safe out there?"

He grinned. "No, but what's the fun of playing it safe?" He lowered his mouth close to her ear. "Come on out of the shadows, Lina. My sword and I will be here to protect you."

She ran her fingers along his scar and over his eyebrows, and his lips. "Then me and my attitude will do the same for you."

When they got to his truck, Lina finally saw who it was that carried her crutches. The idiot boys from last night.

"I know who they are. And they're very sorry. Aren't you?" Dio nearly growled at them and set her down through their apologies long enough to get his keys out and open her door. With a light caress of her hair, he helped her in and closed her door.

Getting in beside her, he started the car and turned on the heat, then leaned over to pull her to him. He gave her a long, deep, intense kiss and ran a hand over her head, pausing alongside her face. "You scared the holy hell out of me. Don't do that again."

"Dio, my foot... It was revenge. Purposeful. And I deserved it. Almost. Not to this extent, but I... Your mom's right, Dio. She is."

"Hey." He rubbed her lips with his thumb. "You're not warm and fed yet. This can wait."

"But I should tell you now so you can make this easier and just tell me to get out here and be done with it."

"Baby, that's not going to happen." He gave her another kiss, a hard urgent wanting kiss. "Buckle your seatbelt, Lina. This is bound to be a wild ride, but it's going to be a nice, long, exciting one. I'm not letting you go."

She drew back at the possessiveness, at the intensity in his eyes, and debated whether to get out, whether she could get to her crutches from the back seat and...

"I won't hurt you." Dio studied her, his voice suddenly as soft as his eyes. "Caroline." He offered his hand, waiting. "If you ever want to leave because of me, because you don't want me, I'll let you go. I won't make it hard on you and I won't ever hurt you. I only mean that I won't let you go because of your past ghosts or because of my past ghosts. I know we'll have stormy times as we get to know each other, as we adapt to each other. But I don't back away from adversity. I confront it head on, like you do, like I've seen you do."

She sighed heavily. "I'm so tired. Deep down soul tired."

"I know, baby. So let me carry you a while until you're not. I get tired often, Caroline. I get to where you are often. Give me your hand and we'll pull each other up. I won't ever hurt you."

She slipped her fingers into his large hand and he carefully avoided her blisters as he raised her hand to kiss her fingers one by one. "Ready?" His beautiful big eyes asked her to know he meant more than just the ride to Harry's.

She nodded. And she let her head relax against his shoulder as he drove. With her body warming, her palms ached more and her foot throbbed. Her arms and underarms and legs hurt. But it was okay.

He had to stir her back to fully awake when they got there, and Harry and Nelda dashed out to the truck as Dio picked her up and kissed her head. Lina couldn't answer the questions, so he did.

Nelda fretted over her hands and threw a warm blanket over her and brought her a heaped up plate of pancakes and eggs and asked if she would be able to eat with her hands like that. Lina assured her she could. And she did. Until she was stuffed.

She listened as Dio made arrangements with Harry to get her car and her things to Dio's house. They worked it every way around Sunday until Nelda jumped in and said to leave Caroline in her care while Harry drove her car to Dio's behind him and they could both just come on back to get her again. Caroline didn't argue. She leaned her head against Dio's strong shoulder as Nelda cleaned and bandaged her hands.

She felt him shift, felt him help her shift, until he was reclined against the arm and several pillows and she was sandwiched between him and the couch, his arm around her, her head against his chest, an arm around his middle. Nelda had ordered him to sleep an hour or so before he got back in the car. Harry said something about him searching all night long.

Caroline was nearly asleep, cocooned against him and covered by a thick blanket when she popped her head up. "Dio?"

"Sleep, baby. I'll have to get to the hospital soon to check on and lecture my mother, but I need to sleep first."

"Yes, but ... did you say you loved me?" At his amused grin, she shook her weary fuzzy unfocused head. "If you didn't, say so. I was so tired. I might have just... and of course I'll be embarrassed if you didn't, but I thought... Did you?"

He shifted again to get closer to her face with a hand aside her cheek, a thumb hooked around her ear. "Yes, I did. And I do. Now go to sleep. If you wake up and I'm not here, I'll be back soon. Stay off your feet, and your hands, and just let Nelda take care of you until I'm back." He kissed her head.

Lina pulled herself closer to him, cringed when she bumped her hand in the wrong spot, and met his eyes. She tried to answer him but her voice wouldn't come; her tongue wouldn't form the words. Instead, she kissed him, on the mouth, the cheek, his eyebrows, his nose, his neck – he had such a glorious sturdy strong neck with stubble that poked her lips and nose, and he smelled like the ocean, like freedom, like forever. She put her focus on his mouth, stuck her tongue inside to taste him, to hook him, to tease him.

"Mm." He forced her head back enough to escape. Still, he looked amused. "Baby, we're not alone. Yet. Hold onto that thought for me." His wet-sand brown eyes sparkled.

She heard a deep voice chuckle somewhere nearby and a woman's voice hush it. Caroline lay her head back against him and turned to teasing his chest with a finger, until her arm grew heavy and she let it fall.

~ Twenty-nine ~

Dio shook his head at the wreck that was Lina's car. The girl either didn't take care of it or she bought it dilapidated. His guess was the latter. It did make it to his place in one piece and he pulled it into the barn. The old Ford could well be usable again with some work. She needed her own car. At least he hoped the foot would heal enough she would need a car and be able to drive it.

She deserved it. Almost. So she said. Vengeance. Someone had hurt her on purpose. Maybe that's why she pulled back from him earlier. Heaven forbid if Dio ever caught the monster who did it.

He wanted to move her things from her car into his house, but Harry was waiting. So was his mother. With a deep breath, Dio went on out to let Harry drive him to the hospital. He wanted to talk to the old woman without Lina there. On the way into Charleston, he debated how much to say, how much to let his anger show.

Harry insisted on going in with him. Dio argued.

"Boy, I've known that woman longer than you have. You just let me deal with her if she gets out of her head again. Take a walk if she upsets you and I'll have her calmed when you get back. I'm not about to let her interfere with this thing. Neddie and I are so darned happy to see you with someone nice and decent but also with the fire to deal with your ass on a regular-like basis, and I'm not about to let the loony bird mess it up. And don't go looking at me like that. Like I said, I known her longer'n you. Ain't nothing wrong with calling what is, is."

Dio supposed he couldn't argue.

A nurse nearly jumped on him when he walked past the station nearest his mother's room. "She's been calling for you all night and all morning. We left messages."

"I wasn't home. You could have called the secondary number. Is she all right?"

"Other than upset that you haven't been here, she's just fine. The doctor's about ready to release her and my nurses are ready for her to go. No offense, but…"

"No, understood. You don't think he could find reason for her to stay a couple more days?"

"Not by my bidding."

With another deep breath, he led Harry in.

"Well, where on earth have you been, Diomedes? And why did you bring that old goat into my room? I don't want him here. Where is that pretty girl who was with you? She up and disappeared this morning…"

"Last night."

"No, it wasn't last night. It was this morning after you brought me my chicken dinner. It didn't have enough salt, by the way. Next time you tell them more salt."

"Mom, it was last night while I was on the way to get your dinner. Why would I have brought a chicken dinner for breakfast? It was last night."

She frowned. "Like I said. Where'd she run off to? We were having a nice chat."

Dio looked at Harry.

Harry moved up to her bed and took her hand. "Now Cleo, you sent the girl off as though you didn't want her here. Said some not nice things to her."

"I surely did not. She was a sweet girl. Beautiful smile. Nice laugh. A nice girl, like I told Diomedes to find. Not one like that little tramp who was here last night. She won't do at all. Dio, you need to stay with that nice one and send the other on her way. Didn't I teach you better than to juggle two girls?"

"Mom … what? There was only one girl here last night. Caroline. The sweet girl with the beautiful smile. That's Caroline, the only girlfriend I have, the only one I want. She's the one you sent away. What are you talking about?"

"Nonsense. I sent away that other one, the one with the bad foot."

"That was Caroline."

"*No*, Diomedes, the *other* one."

He stared. How could he not have realized how far over the edge she'd gone?

Harry took over. "Now you listen to me, Cleo Troy, and you listen good. Dio has found himself a wonderful girl you're going to just love if you'll let yourself. You stop seeing her as two different girls and see her as she is and love her for both sides, just as you loved Dio's father for both his sides and the way Dio loves you, bless his heart, for both your sides. And you be nice to her. She's a good 'un, Caroline is. And she's moving into your house with you and Dio and you're going to be nice to her. I'm gonna be there checkin' to see that you are, you hear? You do this for Dio. He has done bent over backwards for you. You do this for him now."

She looked up into Harry's dark brown eyes, his wrinkled face, his mostly gray hair, and she quieted with a nod.

"That's a good girl now. You know way back when Dio's daddy was working for my daddy, and I saw him start bringing you 'round, I knew you would darn well be trouble for him. I even warned him about you. He just laughed and said he liked trouble and he looked forward to every minute of it. I darn sure think he got himself more than he wanted but it was his choice and I respected that. Now I look at Caroline and think she's getting herself into a whole heap of trouble with Dio, and with you, bless your soul, but I see she can handle it and she'll stick it out the way Dio's daddy stuck it out with you. You make it easier on her. You understand me? I'm gonna tell the girl she can always call me if you get too feisty and I'll take her right out of there and bring her home with me and Neddie till you can behave again. 'Course Dio won't be so happy when she ain't there for him, so you might consider your son and make it easy on the girl so I don't have ta come and get her."

"Just because my husband worked for your father, Harry, that doesn't give you the right to order me like that."

"No it sure doesn't, but my love for Dio sure does. Being his godfather and all gives me the right to look after him. You made that choice years ago. Now you hafta live with it."

Dio moved up to his mom's side. "Are you here again? Can I talk to you now?"

She pulled her hand from Harry's to take Dio's. "What have I done?"

"It's all right, Mom. I've fixed it again. But I need you to try, okay? I need you to be nice to Caroline at least until she gets to know you and gets comfortable with us."

"Has she seen you, Diomedes?"

"Yes. She has seen me. She didn't cringe. She didn't run. She caressed my face the way you used to before this." He shouldn't have said it. A look of guilt crossed her face as she pulled it away. "It's all right, Mom. I understand. All of it. But please, do this for me. Be nice to her, to either one you think you see, you be nice to her. She's had some rough times like we have. I don't want her to leave. I want to keep her."

Her eyes returned. "You can't keep a girl you don't marry, Diomedes. I have told you that over and over. And you can't marry a girl you don't love. You can't. I won't allow it."

"You're right. I love her. I plan to marry her. Then I plan to keep her. Forever."

"She won't do it. She'll run like the others, like every one of them."

"No. She won't, not if you try to be nice. She's tough enough to deal with you. I know she is."

Her eyes watered. "I want a daughter, you know. I have always always always wanted a daughter. Not instead of you. Along with you."

"I know, Mom. I'm bringing you one. Love her the way you love me and she'll be that for you."

"Yes. You bring me a girl who will be my daughter. Then all will be well."

Dio saw the warning look from Harry, but she would. Caroline would accept. "The doctor thinks you're ready to go home, Mom. What do you think?"

She nodded.

"And you'll follow orders so your cough doesn't come back?"

She nodded again.

"Okay. I'm going to go get Caroline and we'll both come back for you. And you'll be nice to her, right? To whatever girl you see with me, you'll be nice?"

Another nod. Dio hoped she would remember it long enough to get Caroline and his mom both home.

Caroline grimaced as she made her way to Harry's front porch using her fingers rather than her palms and keeping most of her weight on her chaffed underarms. She wanted to watch for Dio, to see him pull in, on his way back to pick her up and take her home. She wanted like nothing else to be home with Dio. If needed, she would stay upstairs during the day and avoid the old woman. Until she found a job. She thought again about taking Hayes up on his offer. Even if it was something she could do only on nights Dio worked so she could ride in with him, it would be something. Until her foot healed enough to be able to drive, she had no idea what else she could do.

He loved her. Dio said he loved her.

She looked out across the wide lawn and gravel path to the small street and let her gaze trail over neighbor's houses to the scattered palm trees, up to the bright blue sky and wisps of clouds. She wanted to swim. She wanted to get out of the jeans and tee she'd worn all night and into her bikini and the cold ocean water and release herself into the frenzied abandon of the front crawl as waves tried to slap her back to shore. Maybe if she taped her foot, it wouldn't hurt too much. Maybe Dio would take her.

Caroline brushed strands of stubborn hair from her face as the breeze tugged them from her ponytail. She needed a shower. Long, hot, steamy. Dio's shower was plenty big for both of them. She saw herself in it with him, sudsing his massive chest, playing in his hair and tracing it down to his stomach, sudsing his ... his sword. She felt herself blush.

What was wrong with her? She didn't blush. Ever.

She also didn't let a man take care of her. She didn't let him tell her what she would do, where she would go...

What the hell? There was a first time for everything. She could at least let him be her first that way. To a point. Since he was trying to help, and since, no matter what she told herself, she needed the help by now.

Nelda distracted her with an offered glass of lemonade which Lina gratefully accepted. And she sat next to her on the old porch swing.

"Caroline, before Dio comes back, there are a few things you should know." Grasping her hand, Nelda talked of Dio's mother, of her father, of the way his father's father objected to the woman he chose because she was a *loony bird*. "And you know, he was right, but you should also know she made the man laugh like no one else ever did. His parents, Dio's grandparents, were hard. His pappy needed the laughin'. You see, what we look for in our mate is what we're missing in ourselves. The rest of it doesn't seem to matter and it doesn't need to matter. He found what it was he most needed and he grasped right onto that. People thought he was crazy. Maybe he was indeed, but it didn't matter none to him."

Nelda shook her head. "People will think you're crazy for choosing Dio, not only because of his scar but also because of his parents. They'll say you're walking into trouble. And you will be. That woman won't be easy on you. You gotta know that right off. She's hot and cold and here and ... elsewhere, without more'n half a blink to warn ya. But don't take it personal. Be tough with her. And be tough with Dio if he jumps you about it. I love that boy like he's my own, but he's been too far in denial about his momma. You cain't let him be."

"It runs in the family? So if we have kids, they might be..?"

"You want young'uns with Dio?"

"Well..." Lina blushed again. She hadn't even thought that far.

Nelda gave her a big smile. "Nah honey, her parents and all the rest of the family were all normal enough. They musta just dropped her on her head is all. Kinda the way she... Well now, I guess I better let him tell you about that. Nah, I don't think you have anything such to worry your head about. And I can see the two o' ya having some right beautiful young'uns, too. But if things get too tough now and then, you call me and I'll come help with the old girl. She won't dare smart at me. She knows better. And you will have to teach her better, yourself. She is like a child, Caroline. You need to go in thinking of her that way."

Like a child. But she was... She had no idea how to deal with children. She'd never had to. For Dio, she would figure it out.

She smiled when his car came in sight and pulled herself up on her crutches as he pulled in. If her hands felt better, she'd make her way down the stairs and get to him faster. But all she needed was to fall onto the cracked cement sidewalk.

Harry was out of the car first, but Dio made his way up the stairs first. "What are you doing on those?" He took them away and put his arms around her.

"Well, what do you expect me to do?"

"I expect you to sit still until I can take you where you need to go."

"So I wasn't supposed to pee till you got back?"

"You had to do that on the front porch?" He looked around at the floor.

"I was up anyway, and I wanted to be outside." She wrapped her arms tightly around his neck as he picked her up. "But you might want to be careful. I'm getting kind of used to this. I might never want to get anywhere any other way if you keep it up."

"Somehow I doubt that." He gave her a light kiss. "Ready to go home?"

"Don't you need to be at the hospital? I can stay here if it bothers her to have me there. Or I'll go with you..."

"I was just there. Harry and I had a talk with her. She feels bad about what she said, but Caroline, you should know..."

"Already talked with the girl. She knows better what to expect now, but Dio, I will go out there and get her away from Cleo if I need, so you keep on your mother and don't let her chase this girl off again." Nelda opened the screen door. "Now you bring her in here and let me put clean wraps on those hands before you go anywhere."

Thirty

Caroline appreciated everything Harry and Nelda had done for her, but she was glad Dio got her out of there and glad Harry had convinced the doctor Cleo Troy needed another night at the hospital to be sure she was alright.

Dio took her home, to his home, set her on the front porch on one of the rocking chairs while he unpacked her car, taking her clothes up to his room and everything else to one of the spare rooms until she could go through it. Then he came back to pick her up and carry her upstairs.

She tried to protest, said she could do it, but he insisted her hands wouldn't heal if she didn't stay off them. He'd helped her shower, covering her wrapped hands in plastic gloves to keep them dry and clean, washed her hair for her, dried her, and helped her dress.

They were back on the front porch, on the swing that matched Nelda's swing except with a fresh coat of white paint rather than bare weathered wood. The breeze brushed through her damp hair and made her shiver and he went back in to grab a blanket.

"You honestly think you can be happy out here?"

With a grin, Caroline took his fingers. "It's wonderful. Yes."

"So, if I decide it's time to hire a couple of people to help so I'm less tied down, you think you can help me choose them?"

"Of course."

Silence drifted between them and she watched a pair of wrens hop along the ground and fly back and forth to the base of a fallen tree with a wide crack that made a perfect opening just big enough to get in and out. "They mate all year long, you know."

"Who?"

She nodded toward the little brown birds. "Carolina wrens. Maybe even for life. And they sing together."

"You're an ornithologist?"

"I'm guessing that means bird expert. No, I just like wrens. They're pretty and friendly and they can thrive most anywhere if it doesn't get too cold. And their coloring is beautiful. I love their colors."

"Brown?"

"Sienna and light gold, kind of like the beach and the mix of wet and dry sand. Not here where the beach is so white, but other beaches. I've always thought I'd use that color combination sometime in decorating. Something, somewhere."

"You can do that here. Our room, or wherever. It needs some help by now. One more thing I haven't been able to think about." He watched the little birds flit about up in a nearby tree. "Mom used to keep feeders out and full for them. I've been slacking on that, too, with everything else going on." Dio stroked her leg under the blanket.

"For the wrens?"

"Any bird that comes around. She's not particular."

"Maybe I can start filling them for her, if you'll tell me where to find everything."

"Once your hands are healed. Not before. Caroline, why did you get scared in my car all of a sudden? This morning."

"Um... kind of a flashback. I'm sorry. I'm not afraid of you." She cuddled closer against his side and rested her head on his shoulder.

"Do you want to tell me?"

Caroline felt a deep sigh emanate from her gut and travel all the way through her body in both directions.

"Is it related to your foot? You said it was revenge." His voice was soft next to her ear, his fingers caressed her head, playing with her hair.

"No. Different things. By the time I made it into a ballet company, I'd moved out and had hardened myself well. I learned to do whatever it took to protect myself and to get where I wanted. I um, kind of stepped on some toes, so to speak, but Dio, I was nearly there. I was the understudy for the principal dancer. I'd starred in a couple of big ballets, as an understudy, and I was so close to being a principal."

He shifted, moving to see her face. "A prima ballerina?"

"They call them principal dancers now, but I prefer the old term. Yes. For one of the major companies. It took hours a day of practice from the time I was eight years old. I started classes when I was four, but I didn't start putting that much into it until I was eight and needed... I needed to be out of the house and that was the only thing my mother would let me stay out that long for, so it started as an escape but soon it was so much more. It was my only passion. I didn't care about anything else. I blew off classes to practice. I blew off the friends I used to have. It didn't matter. The only thing that mattered was being one of the best. And I was, Dio. I was so close."

"I would love to have seen you up there."

She bit her lip until controlled enough to continue. "Well, that's not gonna happen anymore, so..."

"What happened, Caroline?"

"I seduced the ballet master. There was finally an opening for a principal dancer spot and it should have been mine, but I thought he was about to give it to the girl he was doing only because he was doing her. It happens, more than you probably want to know. But I figured I could play that game as well as she could. So I did. To keep my chance of being at the top, so the little sleaze wouldn't steal it from underneath me when she wasn't as good, when she spent much of her time running around playing and partying while I was working, giving myself blisters, adding blisters to my blisters, always fighting through pain just to get better.

"I'd worked so hard. I didn't date. I didn't even date, I wanted it so much. I saved all of my energy for that spot that should have been mine. And she... I didn't care anything for him. I didn't even like him. But I wouldn't let her jump in on me like that, with sex. So I seduced him. When I knew she would find us."

"She messed up your foot for doing what she was trying to do?"

"No. Turns out she... I didn't know. She was in love with him. He'd talked of marrying her. I didn't know. They had to keep it a secret. Screwing a dancer is no big deal. It happens all the time. But... I didn't understand why it was so hard to get to him. Until she went off. She had a meltdown. He was her first and only. I didn't know. I never would have..."

"He gave in to you. It was his fault as much as yours."

"Maybe. But she didn't see it that way. At rehearsal the next morning, she came in wild-eyed and wouldn't talk to anyone. I tried to stay out of her way, but I didn't see her in time. She ... grabbed the chair next to me, a wooden chair with sharp square legs, and pounded it down on top of my foot. I heard the crack, and I knew I was done as a dancer. Her second blow was just below that one, and..." Caroline dropped her head on his shoulder. "She crushed so many bones in my foot they said I'd never walk right, and never unassisted. I could have killed her. Literally, Dio. I lay in that hospital bed and figured ways I could do it. Some nights I still do, when the pain gets unbearable."

He wrapped her in close and kissed her head. "Oh, Caroline. I am so sorry, baby. So, so sorry."

"I deserved it. Part of it."

"No." He raised her face to his. "No. You didn't deserve that. You didn't. If he gave in to you, it was better that she found out he would. She had no right." He shook his head. "A prima ballerina."

"Almost. I never made it. I'll never be in toe shoes again. Now I may never be able to dance in any way again, ever. I was... I was almost at the top in the club, too. For the women, not for you. No way I can compete with what you do, but I nearly had that closer position on your off days." She sighed hard. "It doesn't matter anymore, really. I didn't want the job. It was just something I could do. I never finished school because I kept skipping classes and I figured it didn't matter. But now... I don't know what I'll do now with no diploma and a bad foot. I'm smart. I am. I can learn something. I always learned easily when I wanted to, but who's going to give a lame ex-stripper a decent job?"

"Caroline, you were walking well. Dancing. When you first started at DanceOtica."

"Yeah, I kind of proved them wrong. When they gave up on me, I did some research and worked with it myself. It hurt like hell, but I kept pushing it and it always hurts when I walk, but I ignored it. I can ignore it until I push too far and it gets bad again and then it's back to square one and I have to..." Her head shook. "I just don't have the energy for it anymore, to start again."

"Okay." He kissed her head. "So here's what we're doing for now. You are on strict recovery leave for your foot and your hands. Mom will be coming home tomorrow and she'll insist on doing as much as she can. She's always puttering, keeping up with things inside. Cooking. She likes to cook."

"Should she?"

"You don't want to try to tie my mother down. That never leads to a good place, so yes, as much as she feels up to doing, she should do. If you think she needs to rest, find a careful way to make her do it. In the meantime, you are to sit and rest..."

"I don't do that well, either."

"No surprise there. What do you like to do that doesn't involve being on your feet?"

She threw him a grin.

"Beyond that. I get how much you're into that. Not that I mind at all. Works well for me." He kissed her softly.

"To tell you the truth, I've never much liked it before. Before you. I really didn't." Caroline ran fingers down his chest. "It was always just a thing, sometimes a tool. Since that incident, I hadn't bothered."

"Is that why you're so fired up?" Dio grinned and kissed her nose.

"No. It's just you." She pressed into him.

"Hm." He pulled back. "I um, have to get some stuff done around here before work tonight. So..."

"Work?"

"With you and the cowboy out, they're short-handed. Means I'm on every night for a while, but first, the animals need fed and such. So as much as I'm tempted to stoke your fire..." Dio planted a kiss on her forehead. "I've got to get to work. Do you want to stay out on the porch or go inside?"

"I want to watch you work and start learning the routine. Where'd you put my crutches?"

"Not going to happen, Caroline. You have to stay off those hands."

"I have to be able to get around and they hurt less than my foot."

His chest rose and fell. "Well, we're going to have to do something about that. For now..." He stood and picked her up.

As much as Caroline teased about getting used to be carried around, she wanted to just move about on her own as she chose. Still, being sheltered with his large arms against his sturdy chest wasn't anything to complain about. Dio walked across the large yard down a slight hill to a large barn, set her down long enough to pull a wooden stool from the barn, and supported her as she lowered onto it. "Too close to the smell?"

"No. What animals do you have in there?"

"Want to see them?"

"Yes."

Picking her up again, he took her inside.

"Horses. You have... Wait. Is that Degas?"

"That's Titian, Degas' brother, and he's fussing at me because it's past feeding time. Here." He set her beside the wood gate keeping the horse in its pen. "Can you stand on the left foot a minute?"

"Of course." Caroline shifted by hopping and holding onto the horse's rail and reached up slowly, letting him smell her hand, and petted his nose. "Hi there, Titian. Good boy. Oh, you're a pretty thing, too."

Dio rubbed his chin as he watched Caroline stroke the horse's nose and talk to him. He never would have guessed his little Lina would be a horse lover, maybe an overall animal lover. Maybe this arrangement would work a whole lot better for her than he'd expected.

Setting the wooden stool next to her, he set a hand on her back and she turned to smile at him. A beautiful smile. Unguarded. Joyful. "So once you're up and about again, I might put you in charge of feeding the horses since you seem to like them."

"Yes. Of course. I'll find a way to do it. Just show me how. Are these all carriage horses?"

"They are. I rescued them and brought them back to health and trained them for carriage work. They take turns. Degas is working now, along with four others. Titian just came in from working, and after they eat, they'll go run around the pasture and hang out. I never let any of them do more than two weeks at a time in the city."

"They're yours."

"They are." He patted Titian when the horse nuzzled his head.

"You're amazing." She threw her arms around him.

"No, I just find that animals don't care how I look and they're good company, for the most part. Quiet. Unobtrusive."

"If that's the kind of company you want, you may have chosen the wrong girl."

He chuckled and kissed her head. "Quiet does get boring after a while. I also like adventure. Let me get them fed and turned loose and we'll go feed the sheep next."

Unsure what she would think, Dio put a rein on his smallest horse, a gentle mare, threw a blanket over her back, and led her to Caroline. "This is Cassatt, my smallest and sweetest girl. Let me help you up."

"What? Really?"

"Easiest way to get around the farm. She'll be good for you."

"She's beautiful." Caroline ran her hand along the side of the light brown mare and stroked the long white mane. "What is she?"

"A Haflinger. Very social horses, very gentle. Good with kids, but strong enough for a full-sized adult." He helped her onto the horse, gave her a few minor instructions, and kept the reins himself.

Obviously, it was all animals she liked. When the dogs came to sniff her out at the sheep pen, she played with them until they rolled over onto their backs so she could pet their bellies.

"You didn't say you had dogs."

"It's a farm. They're working dogs. Those two are Border Collies. They patrol the yard and pasture to watch for danger and protect my sheep. They're not pets."

"They look like they are."

"Yeah well, don't get them too used to that. I put a lot of time into training them right and I don't have time to treat them like they're kids."

"I do."

Dio tried not to roll his eyes. He scanned the area and chuckled. "Come here, Estrela." At his signal, the dog ran from behind the barn where he'd been watching the stranger at his house and nudged up against Dio's leg. "This one, once he gets used to you, will be glad to keep you company as much as you want. With any luck."

"Oh, Dio. What is he? Look at him. He looks like a big baby."

"He is, with me. I hope he'll warm up to you, but I've had him for six years now and he's never gone to anyone else." Dio scratched his ears. "He's an Estrela Mountain Dog. Got him in North Carolina. This one, if the collies start yapping, will high-tail it out there and take care of whatever the issue might be. Mainly coyotes. He'll take 'em down before they can get my sheep. We'll give him time to get used to you being here and then see if he'll warm up. If not, we may have to get one of your own since they're incredibly loyal and will watch after you well if I'm not around. I'm on their notification list for new pups." He picked her up, put her up on Cassatt, and told the dogs to go on about their business. "Time to clean up and eat before I have to go."

"Come to work with me."

Caroline felt a cringe run all the way through her body as she watched Dio, her Dio get ready to go to the club and show off in front of all of those women.

He came to her, decked out in his tight black pants and nothing else, and ran a hand over her head where she sat on his bed in her capris and tank top. "I don't want to leave you here alone tonight."

"I'm not gonna steal your stuff."

He laughed and gently tugged her chin up to meet her lips. "Not worried about that. I mean because it's a new place, but mainly because I know you'll be running around on your crutches since no one will be here to help you, and I don't want you doing that."

"I don't want to be at the club yet. I'm too... With my hands like this..."

"I get it, Caroline, but..."

"I'll be fine. I'll park my rear in that incredible library and act like I'm on vacation."

"You are. Still..."

"I'm fine, Dio. I'm used to taking care of myself."

He rubbed his chin, went to grab a shirt and regular pants to pull over his costume, stuffed his mask in his pocket, and picked her up. She felt far too vulnerable being carried down the stairs and she gripped him tighter as though it would keep them from falling, until he set her in the big chair in the library. "I'll be back in a minute. Look around and see if there's anything you want me to grab for you."

Before she looked around at the ceiling-high bookshelves, Caroline watched him walk away. Truthfully, she did not want to be in the big house alone, but she would deal with it, and she'd try not to think about Dio on that stage with those women leering at him. She wasn't worried. She knew she had nothing to worry about. Still, it was strange now to think about it.

"How about going over to Harry's tonight?" He was back already, talking as he entered the room. "Nelda just pulled three pies out of the oven and would love for you to come share one. Peach. She makes the best pie I've ever had. Tempted?"

"Very. But I'm not dressed for it." After their shower, she'd pulled on loose shorts and a tank top with nothing more.

"Tell me what to grab for you."

Dio fended off questions all night. Somehow it had gotten around that he and Caroline were together, and at this point he didn't care, but he didn't feel like explaining anything to his coworkers, either. Even several of the club's patrons mentioned it and asked where she was. He told them she quit for personal reasons and left it at that.

It hadn't been until he had dropped her off at Harry's and was headed to the club that Dio realized she'd veered around his question about why she'd seemed afraid of him. She'd hardened herself, had learned to protect herself, she said. From what?

While she'd been out with the animals, Dio had seen what she must have been like as a child, so tender, loving, kind. Such an innocent quality flowed around her even the animals felt it. His dogs... She was going to spoil the hell out of those dogs and he knew it. He would continue to tell her they were not pets, but of course it would not matter in the slightest. The thought made him chuckle to himself on the way back to Harry's. It didn't matter, in reality. They'd still do their job. Still, Dio had to at least make some kind of show about thinking it was his place and his animals and therefore his rules. And then she could carry on ignoring him to do as she pleased, as he knew she would.

Pulling in to the cabin on the other side of Folly Beach from his own place, Dio shook his head. The girl was out on the porch. Alone. Wrapped in a blanket.

She eyed him as he walked up over to her. "Hey. How'd it go?"

"Everyone asked me about you all night."

"Really? Because they care at all? Wait. Why did they ask you?"

"Wondered that myself." He sat next to her.

"Oh. That night I found out your mom was in the hospital. Sandy. She heard me asking how to find you."

"Doesn't matter." He found her hand and raised it to kiss her fingers. "Have you been good tonight?"

"Of course not. You don't know me better than that?"

"So you've been walking around, have you?"

"No."

"No? Then how have you not been good?"

"I ate way too much pie."

He grinned. "Nelda will do that to you. Is that it?"

"So far."

"So far?"

Adjusting the blanket, Caroline moved up onto her knees and straddled him, wrapping her bare arms around his neck. "I missed you, and I was getting awfully jealous thinking about all of those women watching you when I wasn't there to watch you."

"No need to be." He stroked her hair.

"I know." She pulled the mask over his head and set it aside.

"You want me to quit?"

She caught his eyes. "You don't need to. I'm not worried. Once my hands heal, I'll come with you." Her soft fingers stroked his face back into his hair. "Dio?"

He kissed her neck. "Hm." She smelled incredible, a mix of peach pie remnants and the body wash she'd pulled out of her things for her shower.

"I want you."

"I would hope so."

"I mean now."

"Here on the front porch?"

"It's after midnight. No one's about." She pushed her tongue into his mouth, squeezed her legs in tight against his.

Pulling the blanket up around her shoulders, Dio slipped his hands underneath and up under her shirt. Her lace bra barely covered her and he easily pushed it underneath the curve of her breasts, out of the way.

"Take me home." Caroline whispered through the night.

"Shh."

"Dio, I was kidding..."

"Hang on to me." He slid down farther, out toward the edge. As he kissed her neck, he unzipped her jeans. And his own. Lina kept one arm around his neck and reached down to touch him with the other hand. Her fingers only. Her palms were still bandaged.

"Another reason to get those hands healed." He found her mouth again. "Let me do it."

"But it was my turn."

"You can catch up later."

She returned her arm around his neck and nuzzled her face into his shoulder, obeying when he motioned for her to raise enough to let him pull her jeans down her hips, off her thighs. They pulled at her, so she raised her left leg enough to let him pull them half way off. And she moved down over him.

Dio pulled her lace undies aside and entered her quick and hard, gritting his teeth to stay quiet. She took charge and moved him in and out of her, almost out, never all the way. He loved the way her chest rose and fell fast and hard, the way her eyes clenched.

He felt her climax, her body stiffen, and still, and Dio followed suit as she fell against him, her body trembling, kissing any part of his skin she could find until she calmed, until he did.

"Marry me, Caroline."

"Mm, I don't know, Dio."

He pulled back, caught her eyes. "You don't know?"

"Depends. You won't stop treating me like your captive if I do, will you? I don't want you to get all stuffy on me."

He grinned. "Not a chance. Marry me."

"You still know almost nothing about me, about my past."

"Doesn't matter. Marry me." He lowered his face against hers and kissed in front of her ear, her forehead, her nose.

"After what I told you about my foot?"

"Yeah, so you were a bad girl and the angry little bird got even. Marry me, Caroline."

"I may never be a lot of help to you on the farm with this foot the way it is." She slid fingers down his chest, her forehead resting against his.

"Doesn't matter. That's not why I want you. That, I can hire."

"Well, you could actually hire this, too."

"Not legally. And I wouldn't enjoy it even half as much." He nipped her bottom lip. "Say yes."

"I'm... Your mother has nothing on mine. I don't come from a good place."

"Okay. Marry me."

"Dio, I..."

He pressed his mouth up against hers. Pushed his tongue inside. Pulled her closer, holding her hips against his. When he released her mouth, he set both hands aside her face. "I don't care about any of it. Marry me, Caroline. I won't let you up until you say yes. And as a warning, I'm getting ready to take you again."

She groaned when he pressed back up against her.

"Shh. Say yes."

"I may never walk normally again, much less dance. What if I can't even dance with you at the wedding?"

"Then I'll pick you up and rock you in my arms to the beat of the music. Marry me."

"You'll get tired of carrying me around."

"No, I won't. You're far easier to carry than injured lambs thrashing about and bleating in my ear. Say yes."

She traced the lines along his face, ran her fingers across his lips. "Will you walk through town with me? Without your mask? Just ... us, as we are? Me hobbled and you scarred, with all the stares, with all the gossip. Will you?"

"If you want."

"I do. I want you. All of you. All of it. Unhidden."

"Will you be my wife?"

"Yes, Dio. Yes."

He claimed her mouth, held her close for several minutes, and whispered that it was time to go home. Dressing under the blanket was more of a challenge than undressing had been, but they finally pulled themselves back together and she sat next to him cuddling in close.

A knock on the screen door preceded the squeak that said it was opening, slowly.

Harry peeked around the door. "Sorry to bother y'all, but I got a pickup call. Have ta go. What are you two doing out here on my porch so late anyways?"

Dio squeezed her fingers lightly. "Getting engaged."

"Ha, that's what they're calling it these days? Thought that was already settled. Stayin' here all night? You can, but that couch is pretty smallish."

"No, we're going home. Thanks for letting her stay tonight."

"Anytime." Harry set a hand on his arm, gave him a nod, and told them to lock the door as they left and to drive safe.

Dio repeated the caution and took the blanket inside, grabbing the phone she said she'd found in Harry's couch, and locked the big door, pulling it closed. She wrapped her arms around his neck so he could take her to his car.

Thirty-one

"Harry and Nelda are coming to help play interference in case Mom gets out of hand. And so Harry can give her a hand if she needs it so I can keep you off your hands."

"Diomedes, you are not carrying me through that hospital. I'll wait in the car first." Caroline sat at the table in what was now her kitchen, at least part hers, and grabbed another biscuit to dip in the sausage gravy. With Dio's help, she'd managed to make a decent breakfast, as simple as it was.

"So much for wanting to go everywhere that way?" His eyes sparkled. "I figured we'd get you a wheelchair. I can push one and Harry can take the other."

"Nonsense. I'll get around as I always do."

He moved the bandages enough to check her blisters. "Can't let you do it, Lina. You have to heal. I have work for you. I can't leave her alone in the house anymore and I can't work if I can't get outside. Until you heal, you only need to keep an eye on her and give me a call if I need to come. We're stopping on the way in to pick up one of those phones so I don't have to worry anymore about not being reached. I have the thing ordered, so it'll just be a fast pickup, if they don't all have heart attacks when I walk in. But once your hands are good again, there's a ton of work to be caught up with." He took a swallow of coffee, watching her eyes. "This isn't easy street, baby. I expect you to pull your weight."

"Diomedes Troy, I have never in my life had or expected easy street. I'll take care of her fine. But she's going to listen to me and you can't interfere with that."

"You've been talking to Nelda about her."

"Yep. So I'm prepared."

"And you still want this?"

Caroline reached over to run fingers along his face. "I'm keeping you. And sunrise at the pier sounds perfect to me. Of course it's far too late to make me an honest woman, you know, but I doubt you'd be too interested in that, anyway."

He grasped her fingers to kiss them. "I'm getting the best of both worlds: a wife and a stripper. Think I'll be okay with that."

"Yeah? And I'll have the boss, the farm boy, and a husband, not to mention my personal hard body chauffeur. Puts me on top, the way I see it." Even as she joked about it, Lina realized what she'd said. She was on top. The mistress of the house, the boss's wife, and the one pulling the boss's strings. Of course she wasn't his wife yet. "I'll be good, though, so I can hopefully dance with you at our wedding, on my own feet. Tomorrow I'll start working with it again. Maybe I can get it to work that well, anyway."

"Come here." Setting his coffee down, Dio picked her up from her chair and cuddled her onto his lap. "You will, baby. We'll see what we need to do to help it along and we'll do that. We may not ever get you back in toe shoes, but you will dance with me at our wedding."

Caroline pulled herself from her thoughts when Dio turned onto 17, leaving Charleston instead of heading toward the hospital. "Where are we going?"

"After that scene at the phone store, I need to unwind before dealing with my mother. Besides, it'll be lunch time if we go now and she may try to send me out for something before I take her home. I figure we'll let them deal with her a bit longer and have a quiet lunch instead."

"You're taking me out for lunch? During the day?"

"Unless you'd rather not. Could be as bad as the phone shop, you realize."

"Then *they'll* have to deal with my attitude, also. But it wasn't that bad, Dio."

"Not that bad?" He threw her a raised-eyebrows glance. "They looked at me and then looked at you being injured and they were obviously thinking I'd done it and wondering whether to call for help for you. The guy didn't get within six feet of me the whole time. Some of the customers left. In the middle of being waited on."

"Hey, that just made it faster for us. Could be helpful, you know."

"I suppose you could see it that way given he was plenty willing to be close to you."

"Until I opened my mouth and let them know they were being rude. Kind of changed his mind. I'm pretty sure he ended up feeling sorry for you having to deal with me."

He chuckled and raised her hand to kiss her fingers. "Anyway, I figure a little jaunt to lunch will give you a bit more practice with your new toy before you have to walk around in the hospital."

"Toy. Funny." She tossed him a scornful look, but Caroline wouldn't argue. He'd spent too much on the little walker she could use either sitting down or kneeling on. It would definitely come in handy.

In Sullivan's Island, he stopped at Poe's tavern and she couldn't resist teasing. "So, are we eating out on the patio next to the sidewalk?"

"I was thinking more of a to-go order. I'm already pushing this enough for today."

"I was kidding." Caroline unbuckled her seatbelt and leaned over to give him a quick kiss. "You're doing amazing. You are amazing. So, take-out to the beach? Think my new toy will do okay on sand?"

"I figure we can take the boardwalk down as far as you want to go and I'll get you over to a nice spot from there. The blanket's still in the trunk. Sound okay?"

"Perfect. You want me to go in and order? I can do it."

"I'm tempted to let you." He looked out at all of the foot traffic, took a deep breath, and got out to retrieve her walker and hold her door.

Noticing stares as well as he did, Caroline kissed him again to help him relax, with a hand against his face. "You're beautiful, Dio, and I'm incredibly lucky to have found you."

When he could tell her left leg was getting tired, Dio had her sit on the walker and let him push. He took her nearly to the end of the boardwalk, went to spread the blanket on the top of a nearby sand mound, pulled the food from the walker's bag, and carried her over.

She looked out at the Morris Island lighthouse that hadn't been in service for a lot of years and mentioned it was sad that bombing tests way back when had taken it out of commission.

"You know the history of the area well, it seems."

"Yes." She bit into her veggie burger and while Dio waited for more explanation, he did the same with his Gold Bug Plus, named after the story inspired by Poe's time on Sullivan's Island during his service at Fort Moultrie.

She didn't elaborate, so he pushed the thought. "You're a history buff in general or only an area connoisseur?"

"No. Neither. This is incredible. Want to try it?"

"No, thank you. I like meat in my burgers."

She grinned with a shrug and popped one of the slices of the extra avocado he'd ordered into her mouth.

"So?"

She rinsed it with a swallow of Coke. "So what?"

"History. They didn't teach that in school that I remember. It was more world-focused than local-focused."

"No. It was... I've hit all of the historical sites of the area, including Fort Sumter a few times. Back when I was a kid and had no choice. Don't get me wrong, it was interesting, but once or twice would have been good."

"One of your parents was a history buff?"

"Well, my mom's boyfriend. She never married him, but he was there most of the time that I remember. My brothers are his, or so she suggested. I'm not real sure."

"Didn't know you had brothers."

"They moved away long ago, not long after I did. Not even sure where they are now." Her eyes went back to the lighthouse. "Is it silly that I would love to go in there and look around? Probably nothing in it, I know. Still, I've always wanted to climb to the top and..." She shrugged. "Guess that would be pretty tough now. I do love lighthouses because they're beacons, reminders that even when it's dark, there's a light somewhere that will guide you if you look for it. I sympathize with this one since it can't find its light anymore, due to other peoples' actions. I feel kind of sorry for it. Silly thought, right? You don't know what you're getting into, Dio. I did tell you that."

"It's not silly. And you're right, Caroline. I was starting to have doubts about that myself recently, about finding my own light again. Until I met you."

She gave him a sweet half grin and took another bite of her sandwich, her eyes out over the ocean.

"You know they're trying to get it restored. A group of people who care about it, feel sorry for it. Hope it'll work out."

"Yeah. Not holding my breath. Sad, but I don't see enough people caring to make it happen." Caroline pulled her eyes from it, and instead, watched the pelicans searching for fish near the shore.

"What happened to your father?" Dio almost hated to ask since he could see the conversation already triggered some kind of darkness within, but he wanted to know what she'd dealt with, what her fear was about.

"Never met him. Mom was eight months along when he took off, and she blamed me for it. It was my fault he left since I decided to come along unplanned and he didn't want to be tied down. Never mind it wasn't my actions that brought me here. I told her once she should have married him before she let herself get pregnant so at least she could have sued for child support. Didn't go over well. I learned fast to keep my mouth shut so she wouldn't take my dance classes away."

"Sounds like a real winner of a mother."

"Right. Doesn't matter anymore."

"Of course it matters. Is she still around?"

"Guess so. Just after I got kicked out of my apartment, I drove over there thinking I might stay a few days until I found something else, but I couldn't even go in. I'd rather live in my car. It all looked the same, though, with the same badly-painted green wicker furniture out front, so I guess she's there." Her head followed a motor boat pulling water skiers. "Have you ever done that?"

Dio snickered. "No. Not likely to try, either."

"You don't like water sports?"

"I like boats, from inside the boat, and water when I'm under my own volition."

"Meaning you like to swim."

"Right."

"I love swimming. Second only to dance... well, these days second only to you, but mostly..."

Dio watched her face as she talked about how she felt while swimming, how she'd always thought it was far better than sex, although she'd very recently changed her mind about that one. He again saw the carefree little girl in her, although he wasn't sure, from what she'd said so far, that she'd ever been able to be a carefree child. Not that he had too much, either.

"Caroline. Tell me whatever it is you're trying to avoid."

She caught his eyes for a moment and sighed.

So he prodded. "Your step-father. What was he like other than a history buff?"

"He wasn't my step-father. They were never married."

"Okay, so tell me about him."

Her body tensed.

Finished with his burger, Dio moved stuff over and took her side, wrapping her in his arms. "Talk to me."

She put another piece of avocado in her mouth and chewed it slowly, then sighed. "Long story short, he told me once he was only staying with my mom because of me, because as soon as I was old enough, he was taking me away and leaving her the boys that were no use to him. I um... stayed out of the house as much as possible. If I was cooking, he'd come up from behind and press in against me. I started doing laundry at five in the morning before he was awake because it's in the basement and..."

"Caroline..."

"The day I turned fourteen, he came to my room in the middle of the night. Luckily, it was a sleepless night for Mom and she heard me telling him to get off. When he told her to go back to bed and mind her own business and she walked out, I got almost hysterical, but she came back with a big knife from the kitchen and yelled for the boys to get up and..." Her body spasmed in a deep breath. "And threatened to turn him in. So he took off. But again, it was my fault somehow. I'd ruined the *one good thing* she'd had, she said, by walking around the house flaunting myself, which I did not. I stayed too covered for the weather inside the house, because of him. I tried to make it up to her, to thank her for stopping him and sending him away, but nothing was good enough. She did nothing but bitch at me from that time forward.

"The day I turned eighteen, I packed up the few things that mattered, left a note on the table, and moved to Boston to audition for a company. Amazingly, I made it, and I stayed in a shelter until I had enough cash to help with rent and found a place looking for another roommate. One of them was male and we got together for a while until I walked in to find him with someone else. It wasn't really a big deal except I had nowhere else to go and had to see him bring girls in to flaunt in front of me.

"I fought my way up. All the way. All my life. Maybe I went overboard now and then, but I did what I had to do."

Dio pulled her in against him, clenching his eyes against the pain he could hear her trying to stifle.

"So, if I have too much attitude at times, at least you know why." She turned enough to meet his lips. "And I still have enough anger to use it against anyone who's rude to you. But I'm fine, Dio. Really. Other than this stupid foot, I'm fine. I'll find a way to overcome this, too."

He brushed his hand alongside her face and into her hair. "We're going to fix that foot, Caroline. Whatever we need to do. Like I said, maybe not well enough for toe shoes, but well enough to get around on your own. I'll find someone who won't say it can't be done."

"That would cost an arm and a leg, no pun intended."

"I don't care."

"Dio..."

Catching her lips before she could finish her protest, he also kissed her nose. "You'll be more than worth it to me. My mother isn't up for any good parenting awards, either. She's a handful. If you can deal with her..."

"I can."

"Just don't let her run you off again."

"I am sorry about that, but I won't. I'm keeping you. You already said I could."

Thirty-two

Dio threw Harry a look when he suggested it was a perfect night for a campfire.

"Oh, I haven't been to one since I was kid. Can we do that out here?" Caroline had bypassed the lawn chairs Dio set around the front of the house and stretched out on the grass, legs straight out and propped on her fingers this time instead of her palms, as she had just the other day before he took her to the hospital to meet his mother. Except for the two collies beside her, begging for her attention, and the fact she'd been naked then. He wanted her that way again. But Harry and Nelda had no intention of leaving soon. And his mother was being pleasant so far. She talked with Caroline as though she'd never insulted her.

"What do you say, Dio? The girl looks excited as a kid at Christmas by the thought. You'll do it for her, won't you?"

A campfire? His stomach hurt at the thought.

"We don't have to." Caroline tilted her head at him.

"Now don't coddle the boy." Nelda frowned at Dio as she spoke to Caroline. "He's been coddled enough, despite our advice. Time to live in the real world, Dio. Make the girl a campfire and I'll go grab the hot dogs and sausages from the car. We brought 'em for this purpose." She got up and came over to him, crouching at his side. "It's time, Diomedes. You got strength at your side now. You do this and move along. It's time." Nelda rubbed his head and got up to go to the car.

"You haven't had one down there since, have you?" Harry stood and smoothed his pants. "Come then. We'll go get it ready and come back for the womenfolk." He looked at Caroline. "You'll watch over Cleo?"

"I don't need watching over, old man. Go on."

Dio gave her a warning to be nice, told Caroline to call for Nelda if she needed, and not to get up until he came back. He followed Harry, with Estrela at his side, around the side of the house and down the path that led to the bottom of the hill with a small clearing beside the water. It had the effect of an amphitheatre the way it sloped up in a part circle. His father had carved out seats from fallen timber around the property, smoothed them out and sealed them well. Dio had resealed them now and then, often enough they were still usable, although it hadn't been used since he was seven or so and they tried to do a campfire. Dio had screamed at the sight of it and his mother took him up and away, leaving his father to entertain their guests alone.

He stood and stared at the stone circle and dug out pit that was now full of old leaves and small sticks. It looked harmless enough as it was.

Harry set a hand on his shoulder. "Things have changed. It's all okay now, son. Come on. Help me clear this place out."

Dio did the heavy work of lifting rocks to clean around as Harry raked away the leaves and sticks. Once straightened, they set into the trees to find good fallen wood. Estrela prowled the edge of the tree line while Harry gathered kindling and Dio chopped an old rotted trunk into pieces so he could carry it back. He'd built up a good sweat by the time the place looked usable.

"Good enough." Harry slapped his back. "Let's gather the ladies. This old man's ready for some good campfire food. It's been far too long."

"You ought to move out farther where you can do one."

"Well, you know, we're getting too old to be out too far by ourselves now. Not like we haven't thought of it, but we have to be practical. Shame. I envy you this. When you decide to hire more folks, give me a shout. I got good names for you. And Caroline will be darn good at keeping track of 'em, I figure. Give her the chance."

He heard voices as they approached where he'd left Caroline and his mother. She was at it again. Dio sighed and hurried his steps.

"Now don't you give me any grief." Caroline rose onto her crutches to face the old woman. "I'm not going anywhere. Dio wants me here, and I want Dio, so you're just going to have to put up with me. If you want me to be nice to you, you'll have to not give me lip. I won't stand for it. I had enough of it growing up and I won't have it now. So just stop and you talk to me in a polite manner or you don't talk to me."

Dio paused to wait for the reaction. He saw Nelda do the same.

"Fine. I just won't talk then." His mother raised her chin and turned it away, like a spoiled young child.

"So be it. I like quiet. Won't bother me." Lina settled herself in a chair. She glanced over at Dio and gave him a grin.

He waited. Maybe Lina liked quiet, but his mom didn't.

"Do you plan to give me grandchildren?" So much for quiet.

Lina looked over at him again with a sly grin and a dangerous look in her eyes. "Oh, don't worry about that. I have good hips and a nice strong abdomen. I'm sure I'll be able to manage as many children as Dio is willing to father."

The old woman chuckled. "You plan to keep my boy happy?"

"I plan to keep him plenty happy. Don't worry about that, either."

"Well then, I spose I better get along with you okay. I want to live to see my grandchildren and be allowed around them."

"Good plan."

Dio cringed. Allowed around them, yes. Unsupervised, never. He made his way over to Lina and picked up her hands. "Stay off those crutches and let these hands heal. I told you, I have a lot of work ahead for you and I need you well enough to get around."

The old woman snorted. "Sounds like she's got plenty of work ahead for you, too, Diomedes. You better keep strength up enough to keep up with the girl."

Nelda told the old woman to behave, it was no way to talk to her son. Wasted warning. Dio had heard far worse over the years. He ignored it as always and scooped Lina into his arms. "Come on, baby. Let's go make you your campfire."

"A nice big hot one?"

He grinned. "As big and hot as you want it."

Caroline surveyed the area as he carried her down the sandy path with Estrela beside his legs and the two collies tagging along behind. She could see the water. She had no idea the house was so close to the water. Much of it was hidden by a whole line of thick trees, but a small opening between the trees allowed it to show. "Oh Dio, this is beautiful. I could sit at the top of this hill and just look out over it all day."

"I'll have to put a nice bench out here, then, so you can do that."

She kissed his neck. "I'll help you build it. I'm good at building. I used to be."

"Good at building? Miss Classical Ballerina?"

"Before that I was one of the biggest tom boys anyone had ever seen. I even cut my own hair when it got in my way. Made Mom furious."

"On purpose, I would guess."

"Maybe. Can we go all the way to the water? How much is yours?"

"Enough. And yes, the water front is mine. So is that dock I brought you in on from the boat the other night."

She was struck silent. All this and the dock? The water front. And the dock. The boat. He was her water god, as she always wanted. Someone who loved it like she did. "Tell me you can swim here."

Beside her ear, he kept his voice low. "I swim naked. After I work with my sword on the boat, I come back here and cool off."

"Oh Dio, let me do it with you."

"I'm counting on it." With a grin, he settled her on what looked like a hand-cut log complete with slightly sloping back rest made from a second, thinner log propped on its end. A beautiful spot. Nelda grabbed a long stick and pulled out a small pocket knife to start whittling the end to a point. Caroline offered to help. Dio handed her his knife and stuffed leaves and brush under the kindling to get the fire started.

By the time she and Nelda had five long sturdy sticks chiseled, the fire lapped up over the heavy logs and Caroline did feel like a kid at Christmas. She had a campfire and Nelda promised S'mores, she had a beautiful view with the promise of a bench to help her enjoy it, and she had a sexy stud at her side who promised naked swimming and so much more. This was far better than any Christmas she'd ever known.

Mesmerized by the fire, she relaxed against the log chair, her right calf propped over her left ankle to keep weight off her foot. The ache was starting to subside, and she was ridiculously grateful for it.

"Ready for this?" Dio handed her a stick with a hot dog pierced through the end.

"Absolutely." She held it out, but she wasn't nearly close enough.

"Want me to do it?"

"No, I want to do it. I haven't done this since I was young. Just hold on to me while I hop a bit closer."

"You're not hopping around the fire. Let me move the chair closer, but hang on to Harry while I do."

"I'm good with balance. I am trained, you know. Just hang on to my arm and I'll get there."

"Not risking it. Let me move the chair. But step back first."

"Dio, just hang onto me from behind and let me lean on you and we'll do it together. It'll be fine."

He hesitated. She insisted. Harry took his side and helped them get situated just close enough she could reach her hot dog over the nearest flame. Harry handed another one to Dio. They stood back to front slightly to the side and she twisted her head up to give him a soft kiss.

"Your hot dog will burn."

"I like it well done. Kiss me."

He met her lips again. His arm tightened around her stomach. And she gave him a smile. "This isn't so bad, right?"

"*NOOOO.*"

Caroline jumped at Cleo's ear-piercing scream. The old woman ran at Dio and he picked Caroline up around the waist, pulling her back from the fire barely soon enough Cleo didn't knock them both into it. Harry grabbed Cleo.

"You okay?" Dio still held her tight.

"Yes. What was that about?"

His head shook and he let Nelda take Caroline's arm to help steady her so he could go to his mom. "Mom, it's all right."

"*No,* Diomedes, the fire. The *fire*. Get away. *Get away.*"

"Okay, it's all right. I'm fine."

"Come, Cleo, the boy's all grown now. Look at him. He's just fine. Just you relax now and sit." Harry helped Dio lead her back to her chair.

Lina could only watch from the distance. She didn't dare risk hopping. It would scare Dio to death and he didn't need more of that. She tried to put weight on her foot, but the first bit of pressure snapped a pain all the way through it.

The old woman calmed with Dio's voice, with Harry and Nelda assuring her all was well and they were all enjoying the fire as they used to and as they needed to start doing again.

She wanted to hold him, but her crutches and her walker were both back up at the house. Caroline felt suddenly helpless and fully frustrated. It was her fault. She'd encouraged this. She wanted a campfire...

No. Harry encouraged it. It was his idea. He wanted them both to heal. But Dio was doing okay. He'd been out in public with her, during the day. He was...

Maybe it was Cleo Harry was trying to heal. Why?

He'd *seared it all to hell*, he'd said, but not how. A campfire?

Finally, he looked over at her. Standing there perched like a stork, one leg bent up and balanced on the other, with a soft grip on Nelda's arm, she had to look like the stork the little girl said she was, or looked like. And his dog was at her side. Estrela was standing guard beside her.

Dio said something to Harry and he came over. "Sorry. Are you all right? I didn't pull on you too hard?"

"No, I'm fine. Are you?"

"I shouldn't have brought her down here."

"Now Dio, it's time for her to deal with it, too." Nelda let Dio take over hanging onto Caroline and took her stick. She had them both somehow, hers and Dio's. "I kept telling your father she needed to deal with it, you both did, but he wouldn't have it. You can't keep running from it. I'd say these are done enough. I'll go put 'em on plates."

With a deep breath, Dio looked at his dog. "Sense danger, did you?" He scratched Estrela's head. "Good boy. You stayed right here where you should have."

"Odd that he didn't follow you."

"He's a smart dog, can probably tell already that I want you protected." Dio picked Caroline up to take her back to her chair, across the fire from Cleo. Asking what she wanted on her hot dog, he went to fix them and brought them over on the same plate.

"So what happened? With the fire?" Caroline rubbed his arm.

"She dropped me on it. When I was three, nearly four. I was running around it in circles and she told me to stop. I didn't. So she picked me up and took me in very close to feel the heat, to show me the danger. And she dropped me. I burned most of my hair off, my eyebrows. I didn't feel it at the time. I was only startled from the fall. Once I could feel it, it was the most excruciating pain I have ever felt. It hurt for weeks. I haven't done this since."

Caroline glanced to the other side of the fire where his mom stared into the flames. "She dropped you?"

"She only meant to startle me, but I was big already, too big. She should have had the sense to know she couldn't hold me that way while I was squirming to get down."

Nelda brought a bag of chips to set between them. "She ain't been the same since. She was never real stable, but that... Oh, Dio, she loves you so, it just about killed her."

"Her and me both." His chest rose and fell. "If we do have kids, they are never to be left alone with her. Never."

"If?" Caroline leaned in close and stroked his hair. "Diomedes Troy, I meant what I said. I should be able to give you however many kids you want. I'm in good shape, other than being near lame, of course, and I take care of myself well, never starved myself or anything, and you need little ones to help keep you busy and out of trouble. So don't even bother with that *if* thing. We've got plenty of room for them to run around here and a whole second floor you're not using. Might as well fill that old house up."

"And I'm gonna leave the two of you to talk that one out." Nelda chuckled. "But it'll darn sure be nice to have little ones running about again. Caroline, you'll have to let me come help with them, since I surely miss that." With a smile, she wandered back over to Harry and spoke in his ear, making him laugh, also.

"Well, I guess that's already settled." Dio set the plate down, stood, picked her up, and cuddled her onto his lap. "How about we get this party done and over with?"

"Are you alright?" She stroked his forehead.

"I'm ... ready to thank Harry and Nelda and see them off, then see that Mom gets to sleep okay, so I can have you alone." He put his mouth close to her ear. "Naked." He kissed above her ear. "And wet." With a grin, he scooped her up and moved her closer to the others. "Time for dessert."

Thirty-three

Dio woke to a cool breeze brushing his face, Carolina wrens and other native birds calling to each other, the sound of lapping water, and best, soft skin moving against his.

"Morning." Lina kissed his chest.

"Mm, morning, baby. I didn't mean to keep you out here all night. Did you get cold?"

She grinned and maneuvered on top of him underneath the thick blanket he'd brought out the night before so she could stargaze as they dried after their midnight swim. "No. I was too close to you to get cold." She kissed his shoulder.

It was still mostly dark. Only the barest light accented her hair. Dio pushed up against her, and he pulled the blanket off.

"Dio..."

"I want to see you."

"But, your mom..." She looked up the hill toward the house.

"No one can see us from there." He ran his hands from her pale small firm shoulders slowly down her strong fragile trembling back to her round soft sensual behind, and he coerced her down into him.

"I wasn't ready yet." She whispered in his ear and kissed his neck.

"Yes, you were."

"I wanted to tease you a while." She kissed his nose.

"I'm in charge this morning."

"Why?"

"Because you woke me up. That's the rule."

"Is it?"

"Hm." He rolled them over so he could be fully in charge and watched her expressions change, at times with eyes closed, other times open and looking at him, *at him*, directly. Lovingly. Dio was already obsessed with the way she looked at him. He had never in his life felt so entirely wanted.

"Dio..." Her body tensed, a passionate wonderful tension he could see all over her face, and relaxed. Her arms slid up around his neck and held him in close. "Oh Dio. I am absolutely keeping you."

"I love you, Caroline."

She kissed his jaw. "And I am full force, no holds barred, earth shatteringly in love with you. You better never change my mind."

"I will try very hard to never change your mind. Or to change you. I want you just as you are." Moving to her side, he scooped her into his arms and carried her to the water. "Time to cool off. We have a long day ahead."

One week already. Caroline had moved in with Dio a full week ago and yet it felt only a matter of hours. She quickly realized he wasn't exaggerating the amount of work that needed to be done around the farm, and she much preferred being outside with him than inside with his mother and house duties. So when Harry came over with a young woman, nineteen she said, who'd been homeless and drifting for a few months and was willing to work hard in exchange for a safe place to stay, Caroline convinced Dio to give her a chance.

He was wary, as always, but Caroline stayed right with her during the day for three days straight, and Harry took her back to his place at night for Nelda to dote over, so he said, although Caroline knew it was to give them a chance to make sure the girl was trustworthy — "we've got nothing we'd miss not having outside our own bedroom," he insisted — until Caroline said the girl should just stay there with them.

Penny was wonderful with Cleo. She didn't mind the sass, she was endlessly patient, very willing to accept instruction, meticulous with the cleaning, and always looking for something that needed to be done. Caroline often had to tell her to sit and take a break. When she wasn't working, she was kicked up on the big chair in the library reading a book she borrowed.

The girl hadn't looked even slightly bothered when she saw Dio the first time. Of course Harry warned her, but still, it told Caroline that Penny had a sturdy and sweet constitution. Caroline even found herself enjoying Penny's company and she wasn't sure when that last happened other than with Dio.

Angling her crutches under her arms, she left Penny and Cleo in the kitchen and set out to the front porch to meet the men pulling in to the drive. Dio came to her, taking her side as she made her way down the stairs, and she paused to rub his back. Estrela pushed against her hand until she petted him.

Both men paused when they saw Dio and Caroline felt him tense. "Good morning." She crossed the grass, heading toward them. With a glance at each other, they came to meet her, with Dio and Estrela right behind her.

"Morning." The older one gave Dio a nod but focused on her. "We have the right place?"

"Looking to do some farm work?"

"That's right."

"Then you have the right place. I'm Caroline. This is Dio. He's the owner. I'm the new manager." She tossed him a teasing grin. "And his fiancée." She could see their surprise and touched Dio's arm before offering her hand.

They talked enough to outline their experience. The older one had enough; the younger was his nephew and not experienced but strong and willing to work. Dio outlined what he needed done and asked if they wanted to look around the place before making up their mind.

"Do you want your walker instead?" Dio brushed hair back from her face.

"No. These are easier to maneuver through the grass."

"I don't want your hands sore again. They're barely healed."

"I'm fine." Caroline insisted she could keep up with them and her hands would be okay enough, and she explained briefly to the two men.

They went first to the horse stalls and she knew Dio went there first to see how they'd react to the horses, and more, how the horses would react to them.

"*Degas.*" She made her way to the stall and stroked her nose. "When did you get back?" The mare nuzzled her arm as Dio said she'd come home first thing in the morning along with two others. Staying with Degas while Dio took the men around the barn, Caroline watched the reactions. The younger man smiled at the horses that stuck their noses at him and gave them pats on the neck. Only Titian gave them any attitude, but Titian was always full of attitude. Caroline gave Dio a nod when he looked over for her opinion.

"So." He came back to her side. "I've been thinking about keeping Degas here. There's another horse I'm looking at bringing in that can fill her spot at work."

"Yeah? What will she be doing, then?"

Dio went around to where the horse supplies were kept and came back with a saddle. A small one, smaller than his. "This should fit you. Come here, girl. Let's try this." He went into Degas' stall, hooked the thing up on the horse, and brought her out. "She maneuvers well on grass and hills, also. Want to give it a try?"

"You're keeping her here for me?"

"Well, it'll be a lot easier for you to get around this way once you get used to it. Unless you'd prefer Cassatt since she's smaller, but the kids love her, so I hate to..."

"No, Degas and I will be fine together. Won't we?" Caroline petted her nose.

He pulled a step stool over, a large platform with wood railing on each side. "Rest your arms on the rails and you should be able to pull yourself up."

Caroline first threw her arms around Dio's shoulders and kissed his neck. It was a bit awkward getting up the platform and then on the horse, but he kept her side, showed her the special harness for her right knee so there wouldn't be pressure on her foot, held her waist, and soon she was sitting tall petting Degas from her back. "You're sure she won't mind?"

Dio chuckled and took Degas' reins. "She won't mind." With a pat to the horse's head, he gave Caroline more riding tips while taking his new employees around the grounds.

Thanking Penny as the girl cleared the dishes from the table, Dio asked Caroline if she wanted to go out on the porch to watch the sun set. He extended the offer to his mother and to Penny, but they chose to stay in out of the humidity.

She'd done well with Degas, and with their new farmhands, being friendly and very much in charge with both. Dio was relaxed in a way he hadn't been since his father was still around and up to taking control of any situation that popped up.

He carried her from the table to the porch swing and grasped her fingers as he took her side, looking out over their property. The porch faced southwest, more south than west, so they had a nice view of both sunrise and sunset, planned that way purposely, according to his father.

A kitten jumped up into her lap and she chuckled. "Hey, there. Miss me already?" Caroline snuggled the long-haired gray and white thing in her arm.

Dio rolled his eyes. He'd warned her to let the kittens alone, but she'd had him help her down from Degas while out at the sheep's pasture detailing the work to be done, and came back to find her surrounded by the new litter, with the mother cat watching from a distance. She'd been a stray and he took her in but she wanted nothing to do with him. "That's a farm cat, baby, not a pet, like the dogs."

"You said that earlier."

"They catch the mice and keep snakes away."

"Okay."

"Caroline, if you spoil it, it won't do its job right."

"There are plenty of them. I want this one."

He frowned.

The kitten rubbed its head against her chin, purred loudly, and stretched its paws one at a time against her arm. "Oh Dio, I want this one. Those others that wouldn't get close enough to let me pet them can catch mice and scare snakes. I want this one."

"Too late for me to argue, I'd say." He rubbed its head and it pushed up into his hand. "You'll have to give it table scraps like the rest and it can catch mice like it's supposed to. I'm not buying special food for it."

"Okay."

"And it sleeps in the barn with the others."

"We'll see."

He shook his head, knowing darn well she was going to have her way about it. "At least not in our room. Will you give me that much?"

With a smile, she leaned in for a soft kiss. "Yes. Thank you."

"As though I had a choice."

She chuckled. "Can I put music on?"

Dio went in to turn the radio on and switched it to the outdoor speakers. Music drifted out from under the porch.

"This really is paradise." She reached for his hand.

He brushed the other hand through her hair and gave her a soft kiss. "It is now."

When the song changed, she nodded and mentioned it would be a good one to dance to.

"What is it?"

"Pink. I forget who's singing with her. *Just Give Me A Reason.* Beautiful song." Her eyes closed as she listened.

"I wish I could have seen you dance, Caroline."

She opened them again. "You did."

"I mean what you were trained for. I wish I could have seen you in a prima ballerina spot, or anything close to it. I bet you were magnificent."

"I was."

He kissed her forehead.

"You want a taste of it?"

"You stay off that foot. Until your appointment with the specialist, you're staying off of it."

"I will. But I can give you an idea." She set the kitten down. "Help me over there." She nodded to the grass in front of the porch.

"Caroline..."

"Trust me, Dio. I want you to see."

He carried her over and set her down gently, moving back only far enough. With the music, she raised her right foot to her left knee in a perfect triangle, then moved her foot out front, then slowly in a circle to the back, leaning forward. Her arms went from a delicate curve out to her sides to one arm raised and the other back, balancing still on her left foot. With a faster movement, she swiveled her foot around into several turns, her left foot raising to her toes and lowering, ending with her right foot back against her left knee.

She beckoned him to her, pulled him close, wrapped her right leg around his waist and leaned backward, arms extended gracefully, fingers held just right. Moving her arms over his shoulders, Caroline raised her left leg until both legs were circling his hips and bent backward as her hands slipped down his arms, her abs doing most of the work, along with him holding her waist.

Pulling herself back up, her arms circling his neck, she kissed him. "See? We can still dance. I always figure out a way to do what I want to do."

He grinned. "You know what? I bet we can do better than that."

Thirty-four

Caroline held her head up as well as possible as she hobbled along on her crutches. Dio opened the door for her. The front door. Of the club. A few people were there already getting head starts on their night out, but mainly only employees wandered around, joked with the bartenders, talked with Charlie about their music and to Eddie about their lighting.

Their heads turned at the sight of Dio and Caroline together. She wasn't sure if they were more surprised that she was on crutches or that he wasn't wearing his mask. Some didn't recognize him. Others looked like they might but weren't sure.

She had a hard time convincing Dio to go to the club without his mask, to offer to perform without it. But she'd taken hers off, she said. It was his turn. He was who he was and anyone not okay with that didn't matter. He'd agreed in concept. In action, he had far more trouble with it. But his mother helped. She told him also that he was beautiful as he was and only people who were ugly inside wouldn't see that.

So he gave in. They started with a short walk down Center Street and a stop for lunch, and at a jewelry store. People stared. They swerved away. Or they pretended not to see him. He did fine, though. Caroline kept telling him they would soon get used to him and get to know him and stop staring. At least the locals would. He would always have that reaction from tourists, but she would help him not to care. Or she would throw a smartass comment so they'd realize how rude they were.

But he was nervous in front of his coworkers.

Hayes stared a moment. "What is this?"

Lina didn't hesitate. "We have a new act for you."

Hayes focused on her crutches. "Doesn't look like it'll be much. I don't need a lame stripper. And no offense, Dio, but if you plan to go on without the mask, you'll lose your audience. That's not sexy."

Dio rubbed her shoulder. "She won't be stripping anymore. I

won't have it."

"*You* won't have it?"

Caroline stayed silent for the moment. She would know it was meant for the patrons and the other performers. A warning.

"I won't have it. Her body is not a side show. She's a dancer."

"Not like that, she isn't. And who are you to talk for her? I don't remember that she has trouble speaking her mind."

"She's my fiancée. And she'll still speak her mind plenty, I'm sure."

"Fiancée?"

Caroline smiled and touched Dio's face, with her left hand, showing off the big diamond. "You're wrong, Hayes. Dio is very sexy, and you know he is. Everyone here knows he is."

"Not like that."

"Really? Want me to prove you wrong?" She called over to Charlie and pulled the Lita Ford CD out of her bag. "Put this on for us, if you will. Last song." She gave Dio a nod. He set her crutches against a bar stool and carried her up to the stage.

Caroline helped him out of his shirt. He helped her out of her soft sweater, the same one she wore for her first audition. She balanced on her left leg while he pulled his sword from its case. *If I Close My Eyes Forever*, Lina's duet with Ozzy Osbourne, filled the room.

She began by herself, with him motionless behind and slightly to the side. She danced as she had on the grass, position to position, on her left leg. He joined in with his sword movements, around hers, and then she turned and he moved in. Caroline raised herself onto him with a small leap. He used one hand to support her as she leaned back, her legs around his waist, his sword swinging over top of her, beside her, and she pulled herself back up.

Dio held the sword between his legs and helped her flip over his shoulders until she held herself with her legs around his stomach, her head curled in against his neck. He retrieved the sword. It swung close around her, and he twisted his body as she swung around to his side and he cradled her in his arm, her leg wrapped around his waist to help hold herself up, as the sword swished fast and close. Caroline pulled in tight, kissed his chest, held herself there as she left focus on him, on his careful, fast movements around his body and hers, and then she extended an arm and a leg out as far as she could reach in a kind of arabesque, and wrapped back around his body. Dio helped her upright again and she slid down to her left foot, her right leg wrapped around and between his legs, his head tucked into her neck.

He filled the last bars of sensual music with more sword flashes and they held still as the song ended.

Applause broke out. Whistles. One of the girls said Dio was sexy as hell without the mask and they should close every show.

Hayes joined them on stage, eyed them.

Dio took the sword back to its case as she balanced on her left foot and returned to wrap an arm around her waist. "We've barely worked on it. It'll get better. If you have a spot for us."

"Better?"

"We've only had a few days of practice since we thought of it."

"I have a spot for you. Can you be ready by next Saturday night?"

Caroline nodded.

"You're our new Saturday closers. Any other night you want to come in, we'll have space. And congrats. That's some ring. Looks like I've been paying him too much."

"Not nearly what he's worth. Trust me on that." She gave Dio a kiss and asked him to take her home.

~ *Epilogue* ~

Caroline smoothed her shimmery tan dress, took a deep breath, and asked Nelda if she looked all right.

"Oh honey, you make the whole beach sparkle." She reached up to shift a curl aside Caroline's face. "You sure you want to try this already? It's only a few weeks since your operation. The doc said…"

"I want to walk to him on my own. Just for today. Then I'll be good until it finishes healing."

"Well, you just be careful and I'll be right by your side." Nelda pulled the veil down over Caroline's face and handed her the crutches. "Here you are. You go most of the way on these. No need you being in pain on your wedding night."

Caroline gave her a grin and propped them under her arms carefully. Her dress had only two thin straps over each shoulder and the bodice plunged halfway to her stomach, with two even thinner straps holding it together between her breasts. The rest was simple, smooth, flowing to her calves.

She wore tan because Dio mentioned how he loved it on her the first day he saw her at work, so understated on the outside, contrasting heavily with her own intense sensuality. He loved how it flowed into her own skin and covered her but didn't. She wore tan for him, flowing, shimmery, sensual tan with tiny white sparkles to match the sand around them.

Her music started. It was a long piece of music, which she needed in order to get down the pier from the halfway point tent they'd set up, and to the end where he waited. Luckily her arm muscles had developed back to proficiency with the crutches. Untraditionally, her matron of honor walked beside her instead of ahead of her, in case Caroline needed assistance. Nelda carried the large bouquet of wildflowers.

When she got down far enough to see him clearly, she stopped.

"Honey? You okay now?"

She nodded. He was so beautiful. In light brown pants and a

golden-brown shirt, his sleeves rolled up, his collar unbuttoned. A few of their coworkers were there, Dio's mom, Penny, and a few neighbors she'd met since Dio allowed her to drag him out now and then to talk to people. Harry stood at his side.

"Your music will run out, honey. Are you going to keep that boy wondering?"

She shook her head and started again, toward him. He smiled at her. Her pulse reacted. Her Dio. He was keeping her.

Close enough now, she stopped and traded Nelda her crutches for the bouquet. Dio started toward her. Harry put a hand on his arm to stop him. It was a surprise. Caroline wanted to walk to him herself, even only a few steps. She wanted to stand with him without the crutches in her way just as he'd left his mask off. He now had a tan one he wore only when they went into the city.

It took her a little time to get the foot to balance enough to support her and he was ready to move up and grasp her if needed, but she made it, and he waited and took her hand.

Caroline heard the ceremony. The minister's voice. The song. The seagulls around them. But she was captured in Dio's eyes. She willingly repeated her vows and her eyes watered when he repeated his. And they were pronounced husband and wife.

Dio picked her up as he kissed her. Their guests showered them with bubbles, threw congratulations and well wishes, and he carried her to the middle of the pavilion for their first dance.

Caroline grabbed onto his shirt and raised her right leg behind her in a modified arabesque. She teased him with a pirouette. He picked her up, turned her around, brought her down against his body until her leg was wrapped around his waist, her left toes on the floor between his legs.

She sang next to his ear. She was a bad singer but it didn't matter. He gripped her left leg and brought it up around him until she cuddled into his body, her face nuzzled into his neck.

"Where have you always wanted to go, Caroline?"

"Oh Dio, I'm exactly where I want to be. Right now. Here with you."

"Where else? If you could choose anywhere in the world. Where

would you go? You told me once. Do you remember talking about
it?"

"Yes. To Spain. To watch the Flamenco dancers."

"We're heading there first thing in the morning."

"What? Just like that? You need…"

"Already taken care of."

"But Dio, you don't like to travel."

"Only because of the scar, baby, but with you at my side, it'll be
fine. Say yes."

"On crutches? That'll be…"

"You can do it. I'll be with you. Say yes."

"It's so much money, Dio."

"I don't care. Say yes, Caroline."

"Dio?"

"Yes?"

"Yes. I love you."

"And I am breathtakingly, maddeningly, hopelessly in love with
you. So you better never change my mind."

She smiled and teased his lips. "I'll try never to change your mind.
Or to change you. I want you just as you are."

Caroline gazed around her bedroom, their bedroom, now painted
in sienna and light gold to simulate the wrens and the beach. She
focused on the shadow boxes Dio had picked up to protect and
showcase her starfish collection, along with several small plaques with
starfish symbolism written out in pretty calligraphy. The biggest
among them spoke of regeneration and new beginnings.

She fingered the silver starfish necklace he'd given her just before
her surgery that she wore with her wedding dress. She wore it always.
It was a nice strong chain, also in shimmery silver, and she'd picked
up one that matched to wear on her ankle for their wedding. Her feet
had been bare. He'd grinned when he noticed.

Dio offered her a nice hotel for their wedding night, but Caroline
wanted to be home on their first night as husband and wife, in the
place she loved most. With Cleo staying at Nelda and Harry's and
Penny staying at the incredible bed and breakfast Caroline loved, as a

way of thanking her for everything she did for them, they had the place to themselves. They'd spent the afternoon riding Degas and DaVinci, an ornery full-black male that was Dio's favorite, around the property, pausing on a hill for the picnic lunch Nelda packed for them. Evening passed quickly as they sat out on the porch swing watching the little wrens and their friends flit about until the sun descended. Once dark, they went for a swim and sat around a small campfire to warm and dry, wrapped together in nothing but a blanket with her Kitty at her feet and Estrela at his, the little border collies running back and forth between the campfire and the perimeter they guarded, keeping squirrels away.

Showered and barely covered in a long lace and silk tan nightgown, Caroline smiled when Dio came up behind her. He took her crutches, set them aside, and picked her up to carry her to bed. They didn't bother to talk. There was no need. A light, warm breeze came in through the wide open windows, flapping the new white sheers she'd picked out. The wrens were quiet by now with night falling, replaced by crickets and tree frogs and the occasional hoot of an owl in the distance.

They made love gently, tenderly, passionately, and Caroline cuddled into the strong arms of her sexy swordsman-farmer. More content than she figured she had a right to be, she fell asleep looking forward to the coming adventures with her true love and everything that would come with him.

~~ ~~ ~~

EllaMKaye.com

Acknowledgements

This first book of a new line under a new author name started out as "something different" than my usual stories with several characters and subplots, that are sometimes very long and complex. With life situation changes, where I suddenly had less writing and quiet thinking time, and with market changes, where shorter fiction was suddenly in vogue, I decided to experiment a bit and write some "quick read" books, heavier on the romance and lighter on the plot line. *Pier Lights* is the first of that experiment, and it was quickly followed by five other novels and a novella.

Something odd happened, though: with each book, my natural tendency to dig deep and sort out past conflicts that affect present personality quirks and situations forced its way back.

So be it. An artist has to be faithful to herself first. Therefore, the updated editions of those "quick" books. Thank you to those who read the earlier version of this story (and the others) and left reviews and/or shared your thoughts. Reader reviews are the life-blood of an author's marketing and I appreciate the time and effort it takes. Each comment also helped to shape the new versions.

Thank you to my beta readers and proofers, Liz Ferguson & Annette McRoberts, for catching those pesky little things that escaped my notice.

Thank you to Tonya Morris for providing details about Folly Beach and Charleston.

Thank you to my BookSpa group for the constant inspiration, uplift, advice, and encouragement, and to my sister Kathi Hawkins who encouraged and welcomes every book of this new line.

Thank you, always, to my family, for putting up with the days I type away past what should have been dinner time, for helping me promote, for overlooking what I didn't catch because my head was in a story, and for otherwise supporting this career that is not close to a solitary effort.

<3

About The Author

Ella M. Kaye uses her art and psychology background to create contemporary love stories with mental health issues set around the creative arts. Each of her novels and novellas fall under one of three series: Dancers & Lighthouses, Artists & Cottages, and Songwriters & Cities. Kaye has been writing romantically inclined literary fiction that branches into straight mainstream in both novel and short story form under the name LK Hunsaker for more than two decades. After many moves as a military spouse, she is settled in western Pennsylvania where she enjoys the abundant foliage and recreational lakes along with the hilly vistas, and spoiling her grandchildren as often as their parents kindly allow.

www.ellamkaye.com
www.lkhunsaker.com

~~

Shadows of Greens & Memories (2015)
Artists & Cottages Series

Francis Barrett returns to her hometown of Storm Lake, Iowa to take care of the family holdings, such as they are, after her father passes. While turning his garden shed into a small but livable cottage, she runs into an old flame she admired from afar but never dared speak with during their high school days. Using her secret passion of oil painting to unwind from long days of clearing out the mess, Francis finds her father also had a secret passion and left behind a tale of a man she didn't truly know.

George Frederick McKenry never left the Midwest town where he was born other than brief travels with his four children, who he now has custody of since his ex moved into a condo with her new boyfriend. Running into the one girl from school who rebuffed him when he asked her out, G.F. can't help checking on her and making sure she's getting along alright. False assumptions and past resentments fade as Fran and G.F. let down their guards in order to create new memories.

~~

Shadows of Blues & Echoes (2016)
Artists & Cottages Series

Gillian Hart has big ambitions while working as a reporter for a small circulation paper in Denver, Colorado. When her editor and friend assigns a story about some rich businessman who chucks it all to live in the woods alone outside Durango, she does her best to fight it. With no choice but to give in, Gillian determines to use it as a stepping stone.

Hank Dennison wants nothing but solitude while he recovers from a life-changing devastation he has managed to hide from the public. The last thing he wants is another nosy journalist badgering him, especially one who knows nothing about survival in the wilderness and taxes his waning strength. Noticing the darkness of depression that weighs her down, despite her attempt to hide it, Hank determines to keep her off the path that led him to his own illness.

~~

Shadows of Rust & Reels (2017)
Artists & Cottages Series

By day, Holli Jacoby is a jewelry artist in her hometown of Williamstown, West Virginia. Abandoned by her family, Holli mainly stays to herself, preferring her potter's wheel to the risk of letting others see, and take advantage of, the uncontrollable effects of her bipolar disorder.

Isaac Bradshaw is a welder who spends much of his off time assisting his parents due to his father's declining health. While playing pool, he notices a fiery brunette eye him as though she knows him. He soon learns "fiery" is an understatement, and his buddy warns him against the girl, but something keeps him drawn to her.

Despite their earlier crossed paths and a shared love of adventure, Holli's roller coaster life might be more than Isaac is willing to handle. When the bottom falls out beneath her, their relationship hits a critical test.

~~

A Melody in the Dark (2017)
Singers & Songwriters series (a prequel novella)
published by Fire Star Press as part of the *Music of the Heart* anthology

Meladee Lerner is a single mom and struggling songwriter who moved to Pittsburgh to escape a marriage she didn't want. It's 1979, just after the big snow storm that paralyzed the city, when they run into Niall Dillon, a hard-working young Pittsburgher with strong Irish roots. Niall is making plans to travel the US on his own, but one eventful night gives him second thoughts.

~~ ~~ ~~

Watch for more books from both series, as well as from the new Singers & Songwriters series, coming 2019.